Janey's emotions couldn't take another blow.

Her stomach heaved, her shoulders shook and tears gushed down her cheeks.

"God, Janey, don't," Dillon pleaded in an agonized voice.

Then he lunged to his feet and strode toward her, stopping so close that she could feel his breath warm her skin when he spoke again.

"I don't know when to keep my bloody mouth shut."

"It's not your fault," she whispered, her lips accidentally grazing his. Wide-eyed, their gazes held while Janey's breath constricted and her head reeled.

"God, don't look at me like that or—" He broke off again, then added, "Oh, to hell with it."

As before, his kisses started out feather light, on her temple, her cheek, her mouth. They barely touched as he murmured, "I didn't mean to upset you more."

"It's all right," she sobbed, circling her arms around his neck until his lips were locked tightly and frantically against hers.

"Aptly named, Baxter's latest novel boasts sensuality as its strongest feature—the attraction between the hero and heroine sparks fire from the first and keeps on burning hot throughout."

—*Publishers Weekly* on *Sultry*

MARY LYNN BAXTER

TEMPTING JANEY

MIRA

ISBN 1-55166-809-2

TEMPTING JANEY

Visit us at www.mirabooks.com

Printed in U.S.A.

TEMPTING JANEY

One

The quietness bothered him.

It wasn't natural, Dillon Reed told himself as he ambled down the main hall of Brookwood High School, where he was principal. This hall and the others should be teeming with students laughing, talking and slamming locker doors.

All that and more would start again soon enough, Dillon reminded himself with a quirk of his lips. First thing in the morning, in fact. But on this Wednesday evening, just after dark, the students were gone and silence was the order of the day.

Dillon didn't make a habit of cruising the halls when they were empty. His purpose for having stopped by the school on this particular evening was to get his briefcase, which he'd forgotten. After that, he was headed to his sister's, where he was expected for dinner.

But since he had some time to kill, he'd figured he might as well stroll down the main hall and check for new graffiti on the walls and lockers, something that never failed to raise his ire.

Dillon paused, feeling the silence close around him like a tomb. The place was downright gloomy without its usual hubbub.

What was wrong with him? He spent more than

his share of time on the job, arriving way before the
first bell rang and leaving long after the last one had
sounded. In fact, he was on the premises a lot at
night—the only time he could get his paperwork
done—and the silence had never bothered him before.

What was different about tonight?

He wasn't complaining. He loved what he did,
loved every nook and cranny of this new building,
loved every minute he spent walking the halls and
grounds. He'd worked his way up through the ranks
of the system, starting out as a teacher and coach,
then moving up to guidance counselor, and now to
principal.

He wasn't content, though. He had his eye on a
superintendent's position. But he wasn't in a hurry.
Right now, he was content to remain hands-on with
the kids. Keeping up with them kept him young in
mind and spirit. When the time was right to make
the move, he would know it.

However, he wasn't interested in getting too far
away from Hunter. This small South Carolina town
of forty thousand plus, perfectly positioned between
Charleston and Savannah, was home to him. And
since he'd invested heavily in a chunk of land—land
that he hoped to make into a profitable horse farm—
he intended to be picky about future jobs.

A deep sigh escaped Dillon just as he reached his
office and unlocked the door.

That was when he heard the noise.

When he couldn't identify the sound, every muscle
in his body tensed. He didn't move; he almost
stopped breathing as his military background booted
his system into high alert. He listened.

Nothing.

Dillon almost wilted with relief. His imagination was obviously working overtime, which wasn't a bad thing. Blatant mischief and much worse were problems that all schools had to contend with. It never paid to be careless, and he couldn't let himself get overconfident that his facility was different simply because he ran it with an iron fist.

He had the door all the way open and had reached for the light switch when he heard the noise again. He stood still, feeling his heart up its pace and the hairs stand out on his neck. No mistake this time. Something was going on.

Suddenly a crashing sound, like that of glass breaking, interrupted the stark silence.

Someone else was definitely in the building.

The lab. That was his first guess. It was at the opposite end of this hall and full of plenty of breakable objects. Rage rendered him immobile for several more seconds before it hit his body like a shot of adrenaline.

He spun on his booted heels and charged down the hall, careful at the same time not to let the culprit or culprits know they had company.

Dillon had no idea what he would encounter, but it didn't matter. Whoever was responsible for what was going down would pay dearly. No one destroyed Brookwood property and got away with it.

Another crash assaulted his ears just as he rounded the dark corner. He flinched, but his feet never faltered. Hoping to sneak up on the intruders unannounced, he hadn't turned on the lights. That would have sent them scurrying out the side door of the lab before he could get to them.

When Dillon paused at the door and eased his head around, only the glow from a high-powered flashlight greeted him. Still, he was able to see two people, both males, both young, both wearing caps, masks and gloves.

Students, his instincts told him. Smart students, at that, having thought to shield their identity.

They were having a high old time, too, beating the hell out of the equipment. One had a baseball bat in hand, the other had a hammer. Broken glass, microscopes and computers were strewn about.

The place looked like a war zone.

After seeing the havoc the little creeps had wreaked, Dillon's rage threatened to choke him. This was the first time this kind of malicious destruction had taken place at his school. But no more. He was about to bring their party to a halt.

"Hold it, boys. Playtime's over."

"Oh, shit!" one of them yelled, then tore off toward the door. "Come on, let's get the hell out of here!"

The other one obviously needed no second invitation as he shot over the debris like a sprinter and dashed toward the exit, almost running over his companion in the process.

Dillon followed suit, only to curse silently. The door. He'd underestimated their closeness to the side entrance that made a quick exit possible.

By the time he reached their avenue of escape, the boys were through the door and racing across campus. Dillon chased them, but he knew he was wasting his time.

A nondescript pickup was parked in an area of almost total darkness not far from the lab. They jumped in it and took off before he could get near them, much less get a license plate number.

"Damn," he muttered, sucking in a deep breath.

He'd screwed that up royally, he admitted as he turned and made his way back into the building. If he hadn't been so cocky, so sure of his ability to handle the situation, he would have called the cops the second he heard the sound of breaking glass.

By the time he'd have investigated and found out what was going on, the law would have been there. But no, he'd had to plunge in headfirst on his own.

"Dammit," he muttered again out of sheer frustration as he strode into his office. Once there, he called the police, then waited for their arrival, but not patiently.

What was happening to kids these days?

He'd asked himself that question untold times, but he still didn't have an answer. Years ago, when he first entered the fascinating world of teaching children, nothing like what he'd just witnessed had ever taken place—at least not that he could remember.

How times had changed. Breaking and entering was actually considered a mild offense. Now kids were killing kids. Kids were killing parents. God, it made no sense whatsoever.

What it did do, though, was frighten the hell out of him. He was of the opinion that youngsters should behave and be responsible for their actions. He loved "his kids," but they knew better than to cross the line he'd drawn in the sand. Or at least he'd thought so, he told himself, mentally kicking his own rear.

Apparently he'd misjudged his control, refusing to have security guards in the halls of *his* school. After all, he was an ex-Marine whose rough edge would help him handle any situation that might occur. Until now, that rough edge hadn't failed him.

His thoughts were interrupted by two uniformed officers making their way into his office.

Following introductions, Dillon told them what had taken place.

"Too bad you didn't get the plate number," Officer Temple, the taller of the two, said.

When he had first seen them, Dillon had hidden a smile. One was as tall as a giraffe, the other as short as a Shetland pony. Side by side, they reminded him of Mutt and Jeff.

Dillon's eyes narrowed. "I'll admit the little creeps got the better of me. But I thought I could handle them and the situation."

"That's never a wise assumption, Mr. Reed, especially in this climate."

"I know that now," Dillon said harshly, again mentally kicking himself. It was damn embarrassing to make such a gross error in judgment and be caught at it. "Come on, let's take a look-see at the lab."

The officers made notes, then called the lab team to scour the premises, which Dillon knew would be a lost cause. The kids had played it smart. He'd noticed they were wearing gloves.

Officer Riley, the short cop, finally said, "We'll do what we can, but you'll probably have better luck checking around the campus yourself." He paused and rubbed his chin. "That is, if you think it was some of your students."

"Oh, I think that's a real good possibility," Dillon said in a grim tone. "I just hope the break-in wasn't gang related."

"Wouldn't surprise me," Officer Temple said, his voice brusque.

Dillon tightened his lips. "I've suspected we have one trying to form on our campus, but I haven't been able to prove it yet."

"I hope you're wrong," Riley said. "But gangs are springing up faster than cancer."

Dillon remained silent as the lab team completed their work. Once they were gone, he made a quick inventory, then called the janitorial supervisor to clean up the mess. That done, he grabbed his brief-case, flicked off the lights and left the building.

First thing tomorrow morning, he would turn into a not-so-nice Santa. He would make a list and check it twice.

Dillon steered his utility vehicle through the gates of his hundred-acre horse farm. But instead of making a hairpin right turn that would take him to where his sister and brother-in-law lived, he braked and shoved the gearshift into Park.

While the engine purred, he stared into the darkness. At the moment he was lucky. The late-August clouds had drifted away from the nearly full moon, giving it carte blanche to shine for all it was worth.

Dillon took advantage of that treat. To the left, he could see the cabin that sat atop the hill. One day he planned to remodel it so that he could live there. He could envision its homey coziness, with smoke snaking out of the chimney from a wood-burning fireplace on a cold day, and a dog—the Heinz-57 variety—sitting beside him.

The only thing missing from that picture was a woman.

Muttering an expletive, he focused his gaze on the shack, over which towered several huge oak and pine trees that kept it shaded all year long. Beyond, but not visible to him now, was an acre of cleared land. From there, a narrow gravel road wound through the dense thicket like a tunnel. Occasional clearings offered glimpses of the nice-size pond below, which had been filled with catfish. Any time he wanted fresh fish, he just had to cast a line.

Dillon continued to pat himself on the back that he'd had the foresight three years ago to buy the land when it was offered. Despite the hefty bank note he would be paying off for a long time to come, he didn't regret it.

This place was his lifeline. Without it, he didn't know what he would have done. Probably have sunk into the depths of despair and been content to wallow there.

Grimacing, he refused to let his mind wander down that forbidden path. He had too much ahead to look forward to. His horse farm had the potential to begin paying off soon, now that his prized piece of horseflesh was almost ready to be bred. And he was starting a new school year that held a lot of promise.

For a second, Dillon's mind reverted back to the incident in the lab. He grimaced again but refused to let himself dwell on that, either. The school problem he could correct; the past he couldn't.

Suddenly he realized he'd been lollygagging far too long. His sister, Allie, was probably ready to skin him alive. She believed in punctuality, no matter what. Nothing wrong with that, he reminded himself.

Thinking of his sister, a legal secretary for an affluent attorney, made him smile. That smile remained intact as he parked in front of the modest three-bedroom home on his property, a home he'd generously lent to Allie and her husband, Mike, who worked as his foreman.

His smile widened as the porch light flipped on and Allie opened the door. "It's about time, brother dear," she called out, a hand braced on one hip.

Dillon stepped out of his truck and heard the comfortable crunch of leaves and pine bark under his feet. He inhaled, positive he could smell fall in the air, then said, "Hey, sis."

"Don't you 'hey, sis' me. You're late."

"I can explain," Dillon said, walking onto the porch. He put an arm around her waist and pulled her next to him.

A smile flirted with her lips. "I've heard that before."

"Ah, give me a break, will ya?"

"I'll have to think about that."

They parted as they walked into the cheerfully lighted living-dining room combination, where the smell of freshly baked bread permeated the air.

"Before I hear your excuse, how about a hunk of banana-nut?"

"Ah, my favorite," Dillon exclaimed.

"I shouldn't let you have any," Allie said with a mischievous glint in her eye.

Dillon merely grinned, knowing that her threat was empty. She loved for him and everyone else to compliment her cooking, especially her bread. She was known for that specialty all over town.

But then, Allie was known for a lot. She lived to entertain. She enjoyed people, and they enjoyed her. At thirty-eight, two years his junior, her face was still relatively unlined, although she had prematurely gray hair that she didn't bother to color.

Like him, she was tall and rawboned. Yet her height and build didn't make her less attractive. Her vibrant blue eyes and ready smile made for a charming combination.

He loved her dearly and couldn't imagine his life without her, since he had no other family. Their parents had died in a freak auto accident a long time ago. Since then, they had stuck together.

That was why those dark circles under her eyes and that pinched look around her mouth, visible in the light, gave him cause for concern.

"Are you okay?" he asked.

She made light of his inquiry. "Of course I'm okay. Why wouldn't I be?"

"You tell me," he said, not quite ready to let her off the hook.

"I might be coming down with the same virus that struck the office."

"As long as that's all it is."

"Stop nagging," she chastised in a light tone. "You're worse than some old woman. A lot worse than Mike, and he's bad enough."

Dillon laughed. "All right, you win. For now. So where's that bread?"

"Have you had dinner?" she asked, facing him from in front of the cabinet.

"Nope, but I'm not hungry—except for a huge piece of that bread."

"I'll be glad to heat you a plate of peas and corn bread."

Dillon eased down into one of the kitchen chairs.

"Thanks, but I'll pass tonight. Just the bread, ma'am."

A few minutes later, he was rubbing his stomach and grinning at his sister, who was staring at him over the rim of her coffee cup.

"Well?" she asked.

He reached for his cup of decaf and took a sip. "Well what?"

"Jerk," she muttered.

He laughed out loud. "All right, it was the best yet. But then, you know that."

"It's nice to hear it, anyway."

"By the way, where's Mike?"

Allie made a face. "It's Wednesday, remember? He's playing poker with his buddies." She paused and gave him a pointed look. "I wish you had someone to hang out with."

"I've been at the school," Dillon said, intentionally ignoring her last provocative statement.

"Why am I not surprised?"

Dillon told her about the break-in.

"Did it ever occur to you that you could've gotten hurt?" Her tone was incredulous.

"That was the least of my worries. I just wanted to catch the little shits."

She let out a deep sigh. "I wish you worked as hard on perfecting your personal life as you do on that school."

"Now, Allie, don't start," he said, taking another sip of coffee.

She went on as if he hadn't said a word. "Are you still seeing Patricia Sims?"

Dillon curbed his impatience, but barely. "Actually, I'm taking her out Saturday evening. It's her birthday."

"Well glory hallelujah."

"But don't get your hopes up, sister dear. She's just a friend and will never be anything else."

Allie threw up her hands in dramatic fashion. "I give up. You're hopeless."

"Hey, I'm happy with things just the way they are."

"I don't believe that. It's time you were interested in another woman, for heaven's sake. It's been three years since Elaine's death."

Dillon didn't respond right off, thinking that if Allie only knew what a disaster his marriage had turned out to be, she wouldn't be pushing him in that direction again. But she didn't know, and to tell her now would serve no purpose.

He marveled that his dirty little secret had remained just that. In a town this size, he couldn't believe Allie hadn't been bombarded with the truth. He suspected the reason for that oversight was that she and Mike had only recently moved back to Hunter. Mike had worked for an oil-drilling company in Texas until he'd gotten hurt and had to quit.

"I know you'd like to have a child. Lord knows, you and Elaine tried hard enough. If I recall, she miscarried twice."

He made an effort not to wince visibly. But every time that subject was mentioned, it was like someone had scratched the scab off an old wound, leaving it raw and oozing again. "You're right, I would like to have a child, but not enough to remarry."

"Oh, Dillon, I hate to hear you talk like that. You have so much to offer a woman."

He gave her a halfhearted smile. "You're just biased."

"Maybe a little, but—"

"Hey, give it a rest, will you? Like I said, I'm content with my life. I have my eye on being a superintendent one day, plus I have the farm, which I'm determined to turn into a profitable business—with Mike's help, of course."

He paused and reached for Allie's hand, giving it a squeeze. "So you see, you don't have to worry. I'm fine."

"What you are is hardheaded," she said, withdrawing her hand and getting to her feet. "I'll send some bread home with you."

He stood. "Is that a hint to leave?"

"Of course not, silly," she said with a grin. "But it's either do something constructive with my hands or slug you."

He chuckled. "I'd best be going, then. Anyhow, I need my rest. The rest of this week and next is shaping up to be a killer, what with football season officially starting and the break-in to sort out."

"I hope you find out who's responsible."

"Let's just hope it doesn't turn out to be gang related. I've been lucky so far."

Allie shivered. "Kids are not like they used to be."

"You got that right."

They walked arm in arm to the door, where Allie handed him his doggie bag. He thanked her, then kissed her on the cheek.

He was almost to his vehicle when she said, "By the way, don't forget to pick up a box of candy or some flowers for Patricia."

He narrowed his eyes. "You just don't know when to give up, do you?"

She flashed him a smile. "No, brother dear, I don't."

Dillon simply snorted.

Two

What a day.

Janey Mayfield rubbed the back of her neck, then peered at the clock behind the counter in her candy shop, Sweet Dreams. Almost closing time. Thank heaven for small favors, she thought, as she began making preparations to reverse the Open sign in the window.

What was wrong with her? The answer popped readily to mind. She was tired, but then, she had a right to be. In the month since she'd returned to South Carolina, her world had been turned upside down again. She'd had to adjust to another new home and a new career, that of a businesswoman who now owned and operated her own shop. At thirty-seven, that was no easy feat.

Often Janey felt as if she were on a treadmill that wouldn't stop and let her get off, even for a minute.

Yet she wasn't complaining. Her eyes surveyed the premises. This delightful shop, filled with the fanciest to the plainest of candies, was all hers, thanks to the generosity of her aunt Lois, who had chosen to retire to an assisted living facility in Savannah after suffering a stroke.

Even so, repairs of all sorts needed to be done,

both upstairs and down. But they would have to wait.
There was simply no money to make them.

Despite her problems, though, she had so much to
be grateful for. After getting her teenage daughter
Robin up and off to school, Janey always looked forward to dressing, walking downstairs to the smell of
candy, chatting with her customers, then ringing up
their sales.

But this day had been a particularly difficult one.
Perhaps it was the fact that business had been incredibly slow that made her anxious. Sweet Dreams
had to do well. There was no choice. *She* had no
choice.

As a divorced single parent with a seventeen-year-
old daughter to rear, she had to turn the shop into a
profitable venture. Everything depended on it. During
the last year of her aunt's ownership, sales had begun
to lag for no apparent reason, but Janey felt confident
in her ability to swing sales in the other direction by
introducing change and innovation.

Maybe her less than enthusiastic mood was simply
weather-related. Even for the end of August, it had
been cloyingly hot. The two air-conditioning units,
one for the living quarters upstairs and one for the
shop below, had been laboring overtime.

After summer heat so muggy and heavy that the
clouds and mosquitoes could barely pierce it, fall
would be an exquisite relief. Janey suddenly brightened at that thought.

In the years she'd been gone, she'd forgotten just
how bad summers in the South could be. But when
she'd arrived from Colorado, reality had slapped her
in the face.

This, too, shall pass, she reminded herself with

another dig at her neck muscles. Hot weather wouldn't damage her, but a lack of customers just might. Refusing to dwell on that depressing thought, she grabbed the bottle of glass cleaner and a paper towel, and went to work on the counter.

"Mom, I'm home!"

The sound of her daughter's voice never failed to buoy her spirits. Circumstances beyond her control had kept her away from her child for several months. Robin had returned to South Carolina at the end of her junior year in order to be on the drill team her senior year. But nothing would ever separate them again, she vowed fiercely. Life without Robin wasn't worth living.

"I'm about ready to close." Janey made her way to the side door. When she didn't see her daughter, she asked, "Where are you, darling?"

"I'm already upstairs. I'll be down in a sec."

Janey always looked forward to the end of the day, when Robin would come bounding through the door, excited and eager to share the details of her day. Because she was a member of the drill team and had practice every afternoon, she didn't get home until late.

"Hey."

"Hey yourself." Janey smiled, then walked over and gave Robin a quick hug. "So how was your day, young lady?"

Munching on an apple, Robin shoved a swath of shoulder-length, strawberry-blond hair behind one ear, then perched on the stool at the end of the counter. A grin enhanced her features. "Nothing special—except I aced my Trig test."

"Why, that's great, honey."

Robin's grin deepened, and Janey's heart melted. She and her ex-husband Keith had made a lot of mistakes in their marriage, but their daughter hadn't been one of them. Janey marveled every day at this delightful child they had created.

She was tall and slender, with light brown eyes and incredibly long lashes that were dark despite her light-colored hair.

And while Robin wasn't perfect—not by a long shot, Janey reminded herself ruefully—she wouldn't change anything, except maybe her daughter's strong-willed nature.

"How did the shop do today?" Robin asked.

Janey felt her features sober. "Not good. In fact, it was the pits."

Robin took another bite of apple, then asked, "Wonder why?"

It was on the tip of Janey's tongue to tell her daughter not to talk with her mouth full, but she refrained. Robin would merely roll her eyes, then give her that "look."

"I have no clue," Janey said instead. "I've tried to blame it on everything, even the weather."

Robin stood and tossed her half-eaten apple in the nearest trash basket. "Man, oh man, was it ever hot today. We sweated our buns off, practicing."

"So everything's still going all right with the team?"

Robin's face lighted. "Things are awesome, actually. We learned a new routine today that we're going to perform at the first home game. Can't wait for you and Dad to see it."

"Well, you don't have long to wait. Friday night next week, right?"

"Righto," Robin replied, heading toward the door. "I'm going up and drown in the shower. I'm icky."

Janey wrinkled her nose. "I wondered what that unpleasant odor was."

"Jeez, Mom!"

Janey laughed. "Just teasing."

"So what's for dinner?"

"What do you want?"

"Pizza."

"When you get through drowning, call it in."

After Robin had disappeared up the stairs, Janey shook her head. Teenagers—a different breed. At times not human. Maybe that was a more apt description. She didn't know many parents who would argue that point with her.

But she wouldn't want it any other way. She would take the good with the bad and enjoy every moment. As it was, her daughter was growing up much too fast to suit her. She would have liked to slow time down so she would have more moments to savor. Since that wasn't possible, she would make the most of the time Robin still had at home.

If only she didn't have to share Robin with her ex-husband. If only she didn't feel guilty about the divorce because of Robin. Keith had turned out to be a womanizing lush, and theirs was a family ripped apart at the seams. It had been a terribly difficult adjustment for Robin.

"Hey, Mom."

Saved. Her daughter's timing was perfect. She hated it when her guilty feelings resurfaced and she dwelled on them.

"Yes, dear?"

"I'm going after the pizza."

"Be careful."

Noticing that the clock registered five-thirty, she headed to the front door. That was when she saw a utility vehicle pull up. For a moment she was tempted to turn the sign around, anyway, but she didn't. She needed the money more than she needed the time.

She'd barely made it back to the counter when she heard the buzzer on the door. She swung around with a smile, only to feel it freeze on her lips.

Dillon Reed.

Janey's breath caught as she struggled to hide her warring emotions. It had been inevitable that one day she would see him again. For one thing, he was her daughter's principal. For another, this was a small town. Sooner or later, everyone's paths crossed, like it or not.

"Janey?"

She strove to make her voice sound as normal as possible, though she wasn't sure she could pull it off. "Hello, Dillon."

He hadn't changed all that much in the three-plus years since she'd last seen him. His hair was still unruly and night-dark, but now with a few sprinkles of gray—not unexpected, since he was forty.

His blue eyes certainly hadn't changed in intensity. They still had the power to cut straight to a person's soul. Possibly that was why he was so good with kids. He appeared taller and more muscular than she recalled, as if he'd been using the weights.

He was dressed in jeans, a shirt, a casual sports jacket and boots. He looked like he ought to be running a ranch instead of a school. The only thing missing was the Stetson.

Had he always been such a hunk?

Hunk or not, character lines scored his lean features, and there was a rugged hardness about his mouth.

"Is this place yours?" Dillon asked, shattering the tense silence.

"Yes, as of a little over a month ago."

"Well, I have to say I'm shocked. I never expected you to come back to Hunter."

"I never expected to, either."

She turned away, unable to meet the challenge of those deep-set eyes or that earnest gaze.

"So how've you been?" he asked in his caramel-smooth tone.

Was there a slight strain in that voice, or had she imagined it? She faced him again, though with reluctance. Was he as uncomfortable with the situation as she was? No doubt she was agitated and on guard, but she couldn't gauge his reaction at all. He was a master at hiding his thoughts.

"I have no complaints," she said at last, forcing herself to loosen up.

"You look great."

She looked away, then back. "Thanks."

"So how's Robin?"

"Attending your school and performing with the drill team."

He looked sheepish for a moment. "Sorry, somehow that fact got by me."

"That's understandable. You have hundreds of students." She felt as though she was rattling on, but she couldn't seem to stop. "You can't be expected to remember them all."

He shifted from one booted foot to the other, then stared at her out of bleak eyes. "Look, Janey—"

"It's all right," she interrupted quickly, taking a deep breath. "There's nothing else to say. So let's just give things a rest, okay?"

He didn't respond for a moment. Then he shrugged. "It's your call."

"So what can I do for you?"

His eyes had darkened now, and she experienced an involuntary shiver. "Sell me a box of candy."

Janey forced a smile. "Now *that* I can do."

A few minutes later, after she locked up behind him and watched him drive off, Janey leaned against the door, her heart pounding like a jackhammer inside her chest.

Three

"**I** wish I were built like you."

Robin gave her friend Beverly Olson an exasperated look. "You look fine the way you are."

"I look *fat* the way I am," Beverly responded in a sarcastic tone.

Underneath that sarcasm, Robin picked up on the note of despair in her friend's voice. She stopped what she was doing, walked over and sat beside Beverly on the steps of her front porch. An uneasy silence fell between them.

Beverly seemed unusually sensitive about her weight today, Robin thought. Maybe it was because the first big game was imminent, and Beverly was getting nervous about performing in front of the home folks. For whatever reason, Robin was at a loss as to how to comfort her.

She and Beverly had more or less established a set time to practice their routines in Bev's front yard. This Saturday was no exception.

"How do you stay so damn skinny?" Beverly asked, giving Robin a playful nudge on the shoulder. "You eat like you've been felling trees and don't gain an ounce."

Robin smiled, glad to see her friend's good humor

return. She knew, however, that Beverly was really serious when it came to her weight problem.

"You might need to lose a few pounds," Robin said, "but you're still the best one on the squad."

"Baloney."

"No, it's not baloney." Robin stood and peered down at Beverly. "You're as limber as a rag doll and can do any routine perfectly on the first try. Trust me, that counts for something."

"Thanks, but I'd rather be thin and clumsy."

Robin placed her hands on her hips and pretended to be offended. "Are you saying I'm clumsy?"

"Nah," Beverly replied, her grin sheepish. "You've got it all together."

"That's baloney, too. I'm the one Mrs. Morrison's always ragging."

"Well, what do you expect? She's blind in one eye and can't see out of the other."

They both giggled, then sobered.

"I guess we'd better get back to the grindstone," Beverly said, getting up. "This coming Friday's looming large."

"Right. And since I haven't quite gotten the hang of that new step, I need help."

Robin didn't really, but she wanted Beverly to feel needed. In spite of Beverly's weight, Robin thought her best friend was pretty. Beverly was tall, with mid-length, sandy-colored hair that was silky and shiny. Her eyes were a dark gray, and her skin was flawless. Most of all, she had a sharp wit and sense of humor that made her a blast to be around.

Robin adored her, especially since Beverly was the only one who had befriended her when she'd returned from Colorado. Most of the others in the class had treated her like an outcast.

They were just jealous, Beverly had told her, because she was so "everything" they weren't. Robin hadn't believed that for a second—but she didn't know what she would have done if Beverly hadn't become her friend.

Now, in their senior year, their friendship had deepened. They shared everything except clothes.

"What's churning in that brain of yours?" Beverly asked. "You're staring holes through me."

"Sorry," Robin said. "I was just thinking about how tough it was when I came back here, and how you got me through those miserable times."

Beverly chuckled. "I loved it the first day you tried out for the team. You were great, and most of my so-called friends were green with envy. And I enjoyed every minute of their misery."

"You're awful."

"No, I'm truthful. Eloise and entourage needed some competition. And you gave it to them. It was a hoot."

Robin's features clouded. "Most of them still don't like me."

"So what? Who needs them? All they think about is guys—which one is going to get in their panties next." Beverly paused and grinned. "Oops, my mistake. They don't even wear panties."

Robin giggled. "I hate to agree with you, but I do."

"Speaking of Eloise and company, they just drove up."

Robin peered over her shoulder, feeling her heart drop to her toes. The afternoon was ruined, for sure.

She hated the competition that went on among the drill team, mainly the catty jealousy. But it existed, and she had to face it or get sucked under.

"Wonder what we did to deserve such luck?" Beverly muttered, as four girls piled out of a Lexus sports coupe and walked up.

"Hey, what's going on?" Eloise Frazier asked, batting her big brown eyes and smiling her fake smile, appearing as innocent as a newborn babe.

Robin knew better. The captain of the drill team was as innocent as a hooker on Sunset Boulevard. And she was up to something. It was only a matter of time before she and Beverly found out what.

"We're just taking a break from practicing," Beverly said.

"Want us to watch?" Sally, another of the girls, asked.

"Nope," Beverly said. "Not unless y'all want to perform for us."

Another of the girls spoke up. "We don't need any more practice. We've got the routine down."

"Bully for you," Beverly said.

Robin knew a verbal slinging match was not far off, and while Beverly could more than handle the situation, Robin didn't want to be part of it. So she smiled at the fourth girl, Mandy Taylor, then changed the subject. "Is that your car? It's awesome."

Mandy returned the smile. "Actually, it's my mom's."

Of the four girls, all officers on the drill team, Mandy was salvageable, Robin thought. When the girl wasn't around Eloise, she could be sweet.

"Lucky you, to get to drive it," Robin added, thinking of the older, much less desirable model she drove. Her dad worked for a car dealership but he certainly hadn't bought her a new car. And her mother couldn't have, even if she'd wanted to. Robin suspected her mom was just managing to squeak by.

"My parents are getting me a BMW," Eloise chimed in.

"That's nice," Robin forced herself to say in an even tone, though she dared not look at Beverly for fear they would burst out laughing. Eloise just had to be one up on everyone. She was truly a pain in the butt, though sometimes Robin actually felt sorry for her, because she always had to be the center of attention. What a heavy burden to bear.

"Hey, look who just drove up," said Jodie Tipton, the last of the four to speak.

All eyes darted to the street and watched as a truck pulled into the drive.

"That's my brother, Cody," Beverly said. "And it looks like he's got Chad with him."

Robin's heart skipped a beat at the mention of Chad Burnette. It beat even faster when the senior star quarterback climbed out of the truck.

To die for.

That description fit him to a tee. He was big and brawny, with longish dark-blond hair and green eyes. Even though he was cocky and self-assured and knew without a doubt that he was good-looking, Robin didn't care.

He didn't know that she was alive on planet Earth, though, which she *did* care about. She'd had a mad crush on him since the first time she saw him. Although they had been introduced at a party last year, she couldn't recall his having spoken to her since.

Following Beverly's haphazard attempt at introducing her brother to everyone, Eloise asked, "Hey, Chad, how's it going?"

Robin knew the two of them had been an item for several months. Then, rumors had it, Chad had dumped Eloise, but, Eloise, though furious, hadn't stopped caring about him.

"It's going," Chad drawled, his eyes seemingly scoping out each of the girls.

When Robin felt his gaze settle on her, she swallowed hard.

"Do I know you?" he asked.

"Chad, honey," Eloise blatantly interrupted, "how 'bout letting Cody drop you off by my house when you leave here?"

His eyes never left Robin's face, though his words were obviously meant for Eloise. "Not interested."

Robin flinched at his rudeness, while Eloise sucked in her breath loud enough for everyone to hear. Then everyone else seemed to start talking at once.

But Robin couldn't have spoken if her life had been in jeopardy, for Chad had walked over to her and was now staring down into her eyes.

"Have we ever met?" he asked.

Robin licked her dry lips. "Actually, yes."

"I must've had a brain fart, 'cause I sure don't remember."

"Hell, Burnette," Cody chimed in, "you don't even have a brain."

"Cut the crap," Chad said, still not taking his eyes off Robin.

"Yeah, big brother," Beverly said in a firm but good-natured tone. "Butt out."

"So, Robin," Chad said, speaking for her ears alone, "you going with anyone?"

Robin swabbed at her lips again. "Uh, no."

"Can I call you?"

"That would be great," Robin replied in a breathy voice, her insides going haywire.

"Hey, Chad, let's go."

He flicked Robin on the chin and winked. "Later, then."

It was after Chad had turned and walked off that she caught the full force of Eloise's vindictive glare. A chill darted through her.

How did he always manage to wade in the deep stuff?

Dillon had asked himself that question several times already and still had no answer. Before long he was going to need hip boots.

First, he'd discovered he was going to have to be much more patient when it came to finding out who'd broken into the lab. He'd made his list, all right, and even done some snooping. So far, though, he'd come up empty-handed.

Then he'd come face to face with Janey Mayfield, who had treated him as if he had a communicable disease. Her attitude shouldn't have rankled, but it did. Just who the hell did she think she was? She had no right to pass judgment on him, though it was obvious she didn't see it that way.

What a damn awkward moment. When he'd realized who owned the candy shop, he'd wanted to turn around and get the hell out. That absurd reaction, however, had lasted only a moment, his good breeding and common sense coming to his rescue.

Though it had been years since he'd last seen her, she appeared much the same—in looks, anyway. While never beautiful, she had always been attractive—and still was, though she appeared more on the thin side than he remembered. However, her curves were in the right places. He'd noticed that, much to his chagrin.

Of course her hairstyle had changed. She now wore her reddish-brown hair shorter and tousled, giving her a softer, sexier look. But the real change was in her clear brown eyes. They reflected a guarded intensity that hadn't been there before. But then, he couldn't blame her for that.

What he could blame her for was her attitude toward him, and for refueling his own painful memories.

Now he was sitting in a restaurant with another woman, having dinner, when he would rather be at home. Alone.

"Dillon."

The sound of Patricia's irritated voice brought him back to the moment with a start. "Mmm?"

"What's the matter with you?" she demanded. "You've hardly said a dozen words since we got here, and we've finished our meal."

She was right, he admitted silently. His mind and heart weren't in the evening. Crossing paths with Janey yesterday had definitely soured his mood, which was ludicrous, but a fact nonetheless.

"Sorry," he said lamely, feeling more like a heel than ever.

"I don't think so," she responded bluntly.

"I really am sorry if I'm ruining your birthday. It's just that I've got a lot of things on my mind."

She frowned. "Obviously I'm not one of those 'things.'"

He shifted uncomfortably. "Look, Pat—"

She held up her hand. "I know we're just friends. You've made that plain from the beginning, but—" This time she stopped her own flow of words with a shrug. "And I'm okay with that—for right now," she added hurriedly, giving him a teasing smile. "But I'm not giving up, so be warned."

His gut instinct told him to douse that hope with the brutal truth, but he refrained. After all, this was her birthday, and he couldn't bring himself to totally destroy the evening.

He hoped he wouldn't regret his actions later. As he'd told Allie, Patricia was a friend and nothing else. He cared about her, but he felt no chemistry, sexual or otherwise, which he deemed necessary in any relationship.

That was unfortunate, too, since Pat was a woman who had a lot going for her. She was several years younger than he, divorced, with no children. She was attractive, too, with short black hair and dark eyes. And she owned her own business, a successful beauty salon. He sensed she would marry him in a minute. For that reason, he decided it wouldn't be wise to take her out after tonight.

"Hey, I'm still here, remember?"

He gave her a sheepish grin. "I know. All I can do is apologize again."

"How about ordering coffee, instead?"

That was when Dillon realized the waiter was hovering over his shoulder. "Works for me," he quipped, then did just that.

After the waiter had disappeared, his eyes accidentally wandered toward the door of the restaurant. Suddenly he sucked in his breath and held it.

''What's wrong?'' Pat asked, a frown marring her features.

He cleared his throat. ''Nothing.'' *Liar,* he told himself, watching Janey Mayfield and her daughter thread their way between tables, heading in their direction.

Great, he thought with disgust. Just great.

Four

Janey couldn't have ignored him even if she'd wanted to. Despite the fact that he was seated at a table in the far corner of the room, Dillon's muscular body seemed to stand out.

He had on slacks and a sports coat, a far cry from the cowboy look of the other day. Whatever he wore, his strong features were an attention grabber. Not that she was attracted to him or anything like that, except in a purely objective way, she assured herself quickly.

Still, she was irritated that she'd even given him more than a cursory glance. Lowering her eyes, Janey crossed her fingers that the hostess wouldn't place her and Robin anywhere near Dillon and his date.

She wished now that she and Robin had gone somewhere else to dine, to celebrate her lucrative day at Sweet Dreams. She had sold more candy today than any day since she'd taken over.

Robin had told her that called for a celebration. Ignoring the fact that she was dead on her feet, Janey had agreed. Now, however, she was regretting Robin's choice of restaurant, although this one was the most upscale in Hunter—the place to be seen, Robin had said with a grin.

They had barely been seated and ordered their drinks when Robin said in an excited voice, "Mom, did you see who's here?"

"Lots of people," she responded with wide-eyed innocence.

Robin's mouth curved downward. "Oh, Mom, I know you saw him. It's Dillon."

"Mr. Reed to you, my dear," Janey said sternly.

"Well, it used to be just Dillon." Robin's tone was a bit petulant.

"That was a long time ago. Now he's your principal, which sets new ground rules."

"I know."

"Smile when you say that."

"Who would ever have thought he'd be my principal? It's awesome." Robin's eyes twinkled. "*He's* awesome, actually."

Janey barely curbed her impatience with the turn this conversation had taken. "Oh, really?"

"So cool, too. All the kids like him lots."

"I'm glad."

"You don't sound like it."

"That's not true."

"You should see your face, Mom. When I mention him, you look like you've just bitten into something sour."

Clearly flustered by her daughter's astuteness, Janey cleared her throat and peered at the menu. "You're imagining things."

"I don't think so. After all, he and Elaine used to be your and Dad's best friends. Why don't you like him anymore?"

Janey tempered a sigh before she raised her eyes back to Robin. "I like him just fine, okay?"

"Whatever you say." Robin grabbed her cola, which the waiter had just set down, and took a sip. "But I still don't get it," she added.

"You don't have to get it, okay?" Janey's tone was testy, but she couldn't help it. Enough was enough. She was glad that Robin was happy at school—delighted, in fact—but that didn't mean she wanted her evening inundated with Dillon's praises.

To Janey's relief, her daughter's eyes dropped to the menu.

"Good evening, ladies."

Janey groaned inwardly. His deep voice and his up-close-and-personal nearness could no longer be avoided. At least he hadn't brought his woman friend with him. Janey forced herself to look up and say in a pleasant tone, "Hello, Dillon."

His gaze settled on her a tad longer before switching to Robin. "So how's it going?"

"Uh, great."

Dillon smiled warmly at Robin. "I'm glad. I hope you two enjoy your dinner."

"We plan on it," Robin said, giving him a huge smile in return.

His gaze included both of them briefly before he turned and walked back to his table.

"That's the first time he's actually spoken to me since we've been back," Robin said, her voice filled with amazement.

"Unfortunately, the good students like you get lost in the shuffle. While that's too bad, it's the truth."

Robin glanced at Dillon. "I know. You can bet he knows the jerks on campus." She paused. "I wonder if he's in love with that woman."

"I haven't the foggiest idea, nor do I care."

"I still don't know why you don't like him any-more. Did he do something to piss you off?"

"Robin, don't push it."

"Yes, ma'am."

Janey cleared her throat and smiled at the waiter, who had reappeared to take their orders. Once he was gone, she turned that smile on Robin, thinking again what a smart and lovely young woman she was and how proud she was of her—although at times she could certainly try a mother's patience. This evening was one of those times. Janey knew she'd made a mountain out of a molehill when it came to Dillon. In her own defense, she had been caught off guard, first by his appearance, then by Robin's enthusiastic response to him.

But she shouldn't have been surprised. After all, Robin was right: they had been neighbors and friends for years before she and Keith had broken up and she and Robin had moved away. And Robin didn't have a clue....

"Mom."

"What, darling?"

"Are you all right?"

Janey gave her a bright and reassuring smile. "Of course. How could I not be? I had a great day at the shop, and I'm having dinner with my most favorite person in the whole world."

"You don't miss Dad at all, do you?"

Janey clamped down on another sigh. "No, I don't. I have to be honest."

"That's too bad, because I do."

"I know, darling, and I'm sorry, for your sake."

And she was, though she had to admit that Robin's strong tie to Keith was a nagging worry. While she realized she had no choice but to share her daughter with her ex-husband, she wasn't thrilled about it.

The two men she least wanted to discuss or have anything to do with—Dillon and Keith—seemed suddenly to have become the dominant topics of conversation.

"Speaking of Dad, he wants me to spend next weekend with him."

Janey's chest tightened. "But, darling, that's the first home game. I thought we could celebrate together."

"But what about Dad?" Robin asked, a stubborn look on her face. "He feels the same way you do."

Janey tried to hide her hurt. "If that's what you want to do."

"I just wish I wasn't pulled between the two of you all the time."

Janey's heart wrenched. "I know, and I'm sorry about that, too. But that's the way it is."

Their food chose that moment to arrive, for which Janey was grateful. She wished things could be different, but they weren't. Sooner or later, Robin was going to have to accept that, as painful as it was.

They ate in silence for a moment, then Robin looked at her with another grin on her lips. Relieved, Janey answered with one of her own. "So what's up?"

Robin giggled. "What makes you think there's anything up?"

"I know you, especially when you get that certain look on your face."

"I met someone—or, at least, I saw him again."

"Ah, a him."

"Come on, Mom, give me a break."

Janey forced a straight face. "Sorry, I'll be good."

"His name is Chad Burnette. And talk about a side of beef..."

"Robin!"

"Well, that's what he is. He's to die for, and he paid attention to me."

"Tell me something about him."

"I met him at Beverly's. He's a friend of her older brother. And he's our team quarterback."

"My, my, that is a coup."

Robin squirmed in her chair. "Oh, my gosh, Mom, you have no idea how many girls would give one of their boobs to date him."

"I doubt that," Janey said, trying to hide her dismay at her daughter's choice of words. Would her own child never cease to amaze her? Or shock her?

"I'm assuming he hasn't called yet?"

"No." Robin's face lost some of its animation. "But I'm praying he will."

Janey smiled, reached over and squeezed Robin's hand. "Stop fretting. He'll call. After all, you're drop-dead gorgeous. How could he not go for you?"

"You're just biased."

"Who, me?"

They both laughed, then went back to eating. After finishing a bite, Robin said, "Look, Mom, Mr. Reed and his squeeze are leaving."

Janey forced herself not to react, though her gaze did unwittingly drift in that direction. For a split second her eyes and Dillon's met and held. Dillon's appraisal of her seemed deliberate, she thought. What was he trying to prove?

Then he nodded, breaking the link. She flushed before turning away.

"I can't wait to tell Bev I saw Mr. Reed." Robin made a face. "I hate calling him that. It sounds too funky."

"Funky or not, start loving it," Janey snapped, then returned her attention to her meal.

Her mouth slid over his penis.

Keith Mayfield groaned as he grabbed a handful of her dark hair, urging her up and onto her back. Once there, he used his fingers to spread her legs, then shoved his dick hard and high into her.

She gasped, digging her fingers into his buttocks.

While looking down at her, he thrust and kept thrusting until her moans coincided with his. He buried his head in the fullness of her man-made breasts and let go of several deep breaths.

Once their breathing had evened out, he rolled over onto his back and stared at the ceiling.

"Have I ever told you you're the best?"

"Every time we fuck," Keith responded in an impatient tone.

She chuckled, apparently taking no offense. "And that's a lot."

"That it is."

Keith crooked his elbow then and braced his head on his hand. Sabrina Goodness was already staring at him when he peered down at her.

She was pretty, even though she was a little too much on the chunky side to suit him. He preferred his women thin, like Janey. Why had he thought about her, especially now?

Hell, who was he kidding? She was all he'd thought about since he had found out she'd returned to Hunter, though he hadn't seen her yet.

"What are you thinking about?" Sabrina asked, running a long red fingernail around his nipple.

"You don't want to know."

"Of course I do," she said, leaning over and tonguing that same nipple.

His response was instant. Dipping her eyes to his erection, she laughed, then surrounded it with her hand.

For several moments their grunts of satisfaction were the only sounds in the room.

Afterward, Keith got up and walked across to the window, where the blinds were open. He stared out into the inky blackness, but he couldn't see a thing, not even a star.

"I know something's bothering you, so you might as well get it off your chest."

He swung around and faced Sabrina. The lamp burning in the corner of the room allowed him to see that her attractive features were marred by a frown.

"I don't think it's a good idea for you to move in with me."

"Why?" she demanded bluntly.

"Robin, for one."

"She's grown, Keith. She'll understand."

"No, she won't, nor will her mother."

"Ah, now we're getting to the crux of the matter."

He jammed his jaws together, not liking her sarcastic tone one iota. "What's that supposed to mean?"

He knew, of course, but he was stalling for time before saying what he'd needed to say for a long time but simply hadn't had the guts to. He still wanted to ball Sabrina, but he wasn't interested in her continuing to monopolize all his time. He was ready to spread his joy around.

"You know what it means," she snapped. "Your daughter's becoming more important than me." She paused. "I thought we were in love."

"Don't make me choose between you and Robin."

Tears welled up in her eyes. "You can be a first-class bastard when you want to."

He merely shrugged.

"What brought this change about? You haven't always been so high on your bratty daughter."

His eyes narrowed. "I suggest you watch your mouth."

"Or what?"

"Or I'll boot your ass out of my life so fast it'll make your head spin."

Sabrina scrambled off the bed and glared at him. "It looks like you're already doing that."

He shrugged again.

"This sudden interest in your daughter doesn't by chance have anything to do with your ex being back in town?"

"That's none of your business."

"Oh?" She laughed a hysterical laugh, then fumbled to put on her clothes and stormed out.

Five

Somehow she had survived the past week, as well as the weekend.

It wasn't the candy shop that had her in a snit but the fact that Robin had indeed spent the weekend with her dad.

But in truth, it hadn't been quite the traumatic ordeal she had expected. Perhaps it was because the drill team had performed on Friday evening and Robin had been perfect, or at least Janey had thought so. She had sat with several other mothers whose husbands weren't available for various reasons.

Still, Janey had been relieved when Robin had walked into the house last night. Thank goodness Janey hadn't had to see her ex-husband. In fact, she hadn't seen him since she'd returned to Hunter, which was more than fine with her. That wasn't the case, however, with her daughter.

"Dad asked about you," Robin had said the second she dropped her satchel on the sofa.

Janey had kept her voice even. "That's nice."

Robin pursed her lips. "You don't intend to cut him any slack, do you?"

"Robin, please, this is not the time to discuss your dad and me."

"Just when *is* the time, then?" Robin asked. "You never want to talk about him."

"That's right, I don't."

"I just don't understand why you ever split up. I thought you were happy."

"We were, in a lot of ways, but..." Janey's voice played out but her determination did not. "Sweetheart, we've already been over this subject and nothing has changed. Sometimes things just happen and two people stop loving each other."

"I think Dad still loves you."

"Trust me, he doesn't," Janey said, unable to contain the bitterness. Then, changing the subject, she added, "By the way, you were the best Friday night. You didn't miss a beat." She smiled, then walked over and hugged her daughter. "I was so proud of you."

As if Robin realized the subject of her mom and dad was closed, she pulled back and smiled. "You really think I did good? And looked good?"

"Absolutely, to both. In fact, I wanted to stand up and yell to everyone that you were my daughter."

Robin groaned. "Thank heavens you contained yourself."

Janey's lips twitched. "And your friend Chad was good, too."

"Man, was he ever. He's the reason we won the game."

"Actually, all of you did your part to bring about the win."

"Even Mr. Reed was pepped up. He came onto the field as excited as I've ever seen him." Robin's face and voice suddenly turned anxious. "Darn it, I just wish Chad would call me."

"He will, darling. You'll see."

Robin grabbed her stuff and headed for her bedroom. "He'd better, that's all I can say. 'Night, Mom."

"Aren't you forgetting something?" Janey placed a finger against her cheek.

"Sorry." Robin crossed back to Janey and kissed her where the finger had been. "See you in the morning." She paused. "Oh, by the way, Dad wants to take me to dinner one night this week."

Now, as Janey flipped the shop sign to Open, her thoughts remained on Robin and Keith. She was beginning to question her good judgment in returning to Hunter.

The thought of her daughter spending too much time with Keith made her crazy. It wasn't that Keith had been a bad parent to Robin, because he hadn't. He had simply been a bad husband, which had left Janey embittered. She would admit *that*. And, she was jealous of Robin and Keith's relationship. She would also admit *that*.

If Keith had wanted to continue to be with his daughter, then he shouldn't have broken up the marriage.

The buzzer sounded as the door opened. Relieved that she was rescued from her thoughts, Janey smiled and said, "Good morning, Penny."

Penny Giles didn't return her smile or her greeting. Uh-oh, Janey thought as the rail-thin woman walked up to the counter and plopped down a sack. "I'm returning this candy."

"Why is that?"

"It wasn't the right kind."

"I have no problem taking it back, as long as you didn't open it."

Penny gave her an incredulous look, then snapped, "Of course I opened it. I ate a bite, too. That's how I knew I'd bought the wrong kind and that I didn't like it."

Janey didn't know whether to laugh or cry. Dealing with the public could be a nightmare. But, on the other hand, it could also be a hoot. She never knew what a day would bring. However, a few customers like this one made her want to put a permanent Closed sign on the door.

"Penny, you know I can't return your money under those circumstances." Janey's tone was firm but gentle.

Penny's lips tightened. "Well, I don't see why not. You're supposed to stand behind your product."

"And I do. If the candy itself was bad, then there wouldn't be any question, but—"

"Forget it!" Penny grabbed her sack and headed for the door.

Just as she flounced out, another lady walked in.

"Oh, boy, this is going to be one of those days," Janey muttered.

Hazel Bishop, her part-time helper, gave Janey a perplexed look. "What was that all about?"

"I'll tell you, but you won't believe it."

"When it comes to the public, honey, I'll believe anything. I've worked in retail longer than I care to admit."

It was that expertise that had landed Hazel the job in the shop. Besides that, she was a neat lady. Though gray haired and round as a silver dollar, she never seemed to run out of energy. She was a widow in her early sixties who needed a little extra cash to supplement her income. When she'd applied, Janey had known instantly that she was the right one.

Janey hadn't been wrong.

"So tell me," Hazel said into the silence. "I can't wait to hear."

When Janey explained what had happened, Hazel merely shook her head. "This world has more nuts in it than this candy shop."

Janey laughed out loud. "I doubt that particular nut will ever come back."

"Ah, forget her. The likes of her are not worth worrying about. Besides, we have too much work to do."

And work they did. While Janey ran the front, Hazel unpacked several cartons of candy in the back room, then filed the invoices.

The day passed without further incidents. However, Janey couldn't say that it had been a lucrative one. Business was slow all the way to closing time.

After sending Hazel home, she was about to lock up when another car drove up. It was her old friend Gwen Hopson.

"Get in here, lady," Janey said, giving her an enthusiastic hug.

It seemed as if she'd always known Gwen, although they hadn't spent much time together since her return. She couldn't have made it through her divorce without the woman. Divorced herself, Gwen had managed to cross that minefield with surprisingly few wounds. But then, she hadn't had children.

Gwen was short and thin with dark hair. And while she wasn't pretty in the conventional sense, she had an infectious personality and grin. She was a social worker for the local hospital, a job to which she was perfectly suited.

"I'm not even going to come in," Gwen said, standing just outside the door.

"Pray tell, why not?"

"I want to avoid temptation, but I heard something at work today I thought you ought to know about."

Janey frowned. "Bad news?"

"Well, it could be—let me put it that way."

"Shoot," Janey said.

"Word has it that a candy store's opening in the mall."

"Oh, no," Janey cried, feeling her spirits take a nosedive.

"Now, don't push the panic button yet," Gwen advised. "You know how rumors are."

"Don't I ever," Janey said bitterly.

"Hey, don't let it get you down. If it happens, just consider it another bump in the road that you have to get past."

"But I'm getting awfully tired of those bumps, my friend."

Gwen gave her a hug, then said, "I know. Look, I gotta run now. I'll call you."

Thirty minutes later, Janey was upstairs in her bathtub, surrounded by lavender-scented bubbles. But she couldn't relax, despite the tranquil atmosphere. Her insides were wound tighter than a spool of wire.

What next?

Since she had moved back, her life had been anything but easy. If Gwen's news turned out to be fact rather than rumor, then she was in trouble. As it was, Sweet Dreams was barely turning a profit. If it hadn't been for Robin's child support, she would be dipping into her sparse savings. And if business didn't pick up, she would soon have to do that, anyway, because Robin's child support would stop when she turned eighteen.

Still, Janey was determined to count her blessings and not her disasters. Robin was well-adjusted in school, making good grades and having a ball to boot. As long as that was the case, Janey could continue to tread her troubled waters and survive.

Thinking of Robin and school suddenly brought Dillon Reed back to mind. While idly scooping a handful of bubbles, Janey admitted to herself that his lean, hard body as he'd strolled into the shop that day had caught her attention.

And seeing him again at the restaurant had apparently kept it, she realized now, recalling how he'd looked and smelled. Suddenly Janey fought the urge to sink her head under the water to cleanse her mind of such craziness.

Thinking about Dillon Reed in those terms could turn into a real problem—a problem she didn't need.

"Okay, what do you think?"

Janey angled her head. "Mmm, let's see."

"Mom! You're supposed to tell me I look smashing."

"Okay, you look smashing."

"But you're supposed to mean it."

The teasing glint in Janey's eyes increased. "Oh, honey, you look better than smashing. You look breathtaking."

Robin blew out a breath. "I just hope Chad thinks so."

"Don't be so hard on yourself. This is just a date to get a cola, a date that I should have said no to. Even now, I can't believe I didn't."

"That's because you're a good mom."

"Flattery will get you nowhere," Janey said with mock severity.

As a rule, Robin never went out on school nights unless it was to a school function. But when Chad had asked her out yesterday for tonight and Robin had begged to go, Janey had caved in.

"So mind you, young lady, this is an exception. Don't let midweek dates become habit-forming. School before play."

"Speaking of school, have you heard?"

"Heard what?"

"About the break-in. Two guys practically destroyed the chemistry lab the other week."

"Oh, dear, I hadn't heard. Do you think they were on drugs?"

Robin lifted her shoulders. "Who knows? But I'm here to tell you that Dil—uh, Mr. Reed was hopping mad."

"I'm sure he was."

Robin faced the mirror again and fiddled with a piece of hair. "And since then, he and the assistant principal have been stalking the halls."

Janey sighed. "It's getting to where I'm afraid to even let you go to school."

Robin rolled her eyes, her trademark gesture when things weren't to her liking.

Just then, the doorbell chimed. Robin's hand flew to her heart. "Oh, my God, he's here. Are you sure I look all right?"

Janey hid a smile, then shook her head. "Calm down or you're going to hyperventilate."

"I'm calm. I'm calm."

The instant Janey opened the door and Chad Burnette walked through it, something about the young man put Janey on the defensive.

As Robin had said, he was good-looking—model material, endowed with a body made to play any sport. And he was polite, too, extending his hand to Janey immediately and saying that he was pleased to meet her.

Still, there was something about him that didn't sit well with Janey. Maybe it was the look he gave her daughter, followed by the arm he slung around her shoulders. Both actions appeared territorial, as if he were staking a claim.

Janey strove to override those feelings, but she couldn't. She could always count on her gut instincts; so far they hadn't failed her. At the moment, they were screaming at her. She considered telling Robin she couldn't go. But she couldn't embarrass her daughter that way, even if Robin would forgive her—which she wouldn't.

She would just have to tough it out and pray that this one time her instincts were wrong.

"You kids have fun," she said, trying to hide her anxiousness. "But be careful."

Robin took her adoring eyes off Chad and faced Janey. "We will, Mom."

"Be home by nine o'clock and not a minute later," Janey added.

"Don't worry, Mrs. Mayfield. I'll have her back."

Chad's words should have reassured her, but they didn't.

Six

Dillon patted his mare on the neck. "Come on, girl, let's head back to the barn."

He'd been working with Dandi all Saturday morning, something he did most every weekend and on the rare afternoons when he could sneak away from his office a little early.

On this particular morning, he was really enjoying his outing. Since the unsolved break-in at the school and other teacher problems heaped on top of that, he'd been tense. Now he felt some of the stress ease out of his body, leaving him relaxed.

Dismounting at the barn a few minutes later, Dillon shoved his hat back, wiped his brow, then lifted his head heavenward. He was ready for fall. Here it was the beginning of September, but so far no cool weather or rain. Both were needed, but as far as the eye could see, there were no clouds.

Soon, though, summer would ease into fall, and the huge oaks, maples, and sundry other trees would flaunt their foliage like bright pieces of ribbon flowing gracefully in the wind. A sight to behold.

And, cooler weather went hand in hand with football, his favorite sport. The home game last weekend had gone off without a hitch. In fact, he couldn't have asked for it to have gone smoother. On the whole, the kids had been well behaved. Only a few minor incidents had cropped up, which his assistant had taken care of. Not only had the football team done exceptionally well, but so had the cheerleaders, band and drill team.

Thinking about the drill team brought Janey Mayfield suddenly to mind.

He frowned, wondering why thoughts of her continued to sneak up and bite him on the butt. Although it disturbed him to have to acknowledge it, he'd actually thought a lot about her since their last encounter.

He'd seen her at the football game, too, though he'd made sure she hadn't seen him. He'd told himself to look away and forget her. Instead, he'd found himself watching her every move; her slender hands as they had clapped in an exciting moment, the vulnerability of her exposed throat when she'd swallowed, and that hint of sadness in her eyes.

It was the sadness that had remained with him. Perhaps it would never leave her. After all, no one could come through such a horrible ordeal unscathed.

He certainly hadn't, so he couldn't very well pass judgment. But that was exactly what he'd been doing. Hell, at one time he'd been bitter, too. But the difference in them was that he'd put the past behind him and gone on. He suspected she hadn't.

In some ways it had probably been easier for him. He hadn't had a child to consider. Thinking of Robin made him smile. As a young adult, she was already lovely. When she really matured, watch out. She would be a knockout.

In her own way, so was Janey. Robin seemed to have some of her dad's personality, though.

Thinking of Keith Mayfield darkened his mood again. Despite the fact that they had been friends, he'd never felt comfortable with Keith, probably because the man had a controlling nature and drank far too much. Even before the divorce, Dillon had often wondered why Janey stayed with Keith. Robin, of course.

Suddenly he shook his head to clear it. What the hell had gotten into him? Janey Mayfield and her daughter were the last people he wanted to occupy his mind.

But as long as Robin was a student in his school, he was bound to come into contact with Janey. Most likely she would become involved in her daughter's activities, especially the drill team. Eventually all moms did their part, even the working ones.

So she'd better get off her high horse and treat him as if he belonged to the human race. Just the thought of the small-town rumor mill having any more grist sent a chill through him—though that wasn't likely to happen. He and Janey were old news. Still, he wasn't about to take a chance. He abhorred the idea of anyone talking about him in the past or present, except when it pertained to his job.

His personal life was off-limits.

Ah, to hell with it. What did it matter what Janey thought about him? It didn't, not really. Besides, there wasn't one thing he could do about it. He wasn't about to avoid her.

If she had a problem with him, that was her concern, not his. It would all come out in the wash, anyway, as his granny used to tell him. And it usually did.

With that uppermost in his mind, Dillon concentrated on brushing down his mare, then feeding her. He was striding outside when he looked up and saw his foreman and brother-in-law, Mike Townsend.

"How's it going?" Mike asked in his lazy drawl.

"I just finished giving Dandi a workout."

Mike was tall and wiry, with ruddy cheeks and what looked like a beer belly, though he didn't drink. Instead he fattened up on Allie's cooking.

"I just finished taking care of the creek in the upper pasture," Mike said, wiping sweat off his brow with the back of one hand.

"What was wrong?"

"Debris and leaves had the flow blocked." Mike led his horse to the drinking trough.

Dillon noticed immediately that Mike seemed to be dragging his leg more than usual. Thanks to the injury he'd gotten while on the oil rig, Mike now walked with a strong limp. However, that didn't usually slow him down. He was always on the move, looking for new projects to keep the farm in tiptop shape. Dillon prized his work and couldn't have maintained the place without Mike.

Another plus was that Mike loved the outdoors, and so did Allie. With someone living on the property, Dillon never had to worry about anything, especially his horses.

Mike faced him again. "Anything in particular you want me to do? I have several things going, but nothing I can't put on the back burner if need be."

"Not right offhand," Dillon said. "It looks like you're pretty well caught up."

"How did Dandi do today?"

"Fairly well, though she seemed to be moving slower than usual, now that I think about it."

"I sorta noticed that, too. I'll check her over."

"For sure," Dillon said, trying not to push the alarm button. Nothing could happen to Dandi. She was the one he was counting on to jump-start his business.

"Are you coming to the house for lunch?"

"Speaking of lunch, how's your better half? Last time I saw her, she was feeling a bit under the weather."

Mike rubbed his slightly grizzled chin. "Still is, as a matter of fact."

"Has she been to the doctor?" Dillon asked.

Mike snorted. "You know better than that. She'd have to be dying before she'd take off from work and tend to herself."

"She might not have any choice," Dillon said sharply.

"Well, you try and tell her. She's not happy if she's not burning the candle at both ends."

Dillon slapped Mike on the back. "I'll see what I can do."

"Good luck."

"Thanks for the lunch invite," Dillon added, "but I had a late breakfast. Anyway, I'm headed back to town. I'll see y'all after a while."

Later Dillon couldn't say what wild hair had made him head to the candy shop instead of home. He wanted to think his motive was nothing more than to purchase a box of candy for his sister in hopes of making her feel better. However, he couldn't be sure why he'd done something so out of character for him. Maybe it was to clear the air between Janey and him, using Robin as an excuse.

When he opened the shop door, disappointment socked him in the gut. Someone else, an older woman, was behind the counter. But then Janey walked out of the back room. She saw him and pulled up short.

"Hello," he said, then cursed silently because his voice sounded unnatural, even to him.

She looked as good or better than he'd ever seen her, dressed in a pair of print leggings that called attention to her slender legs, and a long pink summer sweater that left no doubt as to the swell of her breasts.

He swallowed hard as he jerked his eyes off that part of her anatomy before he got caught. When he was drawn back to her, he concentrated on her red hair, pulled back in a ponytail with some loose tendrils at the neck.

She looked young enough to be Robin's sister instead of her mother.

"Hi," she finally said, clearly as uncomfortable with him now as she had been before.

The elderly lady's eyes were pinging back and forth between them as if she could feel the heightened tension in the room. Janey was the first to break the awkward silence by introducing her helper. Because Hazel was behind the counter, Dillon didn't extend his hand. Instead, he nodded and smiled.

"What can I get for you today?" Janey asked pointedly.

Though her tone irritated him, he kept his cool. "I'd like something new and different for Allie. She's not feeling so hot."

A slight frown marred Janey's forehead. "I'm sorry."

Is that the best you can do? Dillon wanted to ask. *Especially when it comes to someone you used to consider a friend?* But he didn't. He kept his mouth shut.

"I think we can help you with that," Janey responded in an even tone, though she refused to meet his eye.

That riled him even more. "Whatever you suggest will be fine with me."

Once the purchase was made, Dillon knew he should have turned and walked out, but he didn't. Instead he said, "How 'bout going for a cup of coffee?"

Janey looked startled. "With you?"

He cocked his head and gave her a sardonic smile. "Yeah, with me."

She flushed, then looked quickly over at Hazel, who said, "It's fine with me, honey. I'll watch the store. You take all the time you want."

No doubt Janey was at a loss. The warring expressions on her face told him that. But he wasn't about to back down now. He'd already opened his mouth and inserted his foot. He would have to take whatever came next, then choke on it, if need be.

"I won't be gone long," Janey said to Hazel, her tone tense, as if she were barely hanging on to her temper.

Thank goodness they didn't have to go far, Dillon thought. There was a place that sold doughnuts and coffee a couple of streets over. During the drive there, neither said a word. Had he lost his mind or what?

It was the "or what" that worried him the most.

Once they were inside and the coffee was served, Dillon's lips stretched into a smile.

"What's so damn funny?" Janey snapped.

"Your expression," he responded. "You're pissed."

"I wouldn't have used that word, but it works."

Dillon let out a deep sigh. "This is ridiculous, you know."

"What?"

"Don't put on the innocent act with me. You know what. Us scratching at each other like two cats tied in a sack."

"I hardly think that's the case."

An eyebrow shot up. "I disagree."

"What do you want from me, Dillon?"

"I wish the hell I knew," he muttered harshly. Once he'd said that, he realized he was telling the truth.

Neither had touched the coffee that was sitting in front of them. Dillon did pick his up, only to set it right back down.

"What I wish is that you'd take me back to the store."

That really made him mad. He leaned forward and said, "Not until I say one thing."

"All right, say it."

His lips twisted. "Don't you think it's time you got over the fact that *your* husband had an affair with *my* wife?"

Seven

Janey's first impulse was to slap his face. It was close enough that with little effort she could do just that. Instead, she curled her fingernails into her palms until she felt the self-inflicted pain.

"That was a hateful thing to say," she spat.

As if sensing he was in harm's way, Dillon eased back, his dark T-shirt tightening across his broad muscles.

"It's the truth."

"It is not the truth," Janey stressed tersely, fighting her anger. "And I don't give a damn how you feel." She would hate to make a spectacle of herself. But if he didn't stop taking unfair shots at her, she just might give him a taste of her fury.

Dillon leaned forward again and said in a low tone, "Hey, take it easy. I didn't mean to upset you."

Janey glared at him, feeling an ache in her throat. "Well, you did."

"It's just that every time I come near you, I feel like I'm getting jabbed with a knife. And I don't deserve that."

Janey averted her gaze from his delving blue eyes, sensing that his appraisal of her was deliberate. Was he out to intimidate her, or was he simply testing her?

Either way, she hardened her resolve, determined to regroup while trying to figure out how she'd gotten herself into this situation in the first place. She should have known better than to leave the shop with him, that it would do no good.

In her mind, Dillon's friendship and trust had died along with her marriage. Maybe that was irrational thinking, but that was how she felt. And so far he'd given her no valid reason to resurrect that friendship. Suddenly her thoughts jumped to her daughter, and she flinched inwardly.

He ran Robin's school. She couldn't avoid him indefinitely. Even if that was what she wanted, it wasn't realistic. So where did that leave them? She didn't know, and she didn't think he knew, either.

"Janey?"

His gruff-sounding voice drew her back. For a second, their eyes held, and her breathing increased.

His dark lashes hid his thoughts, but she couldn't suppress the shiver of apprehension that went through her. And annoyance, too, that he had the power to disturb her with those intense looks. Not sexually, she assured herself, but she couldn't deny that she was seeing Dillon in a new and different light.

Dillon coughed lightly. "Your coffee's getting cold."

"I don't care."

"Fine," he said, reaching for his cup and taking a healthy drink from it, though he never took his eyes off her face.

Janey felt herself flush. But she didn't turn away. She wasn't about to let him get the better of her. Maybe it would be a good thing if they did, indeed, clear the air between them. Then she could go on with her life and he could go on with his. And when she saw him again, it wouldn't be such an awkward event.

"You have to know how difficult this is for me," Janey finally said into what seemed a hostile silence.

Dillon blew out a breath. "It's not exactly a piece of cake for me."

"No, I'm sure it isn't." She paused. "For a while, I thought it might be a good idea for us to talk about the past, about what happened that awful afternoon. But I've changed my mind. I don't think it would be productive at all. I want to go back to the shop."

"No."

Janey gave him an indignant look. "No?"

"Of course I'll take you back if you really want to go," he said in an irritated tone, "but I'd rather we got some things off our chests."

"Like I just said, I don't think that's a good idea."

"God, I don't remember your being this stubborn."

"You didn't know me that well."

"Oh, I think I did. After all, our families spent just about every weekend together, plus a lot of time during the week."

"So what's your point?" she demanded, digging her teeth into her bottom lip. She didn't want to do this, so why was she letting him bully her this way?

"My point is that I get the idea you blame me for what happened."

Janey took a deep, shuddering breath, then stared at him. Did she somehow blame him? Was that the reason she felt so antagonistic toward him and uncomfortable around him? "Maybe I do."

"Why, for chrissake?"

"If you'd been a better husband to Elaine, paid more attention to her, then maybe she wouldn't have gone after Keith."

He laughed a mirthless laugh. "Surely you don't really think that?"

"You asked how I felt."

"I could say the same about you, that you should've been a better wife, then *he* wouldn't have wanted to stray."

"Damn you, I was a good wife! And you know that." She felt tears sting the back of her eyelids and turned away, horrified that he would see them.

"Look, I'm sorry."

She whipped her head back toward him. "That's not good enough."

"We both know that we could sit here and throw blame around until doomsday," he said in a softer and more conciliatory tone. "But what good would it do? We both have to move on."

"Have you?" she snapped. "Moved on, I mean?"

"Have I healed completely? No. And I probably never will, but I'm not letting what Elaine and Keith did sour the rest of my life. You can bet on that."

"I'm not, either."

"Then prove it by calling a truce with me, if only for old times' sake."

"I was thinking more about Robin's sake."

"Certainly that, too. Whatever works."

"We could just avoid each other, you know, like we've done for the past few years."

"Only because you left town," Dillon said bluntly.

Janey stared down at her now-cold coffee, then

back at him. "And I'm not sure it was a smart move to come back."

"Why did you?"

"Robin." She paused, then went on. "You knew we went to Colorado at my brother's insistence."

"Allie told me."

"Since our parents' deaths, I always turned to Drew when the going got tough. I was so sure that being near him was the answer. But Robin was never happy there, though Drew did everything in his power to make us both feel at home."

"What about you?" Dillon asked. "Were you happy?"

"Not at first, of course. Keith's betrayal was still too fresh, and I was miserable."

"I know that feeling," Dillon admitted grimly.

She picked up on the pain mixed with bitterness, and questioned his honesty. Had he moved on, or was he kidding himself? Was he still harboring the pain of the past, the same way she was? Fearful of getting involved, she refused to dwell on his feelings.

"However," she said in a rush, "I was able to use my marketing degree and get a really good job with a department store as their head buyer."

"That's great."

"It was, up to a point. But I wanted to spend more time with Robin than the job would allow, so I was torn."

"Still, you wouldn't have left."

"Probably not. Returning to Hunter wasn't easy."

"How did Robin persuade you?"

"She whined a lot."

Dillon chuckled, which seemed to cut the thickness in the air in half. She released a pent-up breath. Maybe she would survive this ordeal, after all.

"That's not exactly true," she continued. "Though Robin did pull several 'poor me' stunts. Really, I guess Aunt Lois was the key."

Dillon's eyebrows lifted. "Ah, I'm starting to get it. Lois owned Sweet Dreams."

"Right, but she wanted to retire. So one day, out of the blue, she called and asked if I wanted to take over the shop, said that it was mine. The catch was, I had to come back and run it." Recalling that conversation, Janey's lips eased into a smile. "Anyhow, Robin talked me into it, only I couldn't sell the house or walk away from my job responsibilities at that point."

"So you sent Robin on."

"I did, which was one of the hardest things I've ever done. But she missed her friends badly and wanted to try out for that blasted drill team, so she talked me into letting her come ahead and live with Aunt Lois." Janey paused, noticing that it had started to rain outside.

"Go on," Dillon prodded.

"Other than being away from her, everything else was working out. Then Lois had a stroke and had to go into an assisted living facility. I had no choice but to come back, which meant I had to take a loss on the house."

"That's too bad."

"I couldn't take a chance on Robin moving in with Keith."

"I can understand that," Dillon added in a harsh tone.

"Have you run into him?" she asked hesitantly.

"Nope."

"I guess that's a good thing."

Dillon shrugged. "At one time I would've decked the bastard, but now I wouldn't bother. He's not worth the effort."

"So far, he's left me alone," said Janey, "but I worry about his influence on Robin."

"Is he still drinking?"

"I'm sure he is, though Robin's careful not to mention it around me."

"At least Elaine and I didn't have any children to get caught up in this mess."

She picked up on that bitterness again and knew that even if he didn't realize it, he was still smarting. "Speaking of Elaine, how did you manage to hold yourself together?"

He regarded her from beneath lowered lids. "You do what you have to."

"Still, it must've been tough to continue living with her after she betrayed you."

"Under the circumstances, what choice did I have? When I found out about the cancer, I couldn't just desert her."

"I couldn't have, either," Janey said, her voice shaking. "If I'd stayed around, that is. At one time Elaine was my best friend."

"I know." His tone was bleak. "Anyway, she didn't suffer long. Her death six months later was a blessing."

"I still can't believe it all happened." Janey felt the back of her eyelids sting again.

As if he sensed she was close to tears, he lightened his tone and asked, "So, have you found someone else?"

"As in a man?"

His lips twitched. "Yep."

She gave a quick, derisive laugh. "Not just no, *hell* no."

"Ouch!"

"I've grown too independent. I'll never depend on a man again."

"Never's a long time."

"That's the way I feel." Janey tilted her head. "What about you?"

"I go out," he said. "But it's no big deal."

The wariness in his voice didn't escape her, but she wasn't about to let him off the hook. This was his party, and he damn sure was going to pay for it. "I thought there was about to be a ring on your finger."

His features darkened. "What makes you think that?"

"The woman you were with at the restaurant."

"What about her?"

"The way she looked at you, like she could eat you with a spoon."

His face lost its color, and he muttered an expletive. "She's just a friend."

"I think you'd better tell her that."

She was obviously rubbing salt in another open wound, and didn't know why. All she could figure was that this whole bizarre outing had gotten to her. Her nerves had had it.

"I have," he said emphatically. "She knows the score. Like you, I'm not particularly eager to get involved in another lasting relationship."

"Whatever."

He tightened his lips before staring at her for a

heartbeat. "It appears the two of us have more in common than we thought."

"Don't count on it."

He shrugged and smiled. "We'll see."

Resisting the urge to lash back with *No we won't,* Janey rose. "I really do have to go."

His eyes made a disturbing sweep of her slender figure, seeming to linger on her moist, parted lips as if fascinated by them.

"No problem," he finally said.

Long after they reached his vehicle, Janey's face was still on fire.

Eight

Just one healthy swig. What could it hurt? Keith asked himself, reaching for the bottle of bourbon. *Who* could it hurt? That was the important question. No one except himself, and he didn't give a damn.

Right now, he wasn't seeing Sabrina. After she'd more or less given him an ultimatum, then walked out in a huff, he hadn't even bothered to call her. But that was all right. The bitch had served her purpose, anyway. They had been together nearly three years. Following the split with Janey, she'd kept his bed warm. That was all he'd cared about.

Now Janey was back.

That thought suddenly panicked him, and he took a drink straight out of the bottle, but not before gazing out from the glass cubicle that was his office and making sure no one was watching.

He felt the liquor burn all the way to his gut. Yet it gave him a much-needed shot of adrenaline. He found he had to have that to begin his day, and to end it.

Selling cars sucked.

He couldn't quit, though. He made too much money at it. He couldn't afford to give it up. Not only were his tastes expensive, but he had Robin's child support to pay. And pay he had, until recently. Suddenly he had fallen behind.

He winced against the prick of his conscience. He'd made some bad investments, and they had come back to haunt him. Even so, he intended to make good on his financial commitment to his kid. He wasn't dead broke, just strapped for the moment.

Anyway, he didn't have much choice. Something told him he'd better adhere to the court orders, or Janey just might file charges.

He couldn't have that. Besides, he wanted to do right by Robin. That was important to him. He might have fucked his wife over, but he would never do anything to hurt his daughter.

Despite what Sabrina had said, he wasn't using Robin to get to Janey. He suddenly felt another prick to his conscience. Well, maybe that wasn't entirely true. But he did care about Robin. He hadn't realized how much until she'd returned from Colorado and they had had time alone, without Janey's mistrustful influence.

Maybe that was why he'd been having these crazy thoughts about getting his family back together again. Raising a teenager hadn't turned out to be nearly as scary as he'd imagined.

And he missed Janey.

Dammit, he hated to admit that, but he couldn't deny it any longer. Since she'd been back, he'd been by the store, had even parked across the street and watched her as she'd worked. Once she'd come out onto the porch to sweep it off, and he'd gotten a good look at her.

The sight of her had actually shocked him. She had lost so much weight, yet she looked great, especially her breasts. They were as voluptuous as ever.

Something he'd thought was dead—his attraction for her—had roared back to life. He'd been hard-pressed to remain in the vehicle. Yet he'd known better than to approach her, fearing she might clobber him with that broom.

Besides, he hadn't been ready, either. He had to be a hundred-percent sure Robin was on his side. She was the key that could reopen the door into Janey's heart.

Although Robin herself hadn't said outright that she would like them to be a family again, he sensed it. However, he was treading softly with her, as well, though he wasn't sure it was necessary.

So far, Robin hadn't stopped loving him.

Should he thank Janey for that, or was Robin enough of her own person to make that choice? He didn't know the answer to that question yet.

He wasn't even sure Robin knew the truth about why he and Janey had gotten divorced. But it didn't matter. If she hadn't found out by now, she probably never would. If she did, he would handle it. When necessary, he could turn up the old charm another notch.

He shouldn't have let Janey go so easily. More-over, he should never have gotten caught with Elaine in his arms. But he had, and he'd paid the price. He'd lost Janey and Robin.

And he was a damn poor loser.

The idea that Janey hadn't and wouldn't forgive him had festered all these years. He'd learned a hard lesson, though, and he was definitely smarter. When he got Janey back, he wouldn't make the same mistake again. If he dallied, he would make sure he didn't get caught. That way he would have his cake and eat it, too.

"Hey, Mayfield, whatcha doing in there?" A co-worker stuck his head around the door. "Playing with yourself?"

"Go to hell, Kendrick," Keith shot back at the big, burly man with a beard and mustache. "I can do what I please. I'm on my own time now."

"So you've clocked out?"

"Yeah, not that that's any of your business."

Kendrick held up both hands and backed out of the doorway. "Hey, man, don't be so touchy."

"Get lost," Keith muttered darkly.

Kendrick merely laughed. "I'll be glad when you get that bug out of your ass. You've been hard to live with this entire month."

Keith gave him another threatening look.

"I figure you're not gettin' any."

"Get the hell out of my face or be prepared to get yours smashed."

"All right already. I'm outta here."

Kendrick swaggered off, though not before Keith saw the strange look he threw him.

Thank God he hadn't seen the bottle, Keith told himself, or there would've been hell to pay. Or had he? The blood in Keith's veins suddenly ran cold. Was that what that look had been about?

Nah, he was just paranoid. Still, he couldn't let anyone get an inkling that he was drinking his break-fast and his dinner. The only meal he was eating was lunch.

So far, he'd managed to keep his drinking problem to himself. However, he was playing a dangerous game. Even though he was not on company time now, he was still on the premises. His boss wouldn't take kindly to his drinking on the job. He would get fired in a heartbeat, which would be another big and stupid mistake.

If he had to work, he couldn't beat selling cars. He was a natural at it, having sold two just today. If that pace kept up, he would be out of debt in no time.

To reward himself, he was about to get his little girl and take her out to dinner.

That reminder gave him the courage to walk away from the drawer that held the booze. Seconds later, he was in the bathroom, straightening his tie while scrutinizing himself in the mirror.

Not bad. At forty-five, he didn't have a speck of gray in his dark hair. He was tall enough, and despite his penchant for booze his stomach was only slightly pooched. He had no complaints about his eyes, either; the whites didn't look like a road map.

But the best thing he had going for him was his gift of gab. More often than not, he could talk his way into or out of anything. His features suddenly turned grim. He was going to need that gift and more to lure Janey back into his life.

But he had no doubt he would succeed—especially thirty minutes later, when he was sitting at a table at Chili's Restaurant facing a smiling Robin.

They had just placed their orders for two bacon cheeseburgers, curly fries and colas.

"So how was your day, sweetheart?" he asked, realizing again just how important it was for him to get Robin on his side. Without her, he knew his chances of getting Janey back were slim to none.

"Great, Dad."

"So you're not having any problems keeping your grades up?"

Some of the light went out of her eyes. "Well, Trig's starting to give me fits, but Chad's promised to help."

Keith's eyes widened. "Chad? That's a name I haven't heard before."

Robin's cheeks turned rosy. "He's the team quarterback."

"And?"

She giggled. "And I went out with him the other night."

"And he's about the coolest thing on two feet."

"How did you know?"

"Your old dad's been there before."

"I wish Mom saw it that way."

Keep your cool, he cautioned himself. "She has a problem with your friend?"

"We haven't really talked about him yet, but I don't think she likes him."

"Oh, I bet she does. She's just being her usual protective self."

"Maybe," Robin replied, her expression still on the glum side. "Chad doesn't think she likes him, either."

"How many times have you been out with him?"

"Once."

"Then give her a chance, okay?"

"Why are you taking up for Mom?"

He forced himself not to react. "For one thing, because she is your mother, and for another, I haven't had the pleasure of meeting the young man."

"Well, he's drop-dead gorgeous." Robin grinned. "And every friend I have is green with envy."

"That's my girl."

"Oh, Dad, I'm so glad I came back. I wouldn't be having nearly this much fun in Colorado."

"How's your mother adjusting?" he asked with what he hoped was casual concern.

Robin shrugged. "I'm not sure. The candy shop's doing okay, I guess. Mom tries to shield me, but I know she's had some problems."

"Problems go with owning your own business. But if I can help, I'm around."

"I just wish you lived with us," Robin whined.

"Me too, sweetheart."

His words appeared to stun her. "Really?"

"Yes, really."

"You mean you still love Mom?"

"And you, too."

"But what about Sabrina?"

He hadn't wanted Robin to know about the other women in his life, but in a weak moment he'd given in to Sabrina's demands and invited Robin to dinner. Only once. Consequently, he was taken aback that Robin still connected them.

"I haven't seen her in a long time," he lied.

"Good. I didn't care for her much."

"Me either."

She giggled again, then her pretty face sobered. "Oh, Dad, wouldn't it be wonderful if we could be a family again—you, me and Mom?" Tears welled up in her eyes.

God, he needed a drink, if for no other reason than to celebrate. His plan was coming together much faster and better than he could have imagined. He could barely contain his excitement. This was the first time his daughter had ever said anything like that to him.

Of course, he had the biggest hurdle yet to jump—Janey. But he was confident he could meet that challenge. Suddenly he felt like Superman. He could do anything—except take a drink.

"Dad, are you all right?"

"Of course," he said quickly, perhaps too quickly. "Why?"

"You look funny. I mean—"

"Now is that a nice thing to say about your old man?" he interrupted, feigning anger.

She smiled, though it failed to reach her eyes. "I didn't mean to hurt your feelings. It's just that you sorta turned green, and I thought you might be getting sick. You know, there's a flu bug going around. Lots of kids at school are out with it."

"I'm fine," he said, averting his gaze while trying to get his shakes under control. "Ah, here comes our food," he added, hearing the relief in his voice.

"Mmm, that looks yummy."

"Once we chow down, I have something for you."

"What?"

"Not now. Be a good girl and eat all your dinner, then you'll get your surprise."

Again her face clouded. "I just wish Mom was here. I remember we all used to have such fun together."

"If I have my way, we will again."

"You mean you want her and me back?"

Keith reached over and squeezed her hand. "You bet I do, sweetheart."

Robin's eyes filled with tears. "Oh, Daddy, that's wonderful."

"But for now, that's just between us, okay?"

She nodded.

"I want to be the one who tells your mother."

"You have my word," she promised, the tears no longer in evidence. "Mum's the word."

"Good girl. So how's your burger?"

"I'll let you know," she said, taking her first bite.

They ate in silence for a few minutes, though it was all he could do to force his food down. He wasn't the least bit hungry. But God, he was thirsty, and not for water. He needed a drink in the worst way.

Robin pushed her empty plate aside, then groaned. "I'm going to have to go on a diet tomorrow."

"Don't even think about it."

"You know we're not allowed to gain an ounce, which makes Mom mad."

"How's that?"

"She doesn't like for Mrs. Morrison to harp on our weight—says it's not healthy, that we're growing girls."

"I couldn't agree more."

Robin frowned in the direction of her plate. "I'm depressed now. I wish I hadn't eaten all that."

Keith reached in his coat pocket and pulled out a small wrapped package. "See if this doesn't make you feel better."

Robin reached for the gift, her eyes wide with anticipation.

"Go on, open it," Keith told her.

Seconds later, she gasped, then stared at him. "Are these real?" Her voice was filled with awe.

"You betcha."

Robin jumped up, ran to his side and gave him a big hug. "Thanks, Dad. You're the greatest."

Nine

This had not been a good day.

Janey almost asked herself what else could possibly happen. But fear of jinxing herself further kept that question at bay.

Robin had left drill team practice and come home, burning up with fever and shaking with chills. After giving her some over-the-counter medication to bring the fever down, Janey had called the doctor. Robin was now on a strong antibiotic.

Janey thought her daughter might need to be in the hospital, but the doctor had assured her that home was the best place for her, that the hospitals were full.

Although he had eased her anxiety somewhat, Janey had kept Robin under close scrutiny, dashing upstairs between customers to check on her.

Now, Hazel had come to work. Since the store wasn't busy, Janey had been certain that would free her up. Wrong. No rest for the weary. Not long after Hazel had arrived, the toilet in the downstairs bathroom had stopped up. Water had soaked the carpet. Janey had cleaned up as best she could, but it remained a mess.

Now she was waiting for the plumber. And not very patiently, either.

"When it rains, it pours," Hazel said, her brows furrowed in concern.

"I won't argue with that." Janey eased onto the bar stool at the far end of the counter and ran her fingers through her already tousled hair, then cast her eyes toward the stairs.

"You should be upstairs yourself. You look exhausted."

"I am, but I'll make it. It's Robin I'm worried about. She's so sick."

"That stuff is everywhere." Hazel shivered. "I sure don't want it."

"Would you rather not be here?" Janey asked, thinking that if Hazel deserted her, she would just turn the sign to Closed and forget it. That was the beauty of owning your own business. Yet she really couldn't afford that luxury.

As it was, Sweet Dreams still hadn't come up to its sales potential, which both worried and aggravated her. If that other candy store materialized in the mall, then she would certainly be in a world of hurt. She had meant to call Gwen and see if she'd heard any more about that, but she hadn't had the time.

"Why, I wouldn't think of leaving you," Hazel said in a rather huffy tone. "If I get the crud, then I'll just get it."

Janey half smiled. "Thanks, Hazel. I owe you one."

"You don't owe me anything, except to take care of your daughter. I'll see to the plumber and the store. Now skedaddle."

Janey didn't hesitate, dashing back upstairs and into Robin's room. Her daughter was sound asleep but her face was still flushed. Janey crept to the bedside and laid a hand on Robin's forehead. The girl was still warm, but her temperature was definitely down.

Sagging with relief, Janey sat in the rocker across the room, leaned back and closed her eyes. Soon they popped back open. Even though she was dead tired, sleep wouldn't come. She was too wired, had too many things on her mind. Robin's relationship with Keith had her nearly crazy, especially after the stunt he'd pulled last week when he'd taken Robin out to dinner.

The second her daughter had arrived home, Janey had known something out of the ordinary had taken place. Robin's eyes were wide and filled with excitement. Janey's heart had taken a nosedive. What was her ex up to now?

Seconds later she knew.

"He did *what?*" Janey realized her voice had almost reached the shouting level, but she didn't care.

"Mom, calm down." Robin's eyes widened even more. "You're stroking out over nothing."

Janey's lips thinned. "You can't keep them."

Robin gave her a dumbfounded stare, then stuttered, "But…but they're diamond studs."

"I know what they are. That's why you have to give them back."

Robin's expression became more confused. "But why?"

Janey drew an unsteady breath, knowing she was probably handling this all wrong. At the moment, she was operating on pure emotion, but she couldn't help it. Damn Keith and his bribes. That was exactly what this was. The only missing piece of the puzzle was the reason. She didn't know what he was up to, but it was no good.

"Robin, those earrings are at least a carat apiece."

"So?" Tears rimmed Robin's eyes.

Janey ignored them. "So, he can't just go around giving you expensive jewelry like that."

"Why not? I'm his daughter." Now Robin was almost shouting.

"It's your turn to calm down," Janey said, struggling to gain control of the eroding situation.

"You're just jealous," Robin cried, tears starting to stream down her cheeks.

"That's not true."

"You're just jealous that he loves me!"

"Oh, honey, I want him to love you," Janey responded with a catch in her voice and a pain in her heart. "It's just that I don't want him trying to buy your love."

"How can you even think that, much less say it?" Robin lifted her head in a defiant gesture, and her eyes sparked. "Anyway, I don't care if he gives me anything or not. I'd still love him."

There was so much pressure in her chest that Janey could barely breathe. She had indeed handled this all wrong. She knew that, but she couldn't call back her words. All she could do was try to make amends, amends she wasn't sure Robin was interested in hearing.

"Look, honey…"

Robin backed up, her lower lip trembling. "No, Mom. Don't say any more. I just don't understand why all this is happening, why you and Dad just couldn't have stayed married. It's…it's all your fault!"

With that, Robin turned and left the room.

Now, as Janey jerked her mind off that awful conversation and back to her daughter, who was still sleeping soundly, she felt that same awful pressure in her chest.

She hated it when there was a breach between her and Robin. And there had been since the brouhaha over the jewelry, which to date hadn't been resolved. Robin hadn't returned the earrings, but she hadn't worn them, either.

Maybe her reaction to the whole thing *had* been jealousy, Janey told herself. But she didn't think so. She would admit, however, that it sometimes smarted that she wasn't able to buy more frivolous things for Robin.

Still, Janey hated to think that she had stooped so low. Closer to the real reason was Keith himself. He was a user and a manipulator. And he wanted something. What that something was, she still didn't know. That was what frightened her the most.

To make matters worse, she and Robin remained at odds over Chad. Robin was smitten with the boy; she chattered about him constantly. All Janey could do was hold her tongue until the phase passed. But it wasn't easy; she still didn't trust Chad. Thank God, she trusted Robin.

She wondered if Robin had said anything to Keith about Chad.

Janey shook her head and focused her attention back on her sleeping daughter, while trying to sort through her own mixed emotions. Perhaps she should have ignored Robin's pleas and stayed in Colorado.

Life there had certainly been much simpler.

Suddenly Janey heard her phone ring. Seeing it as

an escape from her unpleasant thoughts, she crossed the hall to answer it.

"Janey?"

This time her heart upped its pace, and she didn't know why, which added another dimension to her anxiety. "Hello, Dillon."

"I hope you don't mind me calling."

"Of course not," she said with a slight catch in her voice.

What was wrong with her? Why couldn't she behave normally around him, for crying out loud? He was not in any way part of her life now. So why did he matter?

After they had gone for coffee, she hadn't heard from him. But then, she hadn't expected to. Maybe their intense conversation had shaken her more than she cared to admit, made her realize they were forever linked by a past that was sordid and painful— but linked nonetheless.

"Janey, are you still there?"

"Uh, yes."

"How's Robin?"

Though his question surprised her, she answered without hesitation. "I think she's a little better."

"That's good. I was worried."

"How did you know she was sick?"

He chuckled, and for some unexplainable reason her heart acted up again.

"I happened to be talking to the drill instructor, when Robin came up and asked if she could leave. I wanted to drive her home, but she insisted she could make it."

"Thanks, I appreciate that."

Her words were followed by a moment of silence. Then he asked, "So how are you doing?"

This time she heard the hesitancy in his voice and knew that he was as uncomfortable as she was. She wished that made her feel better, but it didn't.

"I'm fine," she said.

"Are you sure? Somewhere in those two words I detected a sigh of sorts."

"You weren't wrong. Robin aside, it hasn't been the best of days."

"Is there anything I can do?"

"Not unless you can fix my plumbing problem," she quipped.

"It wouldn't be the first time, you know," he said in a low, rather raspy tone. "Or have you forgotten?"

Janey's mouth suddenly felt cotton-dry. She licked her lips, which allowed her to speak. "I guess I had."

Dillon had always been good with his hands. Mr. Fix-it, the neighbors—especially her and Keith—used to call him. Anything that went wrong around their house, Dillon was phoned first. Often a professional wasn't even needed.

"I'm serious. I'll be glad to take a look at it."

"Thanks again, but I've already called someone."

"You can always call them back."

Though his voice seemed at ease now, there was an underlying hint of something that she couldn't quite put her finger on. A pleading note? Nah, she was just imagining things.

Yet when she spoke, she noticed her voice wasn't quite steady. "I could, but I don't think that would be a good idea."

Another moment of silence.

"I see. Well, I'll hold a good thought for Robin."

Suddenly feeling contrite, as if she'd done something wrong, she added, "Look, Dillon, I—"

"It's not a problem," he cut in. "I understand why you don't want me around."

He had no clue what he was talking about. She *did* want to see him. That was the problem. However, right now that frightened her worse than did offending him.

"Take care, you hear?"

Before she could respond, Dillon hung up. Frustrated beyond words, Janey slammed the receiver down hard, then folded her arms across her trembling body and blinked back tears.

She had to get hold of her emotions. It was as if she were wearing them on her sleeve. That had to stop.

"Mom?"

Robin. That was who should have all her concentration, not a man. "I'm coming, sweetheart."

Janey peered at the clock. Five-twenty. Almost closing time, and it couldn't come soon enough.

"I hope you have a better day tomorrow, dearie," Hazel said as she grabbed her purse.

"That makes two of us."

"At least the bathroom problem's fixed."

"For which I'm most grateful."

Hazel turned up her nose. "It's probably a customer who's to blame."

"For what?" Janey asked, wishing Hazel would stop talking and just go home. A little of Hazel went a long way. Besides, she still had so much to do, including making Robin the potato soup she'd asked for.

"For stopping up the commode," Hazel replied.

"You're probably right," Janey said idly, her mind already having splintered off in a dozen different directions.

Hazel's nose rose a little higher. "I don't like them using it."

Janey curbed her impatience. "Me either, Hazel, but sometimes it's necessary."

Hazel mumbled something under her breath before shuffling off toward the side entrance. "I'll see you tomorrow."

Relieved that her helper was leaving, Janey followed her to the door, which she locked, then bolted. Once that was done, she walked back into the shop proper, only to pull up short.

Her ex-husband was standing inside the front door, staring at her, a relaxed grin on his face.

She groaned inwardly as Keith stepped farther into the room.

"Hello, Janey, long time no see."

"Not nearly long enough," she said coldly. "What do you want?"

Ten

His only reaction to her abrupt coldness was a muscle tick in his jaw. Still, Janey knew he wasn't happy with her greeting. Surely he hadn't expected her to behave any other way. But knowing him and his ego the size of Canada, he probably had.

Just the thought almost made her laugh out loud. She had trouble even being cordial, much less anything more. However, Robin would always link them, and because of her, Janey had no choice but to be civil.

"I thought maybe you'd changed," Keith said into the oppressive silence. "Mellowed a little."

"Well, now you know."

Keith's lips twisted, but she had to hand it to him, he hung on to his cool extremely well. She wondered why.

"I don't want us to duke it out every time we're together," he said, interrupting her thoughts.

Her eyes flared. "There won't be any togetherness, Keith."

Other than that obvious tick in his jaw, he continued to hold his emotions in check.

"As long as Robin's in the picture, there will be," he said flatly. "By the way, where is she?"

"In bed with the flu."

He sucked in a harsh breath. "Why the hell didn't you tell me?"

"You haven't given me the chance."

"I want to see her."

"She's asleep, but I'll tell her you came by."

"That's mighty nice of you."

She ignored his sarcasm and added, "While we're on the subject of Robin, I told her she couldn't keep the earrings."

This time *his* eyes flared. "You wait just a minute. You're way out of line if you think you can dictate what I can or can't do for my daughter."

"She's too young for earrings that expensive."

"Bullshit."

She flinched against his outburst of crudeness. "You can't buy her love, Keith."

"I know how my daughter feels about me," he said with a calm arrogance.

"That aside for now, I'd think you'd be more concerned about meeting your financial obligations to her than buying expensive jewelry."

A look of guilt changed his expression, but he sounded unrepentant. "I've been a little short lately, but I'll catch up."

Janey clamped down on her bottom lip to keep from yelling at him to get the hell out of her and Robin's life and stay out. She couldn't. Robin was the glue that would always bind them.

But thank God Robin had been spared the ugly truth about her father. She was still under the misconception that Keith could walk on water. And even if Janey had to put up with her ex from time to time, she would do anything to keep Robin from being hurt.

"I won't take them back," Keith was saying. "But if you don't want her to wear them right now, I'll give in to that."

"How nice of you." Sarcasm colored her tone this time.

His eyes narrowed, and he muffled an oath.

Janey had known that if she kept on, his calm demeanor would disappear, and she'd been right. He was losing ground fast. But what would rousing him prove?

Nothing.

It would only leave a bitter taste in her mouth and make her feel bad about herself. She didn't like playing cat-and-mouse games with him, because she was the one who ended up hissing like the cat.

"At least let her wear them when she goes somewhere special with her steady."

"Steady?" Janey frowned. "She doesn't have a steady."

"Hell, call him whatever you want. Anyway, I know she's got a thing for a football player named Chad Something-or-other."

"She's only had one date with him," Janey said, experiencing a moment of alarm. Apparently Robin had gone into much more detail about Chad with Keith than with her.

"Well, she's crazy about him!" Keith exclaimed.

"Maybe for the moment," Janey responded on the defensive. "But it won't last."

"God, Janey, you just won't give an inch, will you?"

A wave of fury washed over her, but before she could say anything, he went on, "How much longer are you going to punish me?"

"Look, you don't want to go there. And *I* sure don't."

"Did you ever ask yourself why I strayed?" he pressed, as though she hadn't said a word.

Of course she had, but she wasn't about to tell him that. "Stop it, Keith!"

"Well, I know. You were so wrapped up in yourself and Robin that I felt shoved out."

"Oh, poor you."

He flushed, but when he spoke again his voice was even. "But I'm willing to let bygones be bygones. I want you to forgive me."

Janey almost choked. "That's good. That's real good. You screw around with my best friend, and you want *me* to forgive *you.*"

"As a matter of fact, I do."

"That's not going to happen. There's a little thing called trust that's involved. But then, that's a word you don't know the meaning of."

"Janey—"

"No!" she cried, shaking her head violently. "You're wasting my time and yours. It's over, Keith. It's been over for years, and you know it. If I had my way, I'd never see you again."

He gave her a twisted smile, then stepped closer, his nostrils flaring.

That was when she realized he'd been drinking. Her eyes widened, and she stepped back.

"I've tried to be a gentleman," he said, "but you're determined to push whatever button you can to make me lose my temper."

"That's not my intention at all."

"Yeah, right. You're still the same vindictive bitch you were three years ago." He paused, that twisted smile growing. "But that's okay. You're much more challenging this way." He pivoted, then sauntered toward the door. Once there, he turned and added, "Give Robin my love."

Janey clung to the counter, her legs feeling as weak as dirty dishwater. Yet she fought the urge to take a quick shower, feeling dirty in another way, too. The thought of Keith ever touching her again turned her stomach.

Somehow she managed to make it upstairs to check on Robin, who was still sleeping. Once she was in the sitting room that adjoined her bedroom, Janey sank into the nearest chair.

The phone rang.

It was Gwen.

"Hey, kiddo, you sound like you're stressed to the max."

"I am. I just had a round with Keith, and Robin's sick."

"Uh-oh. You're on double overload."

"And if you're calling to tell me that mall store's a definite go, I'll put a hex on you." Janey followed her words with a hint of laughter, which took the edge off them.

Gwen laughed back. "This is your lucky day—or rather mine, since I won't get slapped. Actually, I haven't heard any more about it."

"Praise the Lord. But if you do, you have to tell me. I refuse to be caught unawares."

"Absolutely not, though there wouldn't be anything you could do about it."

"I know," Janey replied in a forlorn voice. "Still, I'd have to try."

"Well, it hasn't happened yet, so try not to worry.

But when it comes to Robin and Keith, that's different.''

"Robin's going to be fine, though she's pretty sick at the moment."

"What did that scumbag ex of yours want?"

"To jerk my chain."

"And did he?"

Janey released a sigh. "I'm afraid so. My bones tell me he's up to something." She explained about the earrings.

"Surely he doesn't think pampering Robin will make you go back to him."

"Who's to say what goes through his mind?"

"Bastard," Gwen muttered.

"I couldn't agree more." Feeling a terrible headache coming on, Janey added, "Let's not taint our conversation any more by talking about him."

"Right."

"So when are we going to get together?" Janey asked.

"Call me when you can get away from the shop, and I'll meet you for lunch or dinner. Either one works for me."

"Will do."

"Meanwhile, don't let that jerk get you down."

Janey rubbed her forehead. "Don't worry, I won't."

After she hung up the phone, she tried not to think about how much her head throbbed. She couldn't give in to the luxury of nursing it. She still had to make Robin some soup.

Thirty minutes later, it was done and served, though Robin took only a few bites. Janey hadn't eaten much herself. Now, as she sat at her desk preparing to work on the shop's finances, she found she couldn't concentrate.

Her thoughts, instead of targeting Keith, as expected, turned to Dillon. Without warning. To add insult to injury, she found herself comparing him to her ex. Keith fell far short.

Janey tossed down her pen, swallowing her panic. How could her mind betray her like this? And her body, recalling the way Dillon's staring at her lips had felt like a tangible caress.

Was it loneliness?

Was that responsible for the unwilling pull of attraction she felt for him? A loneliness for the kind of male companionship she'd sworn she would never crave again?

Suddenly Janey lurched out of the chair and went into Robin's room.

"Mom," Robin croaked, "what's wrong?"

"Not one thing, sweetheart. I just thought I'd sit with you for a while."

Robin gave her a smile of sorts, then drifted back to sleep. Janey didn't know how long she sat beside her child and stared at that precious being.

"I better not find out you lied to me, Aimsworth."

The swarthy sophomore with shifty eyes met Dillon's hard stare. "I ain't lying."

"We'll see."

"You can talk to my buddies—"

"Don't you mean 'gang members'?" Dillon cut in, never raising his voice.

"No, sir. We ain't no gang. They're just my friends."

"Rest assured that I've already visited with your 'friends.'"

Dillon paused, letting his words sink in. But there was no guarantee they had. Hal Aimsworth definitely wasn't the sharpest knife in the drawer, yet he was under suspicion for the lab break-in, as well as a gym incident that had just taken place at the beginning of the week.

And Dillon was fast losing patience with the police and their attempts to get to the bottom of the malicious mischief. He had gotten a tip that Aimsworth and the creeps he hung with might be involved. But since Dillon didn't have the concrete proof he needed, he had to tread softly, which irked him.

"I ain't afraid of you, Mr. Reed," Hal said, shoving back his chair and rising.

Dillon arched one eyebrow. "That's not smart, Aimsworth."

"My mamma said that if I didn't do nothing, you weren't allowed to hassle me."

"Your mamma's wrong, son. As long as you're in my school and get in trouble in class, then I can hassle you, all right. And if you're connected in any way to those break-ins, the cops can also give you a hard time."

The kid's face drained of color.

"You'd best keep that in mind," Dillon said, standing. "Now get out of here."

The assistant principal, Wayne Cooper, usually handled the discipline problems, but in this case Dillon had taken over. It galled him to no end that he couldn't put a stop to the kids breaking in and tearing things up.

But sooner or later they would get sloppy or he

would get lucky, and *wham,* he would nail their asses.

Meanwhile, he had enough administrative work to choke a horse. Speaking of horses, that was exactly where he would like to be about now—on Dandi, riding around his farm, freeing his mind of all this garbage.

The day was perfect for a spontaneous outing. Fall was finally pushing summer out of the picture entirely. But no matter how cool and crisp the weather, he was chained to his desk. With that in mind, Dillon walked back to his chair.

The open folder dealt with the fund-raising drive for the drill team trip. It required his approval.

The list in front of him was made up of the team's sponsor and cosponsor, along with parents who might want to be involved. Without the parents, the trip probably wouldn't come off.

He idly scanned the list, stopping when he reached Janey's name. It leapt out at him, and for a second a funny feeling invaded his stomach.

Leave it be, he told himself. Leave *her* be. She'd made it plain she didn't want anything to do with him. He'd thought he'd gotten that through his thick skull.

Why couldn't he feel anything for Patricia? She seemed to have all the right ingredients for a lasting relationship. She was attractive, young, perfect child-bearing age. But she wasn't Janey.

And that was who he wanted. Only the Lord knew why, because he certainly didn't. But something about her tough vulnerability had gotten to him. Closer to the truth was that he was flat attracted to her, which was a helluva note.

So where did that leave him? He answered that question without hesitation. With a hard-on for a woman who detested him.

Disgusted, Dillon shoved his chair back and got up. To hell with paperwork. He needed to move around. Walking the halls and checking on teachers and students, he hoped, would ease that heaviness in his loins and get his mind back on track.

However, Fate didn't see it his way.

The first person he encountered in the hall was Robin, only she wasn't alone. Hal Aimsworth and one of his running buddies, Cliff Jarvis, had her backed against a locker. She had a frightened but determined look on her face.

However, before Dillon could get there, the boys moved on and Robin headed for the rest room. He caught up with her just before she entered.

"Wait up, Robin."

She swung around. "Uh, hello...Mr. Reed."

He heard her stumble over the "Mr. Reed" part, and almost smiled. For so many years, it had been "Dillon and Elaine" to her. God, how quickly and drastically things could change, he reminded himself sardonically.

"How are you feeling?" He hadn't meant to ask her that, but a moment later he was glad he had.

Her face brightened; then she murmured with a hint of shyness, "Fine now, thanks."

"Good." He lowered his voice. "Were those boys bothering you?"

Robin's eyes, so like her mother's, became troubled. "Hal asked me to go to a party with him." She let go of a shuddering breath. "He gives me the creeps. I told him to take a hike."

Dillon repressed his fury. "If he bothers you again, will you let me know?"

"All right."

He patted her on the arm. "Thanks. Tell your teacher you were talking to me and that's why you're late."

She nodded, then walked off. He watched until she disappeared, then made his way back to his office.

Eleven

It was past closing time, but Emma Welch seemed gloriously oblivious to that fact. Any other day, a late customer wouldn't have been a big deal. But this evening she *was*. Janey was due at a meeting at the school in an hour to discuss plans to raise money for a drill team trip.

Her gaze veered off Emma to the clock. She'd hoped to get a quick bite to eat and a shower before she left. Now that Emma had just strolled in, she could kiss both those pleasures goodbye. However, she couldn't blame the old lady.

If she had turned the sign around at five-thirty, this time crunch wouldn't have been an issue. But she'd been busy unpacking a shipment of candy in the back and hadn't realized how late it was. Hazel had worked her hours during the morning and was long gone.

"Afternoon, dearie," Emma said, both her cane and her false teeth clacking as she made her way toward the checkout counter, her gaze dead center on the stool beside it.

Janey groaned silently, realizing that once the old lady parked herself on that spot, it would take a blast of dynamite to get her up. It wasn't because she was overweight, either. On the contrary, she was so thin, one could see her veins through her parchment-like skin. Janey often feared a strong puff of wind might knock her over.

She would bet Emma was in her late eighties if she was a day. A widow with no children, she was quite alone and lonely, though she never complained. Money was a problem, too; Janey's instincts told her that. Yet Emma never left the shop without at least two pieces of candy.

She knew Emma had been one of her aunt's favorite customers, as well as a friend. She also knew that Lois had been good to Emma, that she'd felt sorry for the woman. So did Janey, but she never let her feelings show. She wanted Emma to be able to hold on to her pride as long as she could. But if anyone needed to be in an assisted living facility, it was this old lady.

"How are you, Emma?"

"Can't hardly get around." She grimaced. "My old bones ain't what they used to be. Old Arthur's been visiting me again. The truth is, he's just plumb camped out in my rickety body."

Despite being in a high snit, a smile unwittingly broke through Janey's lips. "Arthritis has a way of doing that to people. Aunt Lois has the same problem."

"Speaking of Lois, how is my friend?"

A pang of guilt shot through Janey. She hadn't been as diligent as she should have been in checking on her aunt, but it seemed like ever since she'd been back in Hunter she'd been in a pressure cooker. Still, that wasn't any excuse to ignore a person she loved and to whom she owed so much.

This weekend, she vowed, she'd try to see her aunt, to rectify her neglect.

"The stroke took its toll on her, Emma. But you know her. Aunt Lois is determined she's going to get all her parts back in working order."

"Bully for her. Hope she makes it."

"Me too."

"Give her my love." Emma rubbed one of her eyes.

Janey noticed that it was watering. She reached over, popped a tissue and handed it to her.

Emma nodded, then said, "Lordy, but I do miss her." Then, as if she realized how that must have sounded to Janey, she added, "Oh, but I like having you here, too. You're such a breath of fresh air to an old woman like me."

"You're not old, Emma, you're just mature."

Emma chuckled, her cataract-clouded eyes taking on a twinkle of sorts. "Mind if I sit for a minute longer? Right now, I'm too tired to choose my candy."

Janey groaned inwardly, though she would have bitten her tongue before she was rude to Emma. "Of course. You can keep me company while I count today's receipts." She cut Emma an amused glance. "But what's this about you choosing your candy? You always buy the same thing."

"One day I might take a hankering to change my mind. You never know."

It was only after Emma had been planted firmly on the stool for a while that Janey noticed something odd about her. At first she couldn't figure out what it was. Then it hit her, along with a pang of sadness, and she fought back the urge to cry. Still, she looked closer, but her own vision hadn't been playing tricks on her.

Emma's dress was on wrong side out.

Janey had known the old lady's eyesight was poor. Obviously it had gotten much worse than she'd thought—all the more reason why Emma shouldn't be left alone in her small house or driving her ten-year-old Ford. But her only niece obviously hadn't had the nerve to take the car away from her, or maybe she simply didn't care enough.

Since Janey had taken over the store, Emma had even sideswiped another car in the parking lot.

"God bless her sweet soul," Lois had said, when Janey told her about the fender bender. "But she never could drive. Never seemed to get the hang of it."

After chuckling, Janey had thought that the pot was calling the kettle black. Aunt Lois couldn't drive a lick, either. Thank goodness, though, she no longer needed a vehicle.

However, Janey's concern was not for Lois—she was well taken care of—but rather Emma. What could Janey do about the dress? Should she tell her?

No. Janey's gut instinct told her Emma would be mortified to the point of tears. Anyhow, who cared? No one, really, or Emma wouldn't have been left alone to fend for herself in her condition. Another pang of sadness dented Janey's heart.

Then anger overtook that sadness, almost choking her. In that moment, Janey made another vow. She would see what she could do to help Emma.

"What time is it, dearie?" Emma asked, squinting her eyes in the direction of the clock.

"It's a little after six."

"Oh, my, I am keeping you late."

"That's all right," Janey lied.

Emma struggled to get up.

"Be careful," Janey said anxiously. "Aunt Lois would never forgive me if I let you take a tumble."

"I'll be all right. It just takes a minute to get these old hips on the move."

Emma didn't appear all right. Her breathing was too rapid to suit Janey. With her help, the old lady finally managed to get up and hobble over to the counter that housed her favorite candy—licorice.

"How 'bout letting me treat you today?"

"Oh, dearie, I can't let you do that."

"Why not?"

"Well—"

Janey smiled. "See, you don't have a reason, so that settles it." She reached inside the case with a tissue and grabbed a handful of the candy, then bagged it and handed it to Emma.

Emma's mouth worked as she grabbed the sack and held it close to her chest. "This'll last me several days. But I'll be back. I can't miss coming here for that long."

Janey fought back another threat of tears. "Of course you can't. I don't know what I'd do if you didn't come visit. But promise you'll be careful when you're out and about."

Emma leaned forward a little, then winked at Janey. "I haven't hit anything or anyone lately, so you needn't worry. I'm back in control."

Oh, Lordy, Janey thought, not knowing whether to laugh or cry. "That's good, Emma. But you still need to be careful, because I *do* worry about you."

"You're a good girl, Janey Mayfield."

After she got Emma in the car, Janey rushed back inside and locked the door. She then washed her hands, checked her makeup and made a mad dash for her own car.

"I'm so glad you're going to head this project."

Janey made a face at Christy Olson, Beverly's mother. "Actually, I think I was railroaded into it."

Christy, who was pleasantly plump like her daughter, grinned. "Whatever. We're grateful to have someone with your intelligence and enthusiasm at the helm. I'm sure money will come in hand over fist."

"Let us pray," Janey said, wondering how she had come away from the meeting as the grand prize winner. Only she didn't want the prize.

She didn't mind helping. In fact, she'd counted on that. But being in charge? No way. So how had it happened?

New kid on the block. Sure bet every time. And, she'd tossed out several ideas, while the other mothers had remained mum.

"The fresh blood, so to speak, will do us good," Christy told her as they walked toward the exit. "I'm thrilled it's you and not me."

"Thanks, Christy," Janey said drolly. "You're all heart."

The meeting in the high school conference room had just broken up, though several of the mothers had remained behind to gab. Janey couldn't wait to leave. All she had on her mind was going home and taking her shoes off. Her feet were killing her.

"Hey, I promise I'll help."

"You'd better," Janey said, giving Christy a fierce

but tempered smile. "In fact, I'm counting on you to be my right hand."

"I won't let you down."

"I'll call you the first of next week," Janey replied, "and we'll get together and pick our committee."

"The girls will be so excited that we're working together on this."

"It'll be fun," Janey agreed, a little surprised to find herself actually looking forward to working closely with the other girls and their mothers. Until she'd owned her own business, she hadn't been able to play a role in Robin's school life. Now she could, and for that she was grateful.

"Talk to you soon."

Janey pulled up short. "You go on. I need to run to the rest room."

Christy waved. "Good night."

A few minutes later, Janey walked back into the hall, only to stop abruptly when she felt strong hands lightly circle her upper arms.

"Oh!" That tiny word came out in a whimper as she looked straight into Dillon's eyes.

They stared at each other for a second; then, as if he suddenly realized he was still touching her, he dropped his hands and stepped back. "For a minute I thought you were going to run over me."

Though his voice seemed unusually low, it was filled with humor.

"Uh, sorry. My mind was a million miles away."

His lips twitched. "I guessed that."

A short silence ensued.

"So how's it going?" he asked.

"It's going," she responded, hating that her heart

was beating overtime and butterflies were filling her tummy. But no wonder. He looked great in casual slacks and a turtleneck. He smelled good, too, the aroma of his cologne swamping her senses.

What was happening to her?

This was Dillon, for heaven's sake! How had a one-time friend turned into a sexual fantasy? She suddenly felt so torn between her body's betrayal, and her mind's determination to remain uninvolved at all costs that she couldn't function.

"So how was the meeting?" he asked.

Janey cleared her throat. "Productive, actually. But I got stuck with chairing the project."

"Are you okay with that?"

She forced herself to meet his still-probing gaze. "Actually, I am. I need to do this for Robin."

"That's great. I meant to join you, but time got away from me."

"Speaking of time," Janey said, pointedly looking at her watch, "I've got to go."

"Me too. I'll walk you to your car."

That wasn't exactly what she'd had in mind, but she wasn't about to argue. To do so would be to make too much of it. He was just being a gentleman, that was all. He would do the same for anyone else.

That was why she was so stunned when he opened her car door and said, "Have dinner with me Saturday night."

Twelve

"Child, you shouldn't have come all this way."

"Oh, Aunt Lois, 'all this way' is only an hour's drive."

Lois lifted her chin just enough to register her disapproval. "Maybe so, but you should be at the store selling candy."

Janey got up, crossed to Lois's chair, leaned down and gave her another hug. "I'd rather be right here in this room with you."

Lois's pinched features brightened considerably. "But it's Saturday, one of our biggest days."

"Trust me, the shop's in good hands. Hazel's there, and you know she's trustworthy. Robin'll be around in a while, too, and she can help."

"I wish she could've come with you."

"She wanted to," Janey said, "but she has some drill team stuff to do today. So you're stuck with me."

"Give her my love."

Shortly after she'd arrived at the assisted living facility in Savannah, Janey had gone to the cafeteria and gotten them some coffee. On her way there, she had been impressed with her aunt's new home. It was lovely—not only Lois's efficiency apartment but the entire place.

It had several parlors crammed with plants and flowers, exuding warmth and cheerfulness. And the large dining area had bragging rights of its own, with lace cloths on the tables set with china and stemware.

Janey was relieved. Her aunt was comfortable and happy, and that was what was important.

Now, as they sipped their coffee, Janey eyed Lois closely. Since her stroke, she was doing well, even though she seemed a little more feeble than before. Still, her skin had a glow, and her eyes and smile were ever ready.

"I'm sorry I didn't get to see Aunt Virgie," Janey said, taking another sip of coffee.

"She'll be sorry, too, but she'd already planned this outing with her friends."

Virgie Weems, Lois's older sister from Savannah, had been the deciding factor in Lois's choice of facility. The two had always been close, and now that they were both widowed they were finally getting to spend time together.

Janey batted her hand in the air. "No problem. I'm glad Aunt Virgie's able to kick up her heels."

Lois smiled, then said, "So tell me what's going on at the store. You can't imagine how much I miss it."

"Oh, yes, I can. Speaking of the store brings up another reason I came to see you. Emma Welch."

"Don't tell me something has happened to her," Lois said in a stricken tone.

"Not yet." Janey explained about Emma's dress.

"Oh dear, how awful."

"I know she doesn't have a prayer of ever getting into a place like this. From what I've gathered, she's poor as a church mouse. But then, you know her and her circumstances much better than I do.''

''You're on target. She doesn't have any money or anyone who cares about her. That niece out in California certainly doesn't.''

''That's what I thought,'' Janey said glumly. ''I wish there was something I could do. In fact, I vowed I'd help but I'm clueless as to how to go about it.''

''Well, child, where there's a will there's a way. And you're not alone. I'll do what I can.''

''Oh, Aunt Lois, I knew I could count on your help. It's just that Emma's yanking on my heart-strings, big time.''

''We'll come up with something, I promise.'' Lois smiled as she changed the subject. ''So back to the shop. And don't leave out any details, either.''

That visit and conversation with her aunt had taken place mid-afternoon, and when Janey thought about it later, she smiled. However, her smile was short-lived because she was unable to outrun her trouble-some thoughts.

Janey stared at herself in the mirror, wondering if she actually looked as if she'd lost her mind. The face that stared back seemed perfectly normal except for a few more fine lines around her eyes.

She wasn't thrilled about that; she was going to have to slow down and get more rest. And stop doing stupid things, like she was about to do.

For a second, a flutter inside her chest slowed her breathing. One hand tightened on the edge of the dressing table, where she was sitting in her panties and bra. She knew she wasn't having a heart attack, but something was wrong.

Anxiety.

She was having an anxiety attack—a mild one, but an attack, nonetheless. Served her right, she told herself. She had no one to blame but herself. She closed her eyes for a second. She wasn't dizzy, but her hands were certainly clammy. Grabbing a tissue, she wiped them before putting the finishing touches on her makeup.

If only she hadn't gone to the rest room before she left the school, she wouldn't be in this predicament. If only she'd walked out of the school with Christy, she wouldn't have run into Dillon. If only she hadn't said yes to his invitation, she wouldn't be sitting here beating up on herself.

But none of those "if onlys" had come about. As a result, she was suffering the consequences of her actions.

When Dillon had issued the invitation, she'd been so stunned that she hadn't spoken for several seconds.

"Gotcha, didn't I?" he said in a gravelly tone. But there had been a hint of humor there, as well.

Janey blinked several times. "As a matter of fact, you did."

"So what do you say?"

She licked dry lips. "No."

"I was afraid you'd say that."

"But thanks, anyway."

"Hey, I'm not going to let you get off that easy."

His big hands were anchored on the top of her car door. She couldn't have closed it even if she had wanted to. She peered up at him, the moonlight allowing her to see his features.

Janey's heart was pounding far too hard. "I don't think you have a choice."

"Look, what's the big deal? We can chalk a dinner up to old acquaintances getting together." He paused, then lowered his voice again. "I know we have our differences. I won't deny that. Yet I'm still your friend."

Man, oh, man, did he have some nerve. He made the invitation sound so innocent. And he knew just how to make her squirm, though God forbid he should ever realize that. Janey forced her own features to show no emotion.

"Come on," he pressed. "What can it hurt? *Who* can it hurt?"

Me, she wanted to lash back, but she didn't. "Oh, all right," she said, sounding more ungracious than she intended. "You win."

He chuckled. "Makes me think you just agreed to have a wisdom tooth pulled."

"Funny."

"I'll pick you up around seven."

"Fine."

She had shifted the car into Drive, so he had no choice but to step back.

By the time she reached home, her nerves were shot. They had pretty much stayed that way the remainder of the week, though she'd tried not to dwell on the ramifications of Saturday night. Now it was here, and she had no choice.

"Hey, Mom."

Janey gave her daughter a thankful and indulgent smile as her daughter breezed into the room and plopped down on the bed, dressed in an old robe that had holes in it.

Robin plucked the covers in silence for a second before looking up, an odd expression on her face.

"Isn't it about time you were getting dressed?" Janey asked, one eyebrow raised.

"I suppose so."

It wasn't like her daughter to lollygag when it came to going out with Chad. Although Janey still didn't approve of his monopolizing Robin's time, she'd held her tongue.

Robin had just gotten over her snit about the earrings, and Janey hadn't wanted to stir up another hornets' nest by harping on Chad.

Besides, she still had no solid evidence on which to base her prejudice. On the surface, Chad remained polite and well-mannered. However, Janey wasn't ready to let him off the hook. Perhaps she would never care for anyone who dated Robin, always thinking he wasn't good enough.

Janey frowned. She hoped that wasn't the case. She wanted Robin to enjoy her senior year, live it to the fullest. Then, when the time came for her to settle down in the distant future, they would both be ready for a great guy to sweep her daughter off her feet.

Somehow, Janey knew that guy wouldn't be Chad.

"Mom, what's bugging you?"

Janey peered at Robin in the mirror and smiled. "I was about to ask you the same thing." She glanced at the clock on her dresser. "You're always dressed long before Chad's due."

Robin didn't respond, seemingly still preoccupied.

"You two didn't have a tiff, did you?" Janey pressed, feeling uneasy.

"Of course not."

"So you're still on for the evening, right?"

Robin nodded.

Something was wrong, Janey sensed, and it had

nothing to do with her. She hadn't told Robin that she was going out, too, even though Dillon was due in less than an hour. Her reluctance stemmed from the fact that she had no idea how Robin would react to the news. Tonight was her first date since the divorce. And with the man being Dillon... She broke that thought off, cringing inwardly.

"Mom."

"I'm listening, sweetheart."

"I don't know whether to mention this or not, but—"

Her uneasiness went up a notch, spilling into her voice. "You can tell me anything. You know that."

"See, you're already uptight."

"No, I'm not," Janey countered lightly.

"These two jerks came up to me in the hall, and one asked me out."

"Define the word *jerk*," Janey said, forcing herself to remain calm.

"I think they're in a gang. Hal, the one who hit on me, is greasy and dirty looking." Robin shivered. "I almost lost my cookies just being around him."

"Did he say anything out of the way, or try to touch you?"

"Ugh, no! I would've nailed his ass—"

"I get the picture," Janey interrupted, "without your being so graphic in your language."

Robin rolled her eyes, then went on. "I told him to get lost, or something to that effect."

"Have you reported him?" Again Janey tried to keep her alarm at bay but she was having difficulty. With all the crazies out and about, one couldn't be too careful. And when it pertained to her daughter..."

"Dillon—I mean, Mr. Reed knows."

Janey refocused mentally. "That's good."

"He saw them talking to me and asked what they were up to."

"I hope you told him."

"I did, but—"

Janey picked up on her hesitation and jumped in. "But what?"

"There's more. Hal's been watching me."

Janey's hand went to her chest, her heart acting up again, but this time for a totally different reason. "As in stalking, you mean?"

"Nah, not that bad. Just sometimes I'll look up and he'll be there, looking at me."

"That won't do. If you don't report him, I will."

"I'll take care of it," Robin said. "Really, though, all I have to do is tell Chad. Hal would end up a greasy spot in the hall when Chad got through with him."

"You leave Chad out of this," Janey said sharply. "It's none of his concern."

"Sure it is."

Janey counted to ten. "He's not your keeper, Robin."

"Oh, Mom, you don't understand."

She understood, all right. She understood that Chad was much too possessive. But she couldn't blame it all on him. It took two to tango, and apparently Robin was willing.

"If that boy so much as looks at you or comes anywhere near you again, you're to hightail it to the office. Is that clear?"

"Yes, ma'am," Robin muttered, then stood. She made it to the door, then turned around. "By the way, where are you going? You don't usually get all dolled up this time of the evening."

Janey felt her face turn red. "Actually, I'm going out."

"To dinner?"

"Yes."

"With Gwen?"

"Uh, no."

"Who with, then?" Robin didn't bother to mask her impatience. "A man?"

Janey's flush deepened, yet she didn't shy away from Robin's suspicious gaze. "Yes."

Robin went slack-jawed. "Who is he?"

"Dillon," Janey responded reluctantly.

"Dillon? You've got to be kidding." Robin's voice had risen, which was not a good sign.

"No, I'm not kidding. But it's nothing, honey. We're just friends." Janey choked those words out, frantic to remove that terrible expression from her daughter's face.

"But...but you've never gone out with anyone."

"I know."

"What about Dad?"

Silence.

"What about him?" Janey forced herself to ask, though she knew she would regret it. But Robin looked so pitiful, she couldn't help herself.

Tears welled up in Robin's eyes. "He'll be upset, that's what."

"Robin, you know—"

"No, I don't!" she cried. "I only want you to be with Dad."

Janey stood and reached out her arms. "Please—"

"No!" Robin cried again, before turning and storming out of the room.

Janey sank back down on the stool and placed her head in her hands.

Thirteen

The stars were so bright and plentiful in the moonlit
night that the sky seemed ablaze with tiny sparklers.

However, Robin gave that beauty only a cursory
glance. She sat reed straight, while Chad shoved his
Mustang into Park in a clearing at the end of a lonely
dirt road. He let the windows down on both sides,
then killed the engine.

They had been to the movies, though she couldn't
say she remembered much about what had been playing across the big screen. She'd been too conscious
of Chad's big body next to hers, a hand either circling her shoulder or tangled with one of hers
throughout the film.

Ever since she had met him, she had anticipated
his kissing her. All during the movie, she could
hardly wait until they were out of the theater and
alone somewhere.

Now that moment had arrived, and she felt suddenly petrified as the sounds of the night drifted
about her. The crickets chirped, and the wind rustled
the leaves, giving this isolated place an eerie atmosphere.

Then she felt Chad shift his body and knew that
he had turned and was staring at her profile. She
could hear his breathing, loud and heavy.

Robin's body reacted. Her heart slammed against her rib cage, and her hands turned clammy. Her mouth was drier than cotton candy.

This was the first time she'd ever been parking. Actually, Chad was the first guy she'd gone out with more than a couple of times. The only one she'd ever cared about, that was for sure.

Of course, she hadn't been able to go out alone with anyone until she turned sixteen. Since then, she'd had several casual dates. But for the most part she'd just hung out with a group of guys and other girls. None had ever been special.

Until now. Until Chad.

And to think he cared about her when he could have any girl in the school. That thought continued to boggle her mind and make her giddy.

Yet there was also a scary side to all this. Her mom. Mom would have a conniption if she knew where Robin was. *No, she would kill me,* Robin corrected herself. Then she tightened her lips. Why should she worry about what her mother thought?

After all, her mom hadn't cared what *she* thought when she decided to go to dinner with Dillon Reed. The idea of her mother becoming interested in a man other than her dad was repulsive to her.

Robin shut her eyes and took a deep breath. She wouldn't think about that right now. She had much more important things on her mind, like what Chad expected of her. Out of her.

Suddenly Chad touched her shoulder, and she jumped.

"God, are you uptight or what?" His voice came out a low growl.

Yet his breath was warm when it feathered her ear.

That warmth created goose bumps all the way to her toes. His hand had begun caressing her slender shoulder blade, creating more of the same.

"Whatcha thinking about, doll?"

"You," she said in a barely audible voice. And it was not a lie. Her thoughts had been on him, and him only, before switching to her mother.

"And how much fun we're about to have, right?"

Robin nodded. For some inexplicable reason, she couldn't talk. It was as if her throat had suddenly become paralyzed. She didn't know if that reaction stemmed from fear or excitement, or both.

"Did you think I played good last night?" he asked, tracing the outline of her ear with a fingertip.

"Uh, great, especially that winning touchdown."

"I thought so, too. I was real proud of myself."

"Me too," Robin whispered, facing him.

His lips were suddenly so close to hers that her breath caught and her eyes widened.

"This is what I've been waiting for," Chad growled again, placing his mouth over hers.

At first the hard wetness of his lips was exhilarating, and she reveled in what was happening to her body. But when the pressure increased and he ground her against the car seat, she shook her head and moaned.

Chad pulled back, his breathing labored. "What the hell's wrong?"

"You...you were hurting me," Robin said in a halting voice.

"Aw, come on. You're the only one who's ever complained."

That jab hurt, but she wasn't about to let him know

that. She desperately wanted Chad to care about her. The last thing she wanted was to turn him off.

"Chad, I'm sorry," she whispered.

"I sure as hell hope so." His lips came closer again at the same time that his hand fumbled with the top button of her blouse. "It's time we got down to some serious business."

Before she could reply, he kissed her again, much easier this time, and she found herself relaxing, actually returning his kisses.

That was when she felt his hand cup her bare breast.

"Oh!" she yelped, and jerked back.

"Shit, Robin!"

"I'm...sorry," she said again, tears clogging her throat. "It's just that—"

"What? It's just what?"

"I—" Again the tears kept her from speaking.

"I thought you loved me."

Love? Did she love him? Of course she did. That was why she thought about him day and night, why she couldn't wait to see him at school, couldn't wait to be with him.

"I...do love you."

"Then why are you acting like this?"

"Because I'm scared."

He stared at her as if she'd just taken leave of her senses. "Scared of what?"

"Of making love." God, she wanted to die right on the spot from embarrassment. Apparently he wasn't used to girls who didn't put out.

"Why? I'm sure my dick's better than any other guy's you've had." He paused and stared at her more closely. "You have fucked before, right?"

Robin flinched at the use of that word. Oh, she'd heard it countless times, mainly from some of her girlfriends. But she'd never had anyone actually say it to her. Again thoughts of her mom came to mind, and she almost tensed again.

"No, I haven't," she said in a small voice.

"Oh, God!" Chad threw up his arms in obvious disgust. "A virgin. Man, oh, man, I can't believe that. And you're seventeen?"

Robin nodded, hot tears almost blinding her. "Do you hate me?"

He cut her another glance. "Nah. It's just that I'm used to girls puttin' out. And knowing what they're doing."

"I care about you a lot, Chad. I'm sure I love you."

"So cut you some slack, is that what you're asking me?"

"Yes, I guess it is."

He boldly fondled one breast, then the other. Robin swallowed hard but didn't so much as move.

He sent her a challenging look. "Are you ever in for some fun."

Janey pushed her plate aside, then reached for her cup of coffee, though she didn't drink any of it. Her gaze met Dillon's intense stare. "Why didn't you tell me?"

"That I was making dinner at my place?"

"Yes."

He pushed his plate away but didn't shift his eyes. "I figured you'd say, 'turn around and take me back home.' Was I right?"

"That was a safe assumption."

Dillon grinned. "Ah, my instincts came through once again."

Though she didn't return his grin, she did smile. "Were you always this cagey and I just didn't see it?"

"Yes to both."

Her smile widened, only to fade. "If someone had told me a month ago that I'd be having dinner alone with you, I would've told them they'd lost their mind."

"Hey, it wasn't that bad, was it?"

"Actually, the food was good. But then, I knew you could cook."

"Thanks for that much, anyway," he said, pushing his chair back and reaching for the dishes. "But I wasn't referring to the food." His voice had dropped an octave, and his eyes were penetrating.

Her chest thumping, Janey averted her gaze. Still, he was imprinted on her brain—how sexy he looked in a pair of tight-fitting jeans and a long-sleeved shirt. His hair seemed a bit longer than usual and somewhat mussed, as if he'd been in too big a hurry to comb it.

And there was a hint of dark growth on his cheeks, indicating he hadn't shaved just for her benefit. She didn't know if that was good or bad, but it sure as hell added to his sexiness.

"Janey, look at me."

That voice, sounding rusty and not quite steady, didn't help any, either. In fact, it made her want to head for the door. Then, realizing how immature that would be, she got to her feet and asked in a breathy voice, "I don't suppose you'll let me clean up?"

"Not on your life."

He continued to stare at her, a knowing look in his eyes. She hadn't fooled him. But it didn't matter. From the moment she'd gotten in the car with him, she had been determined to keep things on a friendly level.

It hadn't been easy, especially when her pulse kept beating madly—a sign of her unwitting reaction to him.

Still, she had kept behind the line she'd drawn in the sand, and the evening had been quite pleasant, though there was tension in the air. She couldn't deny that.

"Take a seat in the living room," he added into the quietness. "I'll be there shortly."

She liked his condo. Like most of the newer ones, it had a combined living and dining area. This one had lots of windows and bookcases that dominated the wall on either side of the fireplace. Lots of plants and other personal items filled the space.

Her first impression was that he might have had it professionally decorated. On closer observation, she didn't think so. It was too haphazardly put together for that.

Instead of sitting, Janey ambled around the room, picking up several pictures from the bookcase and looking at them. All were of horses, obviously his pride and joy.

He had told her during dinner about his farm, how that was his salvation from the headaches of his work. She could understand his needing an outlet. Lord knows, he was certainly in a high-stress job. Plus she had a teenage daughter for whom she was responsible.

As she thought of her daughter, Janey's brows

came together in a troubled frown as she walked toward the span of windows. She peered into the star-studded night. While the stars were breathtaking, the moon was even more so.

For a moment she let the sheer pleasure of both blot out her pain and worry over Robin.

"You're certainly deep in thought," Dillon said from behind, his tone husky.

Janey whirled around, suppressing that quiver in her stomach that his presence brought on. If only she could figure out what was happening to her, how all this craziness had come about, she could perhaps regain her control. At the moment, however, she was more confused than she'd ever been in her life.

"I was thinking that your place is really nice," she said weakly.

"You ought to practice lying if you're going to make a habit of it."

Her chin jutted. "You don't know that I was lying."

"Wanna bet?" Then, as if he realized he was being rude, he tempered his next words. "Thanks for the compliment, anyway."

"Actually, my mind was on Robin."

"Is she okay?"

She hesitated.

"Janey?"

"She's okay, but she's not happy with me, which is not all that upsetting or unusual in itself. Some days Mom is rarely right about anything."

"That shoe fits me, as well. Hell, the students think I'm from another planet."

She gave him a brief smile, then sat in the nearest chair. He sat on the sofa, adjacent to her.

For a second her gaze settled on his long legs, which were sprawled out in front of him. No one could wear jeans quite like he did. His tush and thighs filled them out just right. She dared not let her eyes drift upward to his crotch. Afraid that he would notice her scalded cheeks, her head darted down to her own slacks, where she removed a piece of lint.

God, what had she thought? That he would have a hard-on for her? Get real, she told herself, mortified beyond words.

"She wasn't thrilled you were going out." His words were a flat statement of fact.

Janey jerked her gaze back to him. "How did you know?"

"Just a guess, but apparently I'm right on target."

"That you are."

"Was it me personally she objected to?" he asked, in what she thought was a concerned tone.

"I don't think so. Actually, she thinks you're pretty cool."

He laughed. "That's nice to know. Then why would she care?"

"Two reasons, actually."

He didn't say anything. He just waited.

"One is Keith."

"Figures," Dillon said.

"The other is, I've never gone out before."

That declaration seemed to land between them with a thud, like a sack of cement.

"You mean you haven't been with a man since the divorce?" His stare was incredulous.

Once again she raised her chin defiantly. "Is that so bad?"

"Yeah, for someone with your looks," he said in a low voice.

That personal and unexpected comment threw her yet another curve. She struggled to keep her mind focused. "I've already told you, getting involved with another man doesn't interest me."

Heat filled his eyes as they swept over her. "What a waste."

Fourteen

Another flush tinted Janey's cheeks, something that happened far too often when she was around Dillon. But how did one school one's features to show no emotion?

She wasn't a redhead for nothing. When she was angry, everyone knew it; when she was happy, everyone knew that, too. She wasn't very good at hiding much of anything. But she'd better learn, she told herself, if she wanted to match wits with Dillon and win.

"Do you mind if we change the subject?" Even to her own ears she sounded prim. She wanted to kick herself.

"Not at all," he said in a bland tone, but she saw the twinkle in his eye, which galled her that much more.

Suddenly too fidgety to sit any longer, she rose. She never should have come here. She never should have gone out with him, period.

Every time their eyes met, accidentally or otherwise, something nameless seemed to jump between them. Like now. He was looking at her with one of those intense stares, as if he were searching her soul.

It was all she could do not to shiver.

"Sit down, Janey."

"I'm fine."

"No, you're not. I think we could both use something to drink."

He got up and walked into the kitchen. Shortly, he returned with two glasses of wine and set them on the coffee table.

Sighing, she once again took a seat. She reached for one of the glasses as if it were a lifeline, taking a sip despite the fact that she didn't like wine.

"I know that's not your favorite, but at the moment it's all I have."

"That's fine."

"Relax," he said in a low, husky tone.

Impossible! she wanted to scream. Instead, she said, "As Robin would say, this is far-out."

"What?" he asked innocently.

Innocently? That was a joke. "You and me having dinner, then sitting here sipping wine."

"I think it's kind of nice. That's what old friends do, you know."

"Not old friends with our history," she countered sharply.

He rubbed his forehead. "Let it go, at least for now, okay?"

Janey took another sip of wine, then nodded.

"So Robin wants you and Keith back together."

Her eyes clouded. "She's under the illusion that I moved back here so we could be a family again."

"Do you think Keith might've planted that seed?"

"I haven't the foggiest idea, though he did ask me to forgive him."

A smirk touched Dillon's lips. "So you've seen him?"

"He came by the shop the other day."

"I can imagine that made your day," he said on a harsh note.

"It wasn't pleasant, I can tell you that."

"What's he up to now?"

"Still selling cars and making a barrel of money, I'm thinking."

"With his line of bullshit, I don't doubt it."

"Yet he's behind on his child support. Go figure."

"He's probably throwing it away on booze and women."

"I would imagine."

"Was he drinking when he came by?"

"Yes, but if I hadn't smelled it on him," Janey said, "I wouldn't have known. He's a master at holding his liquor."

"I know he's Robin's father, but I—" Dillon broke off as if he realized he was about to say too much.

"I know. I feel the same way, especially after the earring episode. That's what Keith and I really got into it about."

Dillon looked perplexed, and she explained about the expensive gift.

"You think he's using Robin to get to you."

"Don't you?" Janey asked.

Dillon's features darkened. "Sounds that way to me. But then, who am I to say?"

Right. Who was he to say? Furthermore, what was she doing having this conversation with him? Perhaps because she needed someone to talk to or she would burst inside. Gwen was usually her sounding board, and vice versa, but lately they hadn't had a chance to get together. Things had been too hectic.

But Dillon? Still, she heard herself add more fuel to the fire. "He should know he's wasting his time."

"What if he wants you back? What if he and Robin are in cahoots?"

Janey stretched her lips into a thin line. "Robin's my life, and I'd do anything for her—except take Keith back. That's not going to happen."

"Smart choice."

"And I told him that, too."

"Good for you."

Brown eyes met blue ones for a long moment before both turned away. Janey, groping to make sense of the smothering feeling in her chest, was the first to speak again, though her voice was a tad unsteady.

"While we're still on the subject of Robin—she told me about the incident with the boys backing her against the locker."

"Don't worry, I'm keeping an eye on them."

"Did you know one of them has been stalking her? 'Watching' her, as Robin put it?"

"Hell, no!"

"I told her to tell you, and she said she would."

Anger darkened his features. "It won't happen again, I assure you."

"Are the boys troublemakers?"

"Chronic. You know about the break-ins at the school?"

"Who doesn't?"

"Anyway," Dillon went on, "I suspect they might be part of a gang that's responsible for the vandalism."

Janey gasped. "And they singled my daughter out. That scares me out of my mind."

"Hey," Dillon said, leaning forward so he could

clasp her hand in his. "Look at me. I'm not going to let anything happen to Robin. You have to know that."

Her mouth worked for a moment; then, realizing she was clinging to his hand and how good it felt, she removed hers abruptly and stood. Feeling her face flame, she looked back down at him.

He was frowning. "You do trust me, don't you?"

"Do I have a choice?"

His deep sigh signaled his frustration.

"Look, it's just that Robin's so headstrong herself. She's seeing someone she says will take care of those thugs if they bother her again. And that bothers me."

"Who's the guy?"

"A big man on campus." She couldn't quite keep the sarcasm at bay. "The star quarterback. Need I say more?"

"Robin's going with Chad?"

"She's dating him, if that's what you mean."

"Hey, he's an okay kid."

"Do you know him personally?" she asked.

"You bet. I'm friends with his parents."

Her jaw dropped. "So you do know him."

"Well, I'd like to think so." Dillon paused, reached for his wine and took a healthy sip. "You don't like him, do you."

"Is it that obvious?"

He cocked his head. "Yeah, it's that obvious."

"There's something about him that makes me uneasy, but I can't say what that something is. Maybe it's his cockiness or the possessive way he handles Robin." She broke off with a shrug. "Again, it's just a feeling I have."

"Well, if you ever have any problems with him,

all you have to do is let me know. I'll take care of them *and* him."

"Sounds like you've had to do that before."

"Chad's had his troubles, but you don't need to worry."

"Spoken like a man with no kids."

Dillon's mouth tightened. "I wasn't granted that privilege."

"Look, I'm sorry," she said, feeling terrible. She might be many things, but mean-spirited was not one of them. What on earth had come over her?

This whole scenario, she told herself. Her. Him. Them. Together. It made no sense. Yet...

Janey cleared her throat and continued. "That comment was out of line."

He shrugged. "My hide's tough."

"I know you'll take care of Robin, and I appreciate it. It's just that—"

"You don't want to let go. Despite what you think, I understand."

Though that gentle verbal slap was deserved, it still stung. "I'm afraid, actually. It's a big bad world out there."

Dillon rubbed his slightly bristly chin, making her wonder what he would look like with a beard; what it would feel like to touch it, to have it prick her body. Good Lord! She put a trembling hand to her head, but she couldn't avoid his eyes. They were smoldering.

Her breath caught before she finally managed to avert her gaze.

"Janey..."

"It's getting late, and I should be home before Robin."

His breath was harsh. "I'm ready when you are."

Ten minutes later, she was unlocking the side door that led up to the living quarters above the shop. Then, she turned and looked up at him. "Thanks for dinner," she said softly, licking her lips.

His gaze seemed to home in on that gesture. She wasn't sure, but she thought she heard a deep-seated moan. Then he said, "My pleasure."

They were both quiet for a moment. Somewhere in the distance a car horn honked, followed by the sound of a dog barking. However, Janey was scarcely aware of either. Her thoughts were occupied with Dillon's closeness.

She could smell his cologne and see his chest move up and down with each breath he took. She sensed he was as aware of her as she was of him. In fact, he leaned forward, and for a moment she thought he might kiss her.

Just the idea brought heat rushing to her face. She turned the knob, then murmured, "Good night."

He held her arm. "Wait."

"What?" she asked, her gaze dropping to where he touched her.

"I want to see you again," he said in a raspy tone that further stroked her abused nerves.

"We both know that's not a good idea."

"Look, my sister's having a barbecue. She'd love for you to come."

"Dillon, I've already told you—"

"Just don't say no. Not yet, anyway." He let go of her arm.

"I—"

"Think about it. I'll call you."

* * *

Once Dillon was behind the wheel, he slapped his forehead with the palm of his hand. Of all the dumb-ass stunts he'd ever pulled, this one topped the list.

"My sister's having a barbecue, and she'd love for you to come," he mimicked himself out loud. Then, feeling like a fool, he looked to see if anyone was around. He was in luck. The street was deserted, although it was only a little past ten.

He didn't know how long he sat there before he backed out of the drive and drove off. He couldn't afford to sit there any longer for fear Robin and Chad would drive up.

That would just be another screw-up.

Tensing his body, Dillon's mind turned back to the invitation for a get-together that hadn't been planned, that he'd fabricated.

Allie would clobber him. Though most of the time she loved to entertain, she was still feeling under the weather. He doubted she would warm to the idea of hosting a barbecue right now.

Damn! It was absurd to anticipate his and Janey's relationship turning into anything other than a friendship. And even the friendship was questionable.

When they were together, they both seemed to walk on eggshells. He knew he did, and that was bullshit. While the solid block of ice that had encased his heart for so long had begun to melt, it didn't mean he was ready for another lasting relationship.

So what *did* he want from Janey? A romp in the hay?

He gripped the steering wheel so hard he heard his knuckles pop. He had to admit that on several occasions a gesture here and there had ignited a flame of pure lust inside him. But that didn't mean he had to give in to that lust.

Besides, Janey wasn't about to let him get to know her in the biblical sense. It was ludicrous to think otherwise. So he would just have to get over his longing to lure her into the sack. That wouldn't be a problem—*if* he could leave her alone, he told himself, a feeling of disgust snaking through him.

Suddenly he heard a loud screech of brakes, and not his own. He swerved, just narrowly missing the truck in the lane next to him.

Feeling sweat pop out on his face, he maneuvered his utility vehicle back on track. The driver then darted in front of him, his middle finger working overtime.

Dillon swore.

Fifteen

Although she'd taken a bath before she'd gone out with Dillon, the second Janey walked into her bedroom she peeled off her clothes, then made her way to the shower, pausing long enough to eye the tub with a hint of longing, imagining bubbles all the way to the rim. But she'd already been that route and didn't have the time to indulge again.

She was expecting Robin any time now, and she wanted to be in the living room when her daughter came in. She didn't want to give Robin reason to head straight for her bedroom. Janey knew it was imperative that she keep the lines of communication open between them.

Earlier, after Robin had pitched her little verbal fit, Janey had considered calling Dillon and breaking their dinner date. But then her common sense had reasserted itself. She couldn't let Robin control her life to that degree.

Besides, she clung to the fact that one squabble wouldn't sever that special bond between her and Robin, a bond she'd developed by spending quality time with her daughter, knowing her thoughts, knowing her friends', knowing what was going on behind the scenes of her teenager's life.

And while friendship between mother and daughter was important, Janey never lost sight of the fact that she had to be a parent first and foremost. Being a wife had always come second.

That unexpected thought brought on a sinking feeling. Had that been the reason her marriage failed? No. She had never neglected Keith. He was the one who had strayed.

To this day that failure still weighed like an anchor on her heart. She had replayed every minute, hour, day and month of their marriage in her mind, trying to find that precise moment when sugar turned to shit.

It was only recently that she'd been able to examine her feelings deeply enough to pinpoint the turning point. The drinking. Keith had begun to nurse the booze on a regular basis instead of a social one. At the time, however, she had chalked up his newfound fascination with the bottle to the pressures of his job, of working on commission, of having to meet a sales quota each month in order to maintain their standard of living.

There had been other clues, as well, only she'd chosen to ignore them. Or maybe she'd been too naive at the time to pick up on them. He'd always been controlling, never wanting her to work outside the home. He'd wanted her at his beck and call twenty-four hours a day. Despite the drinking and the long hours he'd supposedly put in at the dealership, she had hung in there, the dutiful wife.

Until that fateful day when her secure world had been turned upside down.

It had all started out innocently enough. The Mayfields and Reeds were having their annual summer neighborhood get-together. That year it had been at the Reeds', at poolside.

Having noticed that the huge bowl of potato salad was empty, Janey had gone into the kitchen to replenish it. Only moments before, she had seen Elaine go inside. Thinking her friend was in the bathroom, Janey was about to open the refrigerator when she heard voices—her husband's, in particular—coming from the bedroom.

She froze when she realized who was talking to him.

"Don't you get it?" Elaine cried in a low voice. "I'm sick. Really sick."

"Dammit, we're both going to be sick if we get caught," Keith responded.

With her heart pounding, Janey tiptoed from the kitchen into an alcove that kept her hidden but brought them into full view.

"I'm not just sick, Keith," Elaine told him, beginning to sob. "I'm terminal."

"God, you can't mean that." He took her in his arms and held her tightly against his chest. "Surely you misunderstood the doctor."

Elaine pulled back. "It's ovarian cancer, and I don't have long to live."

"Oh, no, no," Keith whispered, kissing her hard on her trembling lips. "That can't be."

Janey longed to put her hands over her ears to block out the horrifying words, but she couldn't have moved if someone had hollered *Fire*. She was so traumatized by what she'd heard and seen that the room was spinning. She closed her eyes and took deep, gulping breaths.

Keith and Elaine having an affair! Elaine dying!

Not happening. She was dreaming. But when she heard Keith respond, she knew she was staring brutal reality in the face.

"Don't cry, my love."

Elaine clung to him. "I can't bear the thought of leaving you."

"Shush." Keith kissed her again. "The doctors are wrong. They just have to be."

Janey felt rather than saw that she was no longer alone. Woodenly, she turned and found Dillon standing behind her, his face a mirror image of hers—bloodless.

"What the hell's going on?" Dillon demanded in a strangled voice.

"Oh, sweet Jesus," Keith wheezed, jerking around, looking as startled as a rat caught in a trap.

Elaine merely buried her head deeper into Keith's chest.

"How...how could you...?" Janey couldn't say any more. Her throat closed; her stomach heaved.

Dillon strode forward, his target Keith. "Damn you to hell, Mayfield!"

Somehow Janey found the strength to move, whipping past Dillon and running outside. She didn't stop until she was at home, slumped over the toilet, throwing up her guts.

When she was spent, she felt hands on her waist. Looking around, she saw Keith. She wrenched away and glared at him, though her vision was blurred by tears. "Don't you ever touch me again! Get your things and get out of this house. Now!"

Now, suddenly realizing where her mind had strayed, Janey winced as a new wave of pain and bitterness washed through her, so strong that she leaned against the tile and let the water nick her skin like hot pellets. Only after she realized that tears were mixed with the water did she twist the knobs to off and get out.

Fifteen minutes later, Janey made her way into the living room, a cup of hot milk in her hand, and curled up on the sofa. After taking a drink, she placed the cup down on the table beside her and took a deep breath. God, she was tired, more so in mind than in body. What a day. Her head fell gently against the cushion, and she closed her eyes.

Not a smart move.

Dillon's image appeared front and center, and her eyes popped back open. She had purposely kept thoughts of him at bay, unable to handle this whole other Dillon—a Dillon whom she'd never known, despite all those years when they had been friends and neighbors.

Sexy. Complex. Unpredictable. Pushy. And vulnerable.

The list could have gone on indefinitely, had she cared to continue. She still couldn't believe she'd given him the time of day, much less had coffee, then dinner, with him.

And that wasn't all. There had actually been moments during the evening when she'd enjoyed herself, enjoyed his company, had even wanted him to *kiss* her.

She had to stop this nonsense. She had to stop thinking about him as a man who upped her pulse rate, who made her breathing shallow, who made her palms sweat.

Instead, she had to think of him as taboo. He reminded her of all the things she wanted to forget.

He'd been a major player in her pain, had seen her during her worst moments.

To some extent, she knew that kind of thinking was totally irrational. Their exes were the ones who had committed adultery, not her and Dillon. Well, she couldn't vouch for Dillon on that score, though she doubted he had ever cheated on Elaine.

None of that was important any longer. But Robin was. Her daughter was in the midst of the most vulnerable years of her life. She needed one hundred percent of her mother, leaving Janey no choice but to squelch her growing attraction to Dillon.

So the barbecue was out. Oh, she would love to see and visit with his sister Allie again. One day that would happen. Perhaps they would bump into each other at the grocery store. For now, though, anything else was off-limits.

Once again Janey renewed her pact with herself to deal with Dillon only as the principal of her child's school. Thinking of Robin sent her eyes to the clock. Robin was late—thirty minutes, to be exact.

Anger drove her to her feet. But that anger was soon tempered by concern. What if something had happened? What if Chad had had a wreck? She hadn't heard any sirens, but that didn't mean anything. The movie theater was on the other side of town, though both hospitals were nearby.

Cool it, she told herself. Letting her imagination run wild wouldn't bring Robin home one minute sooner. Still, she couldn't stop herself from pacing the floor or her mind from conjuring up images of all sorts of terrible things that could have happened.

What if those gang members had followed them? *Get a grip,* she told herself. Yet that cold knot of

fear stayed lodged in the bottom of her stomach like
a rock.

At that moment the door opened and Robin
walked in, only to halt in her tracks, a look of guilt
spreading across her features. And something else
that Janey couldn't quite identify. Maybe it was a
hint of defiance. After all, they hadn't parted on the
best of terms.

"Uh, hi, Mom," Robin said in a rush. "I didn't
expect you still to be up. I thought you'd be asleep."

"You know better than that. I never go to sleep
until I know you're in." Janey's gaze landed pointedly on the clock. "You're late, young lady."

Color splotched Robin's cheeks.

"Did Chad walk you to the door?"

"Yes, ma'am."

"I was hoping to see him."

Perhaps she'd have heard the car had her thoughts
not been on Dillon. All the more reason to yank her
life back on track, she thought.

That high color deserted Robin's face. "Would
you have said something to him?"

"In a heartbeat."

"Mom! Talk about embarrassing."

"I prefer to talk about why you're late. The movie
was over hours ago."

Janey wasn't at all sure she wanted to know the
truth. In fact, she didn't, for fear of what she'd find
out. To her knowledge, Robin had never lied to her,
but there was always a first time, especially with a
young man like Chad in the picture. As a result,
Janey was treading on uncharted territory.

Yet she had no choice but to question her daughter. Robin couldn't be allowed to get by with overtly

ignoring her curfew. If she gave an inch, Janey suspected, her daughter would take a mile. She had that much of Keith in her. And what teenager didn't try his or her parents at one time or another? She'd been lucky that Robin was a late bloomer.

"We stopped for something to eat," Robin said, breaking the smothering silence.

"Go on."

"Mom!"

"Don't 'Mom' me. If you hadn't been late, none of this would be happening. Don't lose sight of the fact that you're the one who's wrong here, not me."

"I'm sorry, okay?" Robin responded in a cajoling tone.

"No, it's not okay. Not this time. I have to know that when you give me your word, you'll stick to it."

"You hate Chad." Robin's eyes flashed. "That's what this is all about."

Janey forced herself to be patient. "You're wrong. I don't know Chad well enough to hate him."

"And you won't try to get to know him, either." She paused and toyed with her hair. "It's all right if you go out with a man other than dad, but—"

"I'm the grown-up here, young lady," Janey interrupted. "That aside, we're talking about you, not me."

"That's not fair."

"Fair or not, Chad's off-limits for the next couple of weekends."

Tears sprang into Robin's eyes, and she cried, "But, Mom, I at least deserve another chance."

"I don't work that way," Janey replied softly. "I love you too much to be wishy-washy. One of these days, when you have kids of your own, you'll understand.''

''Mom, please!'' Robin begged. ''Don't do this.''

Janey winced as she felt herself the pain she was inflicting on her beloved child, but she had to remain firm. ''Tell Chad you won't be going out with him next weekend.''

Suddenly Robin burst into full-blown tears. ''Maybe Dad's right. Maybe I should go live with him.''

Before Janey could unlock her frozen tongue to make a comeback, Robin fled the room. Janey grabbed her stomach and sank into the nearest chair, that cold knot of fear spreading throughout her body. Oh, dear Lord, surely Robin hadn't meant those awful words.

But what if she had?

The second Robin entered her room and slammed the door behind her, she fell onto the bed and let the tears flow. Then, when the sobs had subsided somewhat, she reached for the phone and called Beverly.

''Were you asleep?'' Robin whispered into the receiver.

''Nah. Actually, I'm still working on my Trig problems.'' Beverly was silent for a moment, then asked, ''You sound like you've been crying.''

''I have.''

''Did you and Chad have a fight?''

''No, but Mom and I did. I was late.''

''Oops, you're in big trouble.''

''Up to my eyeballs.''

''Just for being late one time?'' Beverly's tone was incredulous. ''You're not serious?''

"Would I joke about a thing like that?"

"Nope. She didn't take the phone away, did she?"

"No," Robin told her in a tight voice. "It's Chad. I can't go out with him for two weeks."

"Oh, man, that's worse."

"Tell me about it."

"He'll be pissed."

"Oh, Bev," Robin wailed, "do you think he'll ask someone else out?"

"Beats me. But if he does, you should beat him."

"Yeah, right."

"Why were you late? You know how anal your mom is. Way more than mine. It's that single-parent syndrome crap."

"We went parking."

"So how'd that go? I want all the juicy details." Beverly lowered her voice, then added, "Did you put out?"

"Beverly!"

"Well, did you?"

"No."

"But I bet he tried."

Robin clutched the receiver for all it was worth while new tears burned her eyes. "Sort of."

"Sort of?" Beverly demanded in an excited tone. "What does that mean?"

"It means it's something I can't talk about over the phone."

Beverly groaned, then said, "I'll meet you in front of the flagpole in the morning."

"All right."

"Good night."

Once the dial tone sounded in her ear, Robin replaced the receiver, then wiped her eyes. Her mom was mad at her, and so was Chad. And she was miserable.

She turned onto her pillow and wept.

Sixteen

"It's about time you got your buns over here."

Duly chastised, Dillon gave his sister an apologetic smile, then leaned over and kissed her on the cheek. When he pulled back, he frowned. She didn't look like she was feeling any better than when he'd seen her last.

The fact that she was home from work bore testimony to that. He had taken a lunch break today, which was a rarity for him. Instead of getting something to eat, however, he'd headed for the farm. He'd just wanted a few minutes of fresh air.

The horse trailer needed some repairs, anyway, and he wanted Mike to attend to it. When he saw that Mike's pickup was gone and noticed Allie's car in the garage, he had come to the house straightaway.

"Why the sudden frown?"

"I'm worried about you," Dillon said bluntly, pulling a chair out from the dining table and sitting on it. Allie was already there, drinking a cup of tea.

"I'm all right."

"Stop saying that. If you were all right, you'd be at work."

Allie made a face. "This is my boss's doing. He's the one who insisted I come home. Said I looked like warmed-over piss."

Dillon pitched his head back and laughed. "Good old Paul. He sure knows how to cut to the chase."

"Yeah, doesn't he?" Allie replied sarcastically.

"Ah, he didn't mean it that way. He's just concerned about you. We all are."

"I wish everyone would stop fussing, especially Mike. He's driving me nuts."

"And well he should. When you get to feeling like your old self again, we'll call off the dogs."

Allie gave him an exasperated glare. "I'm about to undergo some tests. So there."

"It's about damn time." Dillon paused. "Since I've committed you to having a barbecue."

"Excuse me?"

Dillon didn't respond right off. He got up, walked to the counter and poured himself a cup of coffee. When he turned back around, Allie's eyes were narrowed on him.

"I opened my big mouth and inserted my foot."

"Again," Allie said drolly.

Dillon chuckled; then his features sobered. "I told Janey you were having a barbecue and that she was invited."

"Whatever possessed you to do that?"

Dillon let out a deep sigh. "I'm still trying to figure that one out myself."

"You can do better than that."

"I wanted an excuse to see her again," he said flatly.

Allie tapped her blunt nails on the table while giving him a sage look. "I see."

"I wish to hell you'd enlighten me, then."

"First, what about Patricia? Is she completely out of the picture?"

"She was never in it, although I apparently never convinced you of that. She's a friend whose company I enjoy, but—"

"There's no physical attraction, and there is with Janey."

"I'm not even sure that's the case."

Allie made an unladylike sound. "Hey, are you forgetting who you're talking to? It's your big sister, and I didn't just fall off a turnip truck."

Dillon rubbed the back of his neck, feeling more frustrated than he had in a long time. "I'll admit I'm attracted to her, but I swear to God, nothing will ever come of it."

"How can you be so sure?"

"Because it's insane," he said in a terse voice.

Allie shrugged. "Stranger things have happened."

"Is that supposed to give me comfort?" He knew he was glaring at her, when, in fact, none of these crazy feelings churning in his gut were her fault.

"Man, you're really bent out of shape over this, aren't you."

"After all that's gone on, I'd be certifiable if I weren't."

Allie's brows knitted into a puzzled frown. "Hey, am I missing something here? If so, please fill in the blanks."

"It's not that easy."

"I know that your families were friends, and that Elaine and Janey were even best friends—which does make your interest in her somewhat off the beaten track, but not that far off." Allie paused and took another sip of her tea, then made a face. "Yuk, that's cold."

"Want me to get you some fresh?" Dillon asked, glad for the timely interruption.

"No, thanks. I've had enough already."

Dillon walked to the window, where he stared outside. He could see Dandi and another of his horses munching grass. Suddenly he longed to be with them—and not here, closed up in this room, having this bizarre conversation with his sister, who didn't have a clue what was going on. What *had* gone on.

Maybe it was time he told her.

"What's with you, anyway?" Allie demanded, her tone making it obvious that her patience was waning. "I haven't seen you like this in a long time. Why, you're more uptight than a woman going through menopause."

Dillon turned and gave her a sarcastic half smile. "Thanks."

"You're welcome," she responded.

He jammed his hands in his pockets and stared at her with unseeing eyes.

"Dillon!"

Still stalling, Dillon argued with himself. Dammit, now was not the time to drop a bombshell in her lap, especially when she looked and felt like hell. But he'd blown it. She wasn't about to let him out the door without a feasible explanation.

"Dillon!" she said again. "If you ever want another one of my peach cobblers, you'd better start talking."

"I don't know any other way to say this except to say it."

"God, will you stop acting like an ass?"

He stared at his sister for a moment longer, then blurted out, "The reason why I find my attraction to

Janey so bizarre is that Elaine had an affair with her husband.''

"I was wondering when you were going to tell me.'' Allie's expression was deadpan.

Dillon's jaw went slack. "You knew?"

"Have you forgotten how small towns work?" Her tone was firm but kind.

"No," he said grimly. "But since you never said anything, I..."

"I was waiting for you to tell me. I thought that was how it should work. Lord knows I've given you enough rope to hang ten men, but you never picked up on it.''

Dillon made a helpless gesture. "I'm sorry."

"Hey, don't be sorry. There's no right or wrong here. I had no doubt that when the time was right you'd confide in me.''

He gave the back of his neck another quick dig, feeling like his muscles were stretched on a rack. "I thought I had moved on, or at least that was what I told Janey, only when I talk about that nightmare all the bitterness resurfaces.''

"That's why you don't need to talk about it, why I'm not going to ask for the gory details—which, by the way, I didn't hear through the gossip mill. Besides, what's done is done. No point in beating that old dead horse.''

"Unfortunately, seeing Janey seems to have given that old horse new life.''

"Then don't see her.''

He muttered an expletive. "I wish it was that black or white. Unfortunately, there's a lot of gray mixed in there.''

Allie got up, walked over to him and put her arms

around him. After the hug, she stepped back. "It *is* that black or white. Either you can get past that ugly part of your life and see Janey in a whole new light, or you can't."

"She has more of a problem with us than I do."

"Then you both have a lot of soul-searching to do."

Dillon gave her a bleak smile. "You don't think I'm certifiable?"

"For finding Janey attractive?"

"Not so much that as wanting to be with her."

"Well, now that I think about it—" She broke off, her lips twitching. Then she added, "Of course not. I just want you to be happy, that's all."

Dillon's eyes darkened. "I'm beginning to think true happiness exists only in fairy tales."

Allie slapped him on the shoulder. "Stop it!"

He forced a grin.

"That's better. As for the barbecue, as soon as I get those tests behind me, we'll have a blowout like you've never seen."

This time Dillon hugged her. "Thanks, sis. What would I do without you?"

"To be truthful, I don't know." She kissed him on the cheek. "I bet those hoodlums are going wild. You'd best get your tush back to that school and corral them."

"You got that right." He frowned down at his watch. "Damn, I almost forgot. I have a meeting with a detective in twenty minutes."

Five minutes later he was climbing into his vehicle.

"Tell Janey I said hello," Allie called out, an impish grin on her face.

He scowled, then slammed the door.

"Oink oink."

"Me too," Janey said, ginning at her friend.

Gwen didn't grin back. She was too busy massaging her stomach. "God, I wish I hadn't eaten so much."

"Ditto."

Gwen batted her hand. "Baloney. You didn't consume anywhere near what I did. But as you know, Chinese food is my big weakness."

Janey was delighted to have some time with her friend. As luck would have it, Robin was spending the night with Beverly so they could work on a big science project.

At loose ends when she closed the store, Janey had made a few calls to set up the drill team meeting for later in the week, then had called Gwen, taking a chance her friend might have a free evening. They had agreed to meet at a new Chinese restaurant. Afterward, Janey had followed her friend home.

Now as she stared at the full cup of coffee Gwen had placed in front of her, she made a face. "I really ought to get my fanny home."

Gwen sat down on the other end of the sofa. "What's your hurry?"

"Tomorrow's another workday."

"For me, too, but so what?" Gwen stared at her long and hard. "Something's eating at you, and I want to know what it is."

Janey blew out her breath. "Is it that obvious?"

"Yep. Has been all evening, though I've kept my mouth shut."

"It's a combination of things, actually," Janey admitted, tucking her legs under her. "Robin and I had a row the other night when she was late getting home."

"What happened?"

Janey told her.

"Ah, Robin's just blowing hot air. Even though you more or less grounded her, she wouldn't choose Keith over you."

Janey shuddered. "Surely not, but she's changing, Gwen, especially since she's gotten this boyfriend."

"Do you think it's serious?"

"I do, and that's what worries me. She's crazy about him, and I suspect Keith's egging her on."

"Look, Robin's a good kid, never been in any trouble. A virgin at seventeen, for crying out loud." Gwen paused and raised her eyebrows. "Right?"

Janey paled. "God, I hope so. The thought of her not being one—" She couldn't find the appropriate words; fear had dammed them up inside her.

"Hey, calm down. That comment was a compliment to you. I didn't mean to get your panties in another wad."

"You didn't. It's just that we've talked about pre-marital sex and its consequences so many times. She knows I don't approve." Janey shuddered again. "Why, some of her friends' mothers have given their approval for their daughters to get on the pill."

"That's just like saying you have my permission to get it on."

"Exactly," Janey responded in a flat tone.

"You don't have to worry about Robin. She's been raised right."

"But I still worry. There's something about this young man that I just don't like."

"You would feel that way about any 'young man,' Janey," Gwen pointed out gently.

"Maybe so," Janey acknowledged on a sigh. "There's something else, too." She explained about the creepy boy who'd been watching Robin.

"Does Dillon Reed know? He's the principal, right?"

At the mention of his name, Janey felt heat invade her cheeks, and she looked away. "Uh, yes, he does."

"Hey, I see that flush. What's going on?"

Janey hesitated. "I don't know what you're talking about." She hated lying, but she couldn't bring herself to talk about Dillon, even to her best friend.

She should have known she wasn't going to get by with that.

"The hell you don't."

"Okay, so I had dinner with him the other night."

"'Him,' as in Dillon?"

"Yes." Janey's voice was tight.

"And did y'all talk about old times?" Gwen quipped, a sarcastic tinge to her voice.

Janey bit down on her lower lip.

"Sorry." Gwen sounded contrite. "That was uncalled for."

"No, it wasn't."

"So are you two interested in each other?" She was looking at Janey with disbelief. "I have to admit that if you were, it would definitely blow my shirttail up."

"Well, you don't have to worry. He's the last person I'd get involved with."

"Are you sure?" A hint of suspicion remained in Gwen's eyes.

"As sure as God made little green apples."

Gwen scratched her head. "Well, all I can say is that your life is much more interesting than mine. Anything else going on that I need to know about?"

Janey got to her feet, forcing a smile. "I'll save that for another time. Right now, I'm off before I crash."

Later, when she arrived home, Janey didn't know what exactly set off the alarm inside her head after she opened the side door. Maybe it was the scent of cheap cologne that blasted her in the face, or the fact that the door into the shop was ajar. She was certain she'd closed it behind her after work. Without thinking, she pushed it all the way open and switched on the lights.

"Oh, no!" she whimpered, her hand flying to her mouth.

Seventeen

The candy shop had been broken into.

Janey didn't know how long she stood in that petrified state and stared at the mess in front of her. The counters were open, and candy, along with the party goods and favors, was strewn all over the place.

Janey whimpered again, her eyes filling with tears. Who could have done such a thing? *Why?* That was the question uppermost in her mind. Such blatant destruction of property, and for no apparent reason.

Whoever was responsible hadn't gotten a penny; she never kept any cash in the register. Maybe that was the answer to her question. Maybe they had been furious that no money was available.

But there's cash upstairs.

That thought slammed into Janey's head like a fist. She reeled, yet remained rooted to the spot, suddenly too frightened to move. What if the culprit or culprits were still in the house?

Chills racked her body, and she closed her arms across her chest. How had they gotten in? Obviously she'd failed to secure the bolt on the front door. No matter. In a house this old, there were all sorts of ways to get in, if one was determined.

Janey listened for any unfamiliar sounds, but she couldn't discern what was real and what was imaginary. She was too scared. And too angry. Red hot fury suddenly ripped through her. That was what forced her to move, albeit on legs that had the consistency of melted butter.

Still, she made it to the counter, where she found the phone amidst all the debris. She was about to pick it up and dial 911—when it rang.

Janey jumped as if she'd been shot. Noticing that it was the house line, she grabbed it, but didn't say anything. Her throat was jammed with suppressed tears.

"Janey?"

Dillon. Oh, God. *Thank God.* She clung to the receiver as though it were now her lifeline.

"Robin, is that you?"

Even through the fog of fear and fury, Janey recognized the apprehension in his voice, especially when she didn't answer. If he thought he'd gotten the wrong number, Dillon was bound to hang up. She didn't want that. He represented the solid rock of security that she needed.

"Don't hang up," she finally said in a strained whisper.

"Janey?" he repeated.

This time his gruff voice had risen, leaving no doubt that he was alarmed. "Is that you? If it is, say something, dammit!"

Janey coughed. "It's me."

"Are you all right?"

Before she cleared her throat again and responded, he fired off another question, "Has something happened?"

"The store."

"What about it?"

"Someone broke in." Her voice caught again.

"I'm on my way."

Somehow Dillon's strong, abrupt words managed to penetrate the mist that surrounded her brain and she was able to say, "That's not nec—"

Before she could complete her sentence, the offensive sound of the dial tone buzzed in her ear. When the receiver was back in place, she bit down on her lower lip, trying to hold off the sobs that were threatening to erupt.

She had to get control. It seemed as if she had completely fallen apart, though she'd been through worse things. Her divorce, for one. That had been like a death.

This malicious destruction was nothing compared to that, except that she felt so violated, so used.

911.

She had to call the police. With trembling fingers, she punched in the numbers. Once she'd painstakingly given them the information they asked for, she sank onto the stool at the end of the counter.

She didn't have long to wait, at least for Dillon. She saw his vehicle when it pulled in to the parking lot. She didn't have to get up to let him in, either, she reminded herself. Like the intruders, he could waltz right in.

He crossed to her immediately. "Are you sure you're all right?"

Though he didn't touch her, it was obvious he wanted to. He reached out his arms, only to drop them instantly back to his sides.

Janey clung to the side of the counter. "I'm fine. But look what they did." Her voice broke, and she bit her lip again.

"Hey," he said in a low, raspy tone. "It's going to be okay."

"How can you say that?" she wailed.

"Because no one was hurt, and that's the main thing." He paused. "Where's Robin?"

"Spending the night with a friend."

"You've called the police."

"Right after I hung up from you."

"What about the upstairs?"

Janey's eyes darted in that direction. "I don't know. I just got home and saw this. I was afraid to go up there."

"Smart move."

Before Janey could say anything else, a police car pulled up in front. The investigating officer was Sergeant Hanks, a short, wiry man who was all business. First off, he headed upstairs, his pistol drawn.

Wide-eyed, Janey remained with Dillon, who continued to stand at her side as if on guard. "I can't believe this is happening," she whispered, watching the officer until he disappeared from sight.

"I'm keeping my fingers crossed the bastards didn't make it that far." Dillon's face was filled with as much fury as his voice.

"Me too. I can't bear the thought of them touching our things."

"I'd like to get my hands on the bastards. That's all I can think about."

Janey peered up at him. His jaw was clamped so tightly that she feared the bones might crack. This was yet another side of Dillon. At the moment, he looked capable of taking someone's head off. She didn't know if that was comforting or not.

"I've been through this at the school. Twice now."

"That's right. I'd almost forgotten."

Before Dillon could respond, Sergeant Hanks made his way back into the store. "All's clear upstairs, ma'am."

Janey went weak with relief. "Thank God for that."

"It's a good thing," Dillon muttered harshly.

The fingerprint team arrived about that time and set to work.

"I don't think we'll find a thing in the way of prints," the sergeant said, walking back to the front and checking the lock. "Whoever's responsible probably had enough sense to wear gloves."

"I'm sure," Dillon said, his features still grim.

"Do you have any idea how much candy was taken?" Hanks asked.

Janey took a breath. "From the looks of the empty containers, I'd say most of it."

"I hope they ate it and are puking their guts up about now," Dillon muttered.

Sergeant Hanks cut him a look, then smiled briefly before closing his notebook. "I'm sorry about all this, ma'am. I'll let you know something as soon as possible."

Janey held out her hand. "Thanks for everything."

"Good night."

Dillon followed Hanks and the others out, then locked the door behind them. He faced Janey and said, "First thing in the morning, you should call a locksmith and have all the locks changed."

Janey rubbed her temple, feeling as though a piece

of steel had lodged there. "After I clean up all this mess."

"Before." He paused. "Promise?"

She nodded.

"Good. Another thing—why don't you have an alarm system?"

Janey frowned. "I never even thought about one, and I'm sure Aunt Lois didn't, either." What she didn't tell him was that even if she had, she couldn't have afforded one.

"That's not smart."

"The thought of anyone breaking in never crossed my mind—not in a town the size of this one, for heaven's sake."

"You know better than that. Hell, it happens in Small Town, USA, the same as it does in big cities."

"You're right, of course," she responded in a weary tone.

"Hey, I think it's time you headed upstairs. I'll stay here and clean up this mess."

She was incredulous. "Oh, please, this isn't your problem."

"I'm making it my problem."

"But—"

"You look like you're about to drop in your tracks. Let me take care of it."

"All right," she said, releasing a deep sigh. "I'll help, though. I'm not about to let you tackle this chaos alone."

"Never argue with a strong-minded woman. That's my motto."

That almost brought a smile to her numb lips, but when Janey looked around her, even the thought of a smile died an instant death.

In the end, it didn't take nearly as long to put things back in order as she'd first thought. Still, by the time they were finished, long past midnight, she was exhausted.

"I can't thank you enough," she said when they were done, suddenly feeling awkward for the first time since his arrival. "You didn't have to do this."

His gaze was penetrating. "I know, but I wanted to."

"I guess I'd better go up, and let you get home." Yet Janey didn't budge. The thought of being alone filled her with dread.

As if he could read her mind, Dillon said in a somewhat gruff voice, "Come on, I'll go up with you."

Relief surged through her. "I'll make us some hot chocolate."

"Works for me."

While she was making the cocoa, he stood in the doorway of the kitchen, somehow further shrinking the already small room. She'd never thought of him as such a big man. But then, she'd never thought of Dillon as anything other than her best friend's husband. Now...

Janey jerked her mind off that forbidden thought and blinked rapidly, trying to ward off a new threat of tears. It wasn't Dillon's unsettling presence that was responsible, she told herself fiercely, but rather the circumstances. She'd just suffered a trauma; she had a right to be weepy.

Liar.

At the moment it was him that had her all maudlin. He was too damn sexy, leaning against the doorjamb, dressed in old jeans, a sweatshirt and running shoes, his eyes tracking her every move, a dark glitter in them.

In order to relieve the building tension, she said the first thing that came to mind. "Why did you call?"

"Do I have to have a reason?"

"Yes."

The expression in his eyes didn't change in intensity. "I wanted to let you know the barbecue's on hold."

She blinked. "Barbecue?" Then it sank in what he was talking about. "Oh, right."

"You were so excited you forgot, huh?"

Embarrassed, she was about to try to make amends when she realized he was teasing her. "It's just that I've had a lot on my mind lately," she said in a mock huff.

"I understand. But when Allie gets to feeling better, you're still on the hook." His smile was challenging.

"We'll see."

"That we will."

Their gazes tangled for a moment longer; then he changed the subject. "I hate that this had to happen to you, but I'm so grateful you and Robin weren't here."

Casting her gaze downward, Janey thought about how many times she'd already thanked the Lord for that very thing. Until now, she hadn't allowed herself to think about what might have happened if her daughter had been in the house alone. The hair stood up on the back of her neck. And to think she hadn't wanted Robin to go out, it being a school night and all.

But in a weak moment Robin had won her over—another gift from God. Still, a chill darted through Janey and her teeth began chattering.

Two long strides and Dillon was in front of her, again stopping just short of touching her. "The worst is over," he said in that still raspy tone.

Tears pooled in Janey's eyes as she gazed up at him. "When...you mentioned Robin..."

"Shhh. I didn't mean to upset you."

"It's not your fault." Yet she couldn't stop her body from betraying her. She began to shake all over.

Without saying a word or asking permission, Dillon reached for her and drew her against him. For a moment they both seemed to stiffen, as if realizing this was the first time they had ever touched each other.

Then the tightness of his arms seemed to melt Janey's resistance, along with her fear and anger. She clung to him, sobs wracking her body.

"Don't. Please don't," he said, placing his lips first against her temple, then on her cheeks, leaving moist, featherlight kisses behind. "It's okay."

She had lifted her head just as those last words were spoken, bringing her mouth in line with his.

"Janey..."

His thick, husky voice was her undoing. Her lips parted, and their gazes held while the seconds stretched into a taut minute. Oh, dear Lord, he was going to kiss her. His fractured breathing, combined with the heavy thud of his heart, told her that. And she wasn't about to stop him. She moaned with anticipated pleasure as his lips made contact with hers.

Janey went weak under the intense pressure, as he nudged her lips farther apart so he could gain full access to her tongue. Then he sucked on the tip, making her head spin and her knees buckle.

Oh, mercy! she thought, clutching at him, reveling in the burning intensity of his mouth, giving in to the frantic need expanding inside her.

She arched against him, his erection nudging her stomach even as his hand loosened her blouse and sneaked under it, making contact with bare skin.

Moaning, she dug her fingers into his shoulder blades, while he unclasped her bra, then circled a full breast and engorged nipple.

Raw danger. That was the game she was indulging in. But she was unable or unwilling to do anything about that, too caught up in the feel of his devouring lips and his hands on her skin.

Only when she suddenly felt those same hands thrusting her away did the world right itself. She stared at him, the ringing of the phone and his curses stinging her ears.

"You might as well answer it," he said in a harsh, unsteady tone.

It was her elderly neighbor, Mae Shepard.

"Are you all right, Janey? I saw the police car and was wondering what was going on."

Somehow she found the strength to answer. "Everything's under control, Mrs. Shepard."

Eighteen

"When the officer gets here, beep me, please."

"Will do, Mr. Reed," Mildred Wayland, his secretary, said, a bright smile on her otherwise plain face. Attractive he could do without. Efficient he could not. Mildred was a whiz at handling the computers as well as the faculty.

And she sure knew how to keep him in line, a full-time job in itself. "I'm heading to Mrs. McCurry's room."

"I'll organize your notes on the break-in and have them ready."

Dillon felt the furrow between his brows deepen. "After I talk to the officer, I hope we'll have even more info."

"We'll soon know, I guess."

Dillon nodded, then made his way out into the hall. Classes were in progress, and all was relatively quiet. For once he saw no students in the main hall, a good sign. Supposedly they were where they should be—in their classes, soaking up knowledge.

A sardonic smile touched his lips. Dream on. That was when he heard a cat-call coming from a room midway down the corridor.

He didn't have to enter the classroom to see what was taking place inside. Each door had a slender glass pane. When he peered through, his mouth tightened.

Bedlam. That was the word that came to mind. And the teacher apparently could not care less. Mrs. McCurry's back was to the students while she put information on the blackboard.

Two seniors were in the back of the room, standing, jiving to imaginary music, their pants riding so low on their hips that Dillon feared their clothing would soon be around their ankles. He would bet neither one had on any underwear.

Chad Burnette and another kid whose name he didn't know were the ones holding court. The other students were snickering and rallying them on.

Damn Mrs. McCurry. He would have liked to throttle her. How could she be so oblivious to the pandemonium and maintain her own sanity? Already she had enough citations in her folder to mount a solid case for dismissing her. However, he knew he would meet opposition if he tried. Her parents were bigwigs in this town.

So what? He had never backed down from a challenge yet, and he wasn't about to now. If she didn't clean up her sloppy classroom habits, he was determined to go for her jugular.

Dillon eased the door open and stepped inside. All eyes riveted on him, except the teacher's. She continued to write on the board. The two boys froze mid-action, and the tittering stopped cold.

"Having fun, boys?" Dillon asked in an even tone.

Stark silence greeted him, while his gaze scanned the room, mentally noting that Robin occupied one of the desks. He also noted the condoning and ador-ing look she was giving Chad.

"Hiya, Mr. Reed," Chad said, almost choking on his grin.

"You think this is funny, Chad?"

The boy's features turned sullen. "No."

"No *what?*" Dillon demanded.

"No, sir," Chad muttered. "But we weren't hurt-ing anything."

He ignored Chad's defense of their behavior and said, "Both of you. In Mr. Cooper's office. Now."

Without saying another word, they slunk out, though not before cutting him with razor-sharp glances.

"I suggest you get back to your work—unless some of *you* want to join them," Dillon told the re-mainder of the class.

The students' heads ducked back to their books.

The teacher followed him out into the hall, all but wringing her hands. "I know what you're think-ing—"

"Apparently you don't," he said tersely. "But we'll talk about this later in my office."

"But, Mr. Reed—"

He ignored her and spun on his heels, just as his beeper went off.

"So you really think it could be the same hood-lums?"

"The two burglaries certainly have similar ear-markings."

For the past fifteen minutes, Dillon and Officer Riley had been discussing the school vandalism and the fact that no one had yet been arrested.

Then Dillon had explained to Riley why he'd called him back to the school. Ever since he had witnessed the destruction of Janey's candy shop, his gut instinct had been giving him the devil. He finally decided to listen to it.

Hence, this meeting.

"I'll talk to Hanks when I get back to the station," Riley said. "We'll compare notes."

Dillon swiveled in his chair, then leaned back. "I hope it won't be a waste of time."

"I'm not concerned about that. But what makes you think the two are connected?"

"I've already told you who I suspect—members of a gang headed by Hal Aimsworth, a little creep who's always in trouble. That aside for now, Hal approached the daughter of Janey Mayfield, who owns the shop, and asked her out."

"Ah, I'm beginning to get the picture."

"She told him to go butt a stump, which didn't set too well with Aimsworth, of course."

"So you think breaking into her mother's store might be his way of getting back at her?"

"I sure as hell do. The MOs are too much alike."

Riley stood. "Let me see what I can find out."

Dillon stood also, shaking the other man's outstretched hand.

"You'll be hearing from me," Riley said, then strode out.

Once the door was closed behind the officer, Dillon sat back down, ignoring the papers that Mildred had so meticulously spread across his desk. He was too uptight to focus.

But that was nothing new.

Again his thoughts roared back to Janey, the store

break-in, the kiss they'd shared. A groan erupted from deep in his throat. Good thing he'd closed the door, he thought without humor, or Mildred would have run in to check on him.

"Shit," he muttered, swinging around in his chair, his gaze settling on a blank wall. He had shit for brains—and they were tucked in his shorts, to boot.

He'd taken advantage of her vulnerability, and he hated himself for that. But hell, he was only human, or so he kept telling himself.

Poor excuse.

But when she had started shaking, looking so fragile and helpless, his willpower had evaporated like dew at sunrise. Even now, a week after the fact, he could still taste her sweet lips, feel her pliable body against him—a perfect fit, like it belonged there.

He lunged out of his chair, feeling sweat above his lip despite the fact that it wasn't all that warm in his office. That didn't matter; it was his body temperature that was the problem.

He was hot and horny as hell.

When he'd started seeing her, he truly hadn't meant for things to progress so rapidly or to get this far out of hand. But when she'd treated him as if he had a dreaded disease, she'd gotten his ire up, and he'd wanted to get back at her.

Then something had changed.

He'd noticed what a damn good-looking woman she was and had started seeing her in a different light.

That was when he should have run the way he would have from a mugger in Central Park. Instead, he'd hung around until he wanted more than he should, more than she was prepared to give.

Hell, she didn't seem to like men at all anymore,

much less trust them. A crazy notion zinged his brain. Could he change that? More to the point, did he want to? As he'd told his sister, he didn't want to remarry, though he would like to have a child.

Sometimes, though, he was no longer sure about that. Suddenly a vision of Janey's stomach visibly swollen with his baby jumped to mind.

He groaned. How could he even think about putting himself through that kind of hell again, especially after what had happened with Elaine? If she hadn't lost that second baby, would things have turned out differently? He knew that had been the beginning of the end of their marriage.

Elaine had changed the instant the doctor had given them the bad news. He'd been affected, too. He couldn't deny that. The loss had been a blow that had knocked him out emotionally. For a long time after the doctor had left, he and Elaine had remained silent, each locked in a private hell.

Then she had asked him to leave, telling him that she wanted to be alone. Respecting that, he'd left and gone straight to the farm. Once there, he'd saddled Dandi and had ridden until he couldn't push the horse any farther. Dismounting, he'd fallen to his knees in a bed of grass and had let the tears rain down his face.

"Why? Why? Why?" he'd cried into the soft breeze. "Why couldn't my son have lived?"

The only answer had been the sound of his own choking sobs.

Later, he'd returned to Elaine to tell her that he didn't blame her, that their loss was no one's fault. But his words had fallen on deaf ears. She had become remote, withdrawn, uninterested in him or anything else around her. Maybe she'd sensed that he was as devastated as she was, even though he'd tried his best to mask his broken heart.

Dillon closed his eyes and allowed a wave of despair to sweep over him. Scar tissue on the outside and vulnerable on the inside—that was him.

The door suddenly burst open. "Mr. Reed!"

Mildred's frantic cry and wide eyes yanked him back to reality.

"What—?"

"Oh, God, I just had a call saying there's a bomb in the building."

The past week had been a busy one. In fact, Janey hadn't stopped, which had been a godsend for her, as she'd wanted to be so drop-dead tired at the end of the day that she would fall into bed and sleep.

She had met with her drill team committee twice. A car wash was the first project the girls would do to make money for their trip. The second was a bake sale.

The shop had kept her busy, as well, not so much with customers as continuing with the cleanup following the break-in. She hadn't realized until the next morning the true extent of the damage.

The highlight of her week had been the Friday night football game, another one out of town. She had gone with Christy Olson, Beverly's mother.

Aside from watching her daughter perform, the game had been a disaster: the first person she had seen when she walked through the gate was Dillon.

Immediately her heart had betrayed her; it had raced out of control. Although she had pretended not to notice him, her heart didn't settle until long after the whistle had blown to start the game.

Toxic. That was the word that fit him. And normal people, which she considered herself to be, avoided being around anything or anyone that was harmful.

Though it galled her to admit it, her body had gone into meltdown when his lips had touched hers, leaving her with a craving for more. It was only natural, she told herself. After all, she and Keith had had a normal sex life. It was to be expected that she would miss sex, miss a man's touch.

But Dillon? It still made no sense to get involved with a man who was so irrevocably linked with her past and the pain associated with it. Sensible or not, that kiss had turned her inside out and made her ache for more.

And even now, on Monday, the day Sweet Dreams was closed, she was fixated on him instead of the many other things that required her attention.

"Mom!"

Frowning, Janey scrambled off the chaise longue in her room as she heard Robin making her way down the hall. What on earth was the girl doing home at three o'clock? Practice wasn't usually over until after five.

"Surprised?" Robin said lightly, sailing through the doorway, letting her backpack slide to the floor.

"You know I am. What's the matter? Do you still have cramps?"

Robin had spent the weekend with Keith, another thing that had put Janey on edge. She hadn't come home until last evening. Then, after giving her mom a hug, Robin had gone straight to her room, complaining about menstrual pain.

"No. Some idiot called in a bomb threat and school was dismissed."

Janey gasped. "I hope it was a hoax."

Robin plopped down on the end of the lounge. "Yeah, but it was still kinda cool."

"I'd hardly use that term, if I were you," Janey said in a stern voice. "It could've been serious."

"I doubt it. Some pervert just wanted out of class, or at least that's what Chad said."

"Speaking of Chad, when were you going to tell me?"

Robin gave her a look that was as innocent as fresh-fallen snow. "Tell you what?"

"That he acted a fool in class and got sent to the office."

"How did you know?"

Christy Olson had told her about the incident on the way to the game, but she wasn't about to inform Robin. "Never you mind about that. I don't approve of that kind of behavior."

"He was just horsing around in Mrs. McCurry's class. Her elevator doesn't go all the way to the top, anyway."

"That's a terrible thing to say about your teacher."

"Well, it's the truth."

"That may be so, but that still doesn't excuse what Chad did."

"Please, Mom, give it a rest. Mr. Cooper just gave him and Albert some swats, then let them go."

"So Chad wasn't upset when you couldn't go out with him?" Much to her own disappointment, Janey wanted to add, but she didn't. She had hoped that when she grounded Robin, Chad would seek company elsewhere.

"He wasn't happy, but he understood."

"I just wish you'd date other people, honey."

"It's okay for you to have a boyfriend, but not me?" Robin's tone held a hint of hostility.

"Boyfriend? Now who on earth would that be?"

"Dillon."

"Mr. Reed."

"Well, whatever," Robin countered.

"Hey, young lady, watch it."

Robin's mouth thinned. "Look, Mom, I'm crazy about Chad, and he wants to give me a promise ring."

Janey sucked in her breath and held it.

"And Dad thinks that's super."

Nineteen

Robin leaned against the side of the building and stared up at Chad. He wasn't watching her, though. His eyes were elsewhere, scanning the campus as if waiting for something or someone. But that was Chad—always fidgeting, always on the move.

That made her nervous. But she didn't dare say anything for fear he would jump down her throat. Lately he'd been in a rotten mood, and she'd been treading softly. She figured it was football that had him so uptight. He hadn't played well the last game, and the team had gotten beaten.

He blamed himself, which was ridiculous, but Robin didn't tell him that for the same reason—fear of repercussions.

"So did you talk to your mom about the ring?" he asked, turning back to her.

Jeez, but he was a big guy, Robin thought. He always seemed to loom over her. That made her feel small, something she yearned to be.

Until Chad, she'd felt self-conscious because she was tall with such long legs. But those legs served her well on the drill team, so she wasn't complaining. She knew she could dance, and that gave her some much-needed confidence.

"Robin?" he said impatiently, thrusting a hand through his thick hair.

"Uh, yeah, I talked to her." Her words came out breathy, as if she'd been running uphill.

"And?" he pressed, leaning closer and massaging her shoulder with a big, beefy hand.

She swallowed against the heat that flooded through her. "She's...uh, thinking about it."

No way could she tell him the truth about the conversation she'd had with her mother. He would go ape-shit.

"Thinking about it?" he exclaimed, his tone colored with anger. "That's crap. What's there to think about?"

"You know how moms are," Robin replied, for lack of anything better to say. "They have to think about everything, or at least mine does."

"So fire her." He didn't crack a smile.

"Sure."

"Your dad said it was okay, right?"

"Right."

"No problem, then." Chad leaned over and brushed her lips with his.

Startled, Robin pulled back, her eyes darting from side to side. "Don't, Chad."

His face darkened. "Why the hell not?"

"You know why not. If we get caught, we'll get in trouble."

"Aw, you worry too much."

"I know, but—"

"So are we on for this weekend?" he cut in abruptly.

Robin was relieved he'd moved off the subject of the ring. "Of course. Why wouldn't we be?"

"Your crazy old mother, for one thing," he said in a nasty tone.

Robin flushed. She hated when he talked like that. He just didn't understand her relationship with her mom. Apparently his parents let him do what he pleased. In some ways, she envied that.

"Whatcha thinking about?" Chad asked in a sultry tone.

He was looking at her as if she were some kind of rich cream that he could lap up. She went weak in the knees.

"I hope us." He circled her lips with a finger as he spoke again. "And how much fun we're going to have and how good you're going to feel when we do it."

Robin's flush deepened at the same time that the first-period bell rang. *Saved by the bell, literally,* she thought inanely. Breathing deeply, she stepped to the side and said hurriedly, "Hey, I'll see you later."

"Later."

Robin watched pensively as Chad swaggered off in the opposite direction.

"Emma, I wish you didn't have to go, but I'm so glad you stopped by."

The old lady winked one of her cloudy eyes at Janey. "Coming here makes my day." She grinned. "Isn't that what what's-his-name says in those movies?"

"You mean Clint Eastwood?"

"That's my man, dearie. Only half the time, I can't remember his name."

Janey pushed back her laughter and tears as she painstakingly helped Emma get out the door. "Don't worry. Half the time I can't remember my own name."

"It doesn't get any better, either. Just wait'll you get to be my age."

"I'll never make it," Janey said, finally getting the old lady behind the wheel of her car, a car that Emma still shouldn't be driving. "I'm not made of the right stuff."

"Now where'd you go and get a notion like that?"

She heard the anxious note in Emma's voice and immediately forced a lightness into her own. "Just kidding."

"That's better." Emma cranked the old heap, then gunned the engine.

Black exhaust fumes colored the air, and Janey stepped back, holding her breath. She raised her head toward a sky that looked nasty. A cold front was due to blow in that evening. From the looks of the heavy cloud cover and the feel of light drizzle against her skin, the front was close, all the more reason why Emma shouldn't be on the roads.

"You can't keep giving me candy, dearie," Emma was saying, gunning the engine again, "or you'll soon be in trouble."

Janey coughed to clear her throat, but her eyes still burned. "You let me worry about that. You just enjoy. Be careful driving home. When you get there, call me."

Emma nodded. "I'll do my best to remember."

"If I don't hear, I'll call you. Please drive careful."

Janey remained in the parking lot until Emma's old jalopy was no longer in sight. Shaking her head, she trudged back into the store, where she glanced at the clock. Almost closing time—and she hadn't done much as far as sales went. Overall, business was not good, which frustrated her.

She wanted to help Emma so badly it hurt, only she couldn't. Recently, she and Aunt Lois had discussed Emma's plight once again, with no conclusion reached.

Lois's financial situation wasn't solid, either, though it was much better than Janey's. Still, Lois didn't have the kind of cash that it would take to help Emma. Even if she did, Janey reminded herself, Emma had too much pride to take their money.

Oh, she would take candy from Janey, but that was different. That was small stuff. When it came to uprooting an old woman set in her ways, that was big stuff.

But Emma couldn't keep living by herself much longer in the shape she was in. Each time Janey saw her, Emma appeared more feeble and less able to see. The thought of the old woman behind the wheel was a nightmare.

The idea of sending her to a nursing facility was another nightmare.

But for the time being, Emma's fate was out of Janey's hands. She would just have to keep trying to come up with a solution.

Meanwhile, she had other worries gnawing at her: Robin was at the top of her list. Pausing in her thoughts, Janey went to the small goodie bar at the back of the shop and poured herself the last of the coffee. Battling back a headache, she eased down on the stool and sipped the now-tepid liquid. Disgusted, she put the cup down, then pushed it away.

Figuring out what to do about Robin and Chad was

driving her nuts. When Robin had told her about the promise ring, Janey had mentally gone into orbit, though she had tempered her tone and her words. But right away Robin had picked up on her displeasure.

"I knew you'd have a cow," she said, her mouth tight.

"I'm not having a cow."

"Yes, you are."

"Okay, so I'm not happy. In fact, I don't think that's a good idea at all."

"Oh, Mom," Robin wailed. "Everyone's getting one."

"I doubt that."

"All my friends are," Robin maintained stubbornly.

"Well, like I've always told you, I don't march to the beat of your friends' drums."

Robin rolled eyes that were filled with tears. "Does that mean you won't let me have the ring?"

Just that word made Janey flinch, and her first inclination was to lash out, *No, as in never.* However, she still felt on precarious ground with Robin, unsure just how best to handle this latest crisis. Of late, they had been too much at odds to suit her.

She suspected Keith had a lot to do with Robin's change in attitude. She couldn't prove that—not yet, anyway. However, he had condoned the ring deal, which upped her anger twofold.

"I didn't say that." Janey forced herself to move cautiously through these uncharted waters. God, being a parent of a teenager was so difficult; it took more patience than Job ever had. "I would rather you weren't obligated to just one boy. This is your senior year, darling. I want you to be free to—"

"Oh, Mom," Robin said again, "that's corny. Besides that, being free is not what it's all about. You know how lucky I am?" Robin paused. "Chad's hot stuff."

Janey smiled, reached over and gave her daughter a big hug, then pulled back with a smile. "I think *you're* hot stuff."

"Does that mean I can have the ring?"

"Not right now."

"Then when?" she whined. "Dad said I could. Doesn't that count?"

"Sure it does."

Robin's features turned sullen. "I wish you knew Chad. If you did, you'd like him."

"I'm not prepared to argue with you about this."

"First it was the earrings, now it's the ring. What's with you, Mom?"

"I love you, that's what's with me."

"I love you, too," Robin muttered. "Only sometimes I don't like you."

With those choice words, she left the room, taking a slice of Janey's heart with her.

Now, as Janey jerked her mind off that disturbing dialogue with her daughter, she sighed in despair. If she survived Robin's senior year, it would be a miracle. If she survived what was going on in her own life, period, it would be an even greater miracle.

One thing preying on her mind was the fact that Keith still had not paid his child support. She almost choked on an all-consuming fury that suddenly rendered her useless. She hadn't said anything more to him, having assumed he would have the decency to get the money, no matter what it took.

Damn him.

Too many women and too much booze. And to think his daughter thought he could do no wrong. God forbid that Robin should ever find out the truth.

That aside, Janey couldn't let her ex shirk his duty to his daughter much longer, not if he wanted to continue having a say in her life. Still, she abhorred the thought of approaching him and taking him to task over his continued neglect.

And then there was Dillon. He was a burden all his own. She couldn't get him or that kiss off her mind.

She wondered if and when she would hear from him again.

The thought made her head pound that much harder. What had she done to deserve all this confusion? She was feeling sorry for herself, she knew, as she bent her head and rubbed the back of her neck.

The buzzer sounded, and she looked up.

Keith. She opened the door and, for the first time in eons, was glad to see him. "I take it you have the check," she said without preamble.

He gnawed on the side of one cheek. "That's what I came to talk about."

Twenty

She knew what was coming. He didn't have the money. *Bastard!* That unflattering word suddenly popped to mind, and she wanted to voice it. But she hung on to her control.

"When it comes to child support, there's nothing to talk about."

"Now, Janey—"

"Don't, Keith." She felt her control slipping and reined herself in. It wouldn't do any good to start another verbal slinging match with him.

Besides, she was beyond that point. She didn't care what he did or thought unless it pertained to their daughter. His betrayal had truly killed all her feelings, leaving an empty place in her heart where her love for him used to be.

"God, but you're the stubbornest woman I know," Keith spat.

"And you know a lot of them, no doubt." Those insulting words seemed to fly out of her mouth of their own volition. She wanted to kick her own backside for opening that can of worms when she truly didn't give a damn if he had a whole harem of women every night.

"Dammit, Janey!"

"Sorry. I didn't mean to go down that road. Let's just stick to business."

Keith didn't respond for a moment, which gave her a chance to study him from under her lashes.

He had jammed his hands in the pockets of his pants, and his features were strained. Even though he was dressed to the max in what she figured was a custom-made suit, it couldn't mask the obvious. He was burning the candle at both ends and looked like hell. He seemed to have shrunk, his stature no longer robust and healthy.

Her thoughts suddenly conjured up Dillon, who was just the opposite—physical fitness personified. Angry that *he* came to mind, she forced herself to concentrate on Keith.

No doubt her ex was heavily nursing the bottle again, which terrified her, for her child's sake.

He had all the signs—signs that had escaped her for so long. Oh, she had known Keith loved his beer after work, and she hadn't minded that—until she noticed he never seemed to *not* have a beer in his hand.

When she'd tried to talk to him about it, he'd gotten furious, saying she was making much ado about nothing. And maybe she had been, she'd told herself, wanting to believe that everything was all right, that he *wasn't* exerting more control over her physically while shutting her out emotionally.

In retrospect, she realized it was during the affair that his drinking had become a problem.

"Janey, I still don't have the money."

"Why not?"

"What difference does it make?"

She felt her eyes flash fire. "I can't believe you

had the nerve to actually come here and tell me that."

"I didn't think it was something we should discuss over the phone."

"Discuss? What's there to discuss? This is your daughter we're talking about here, your responsibility to her."

"I know that, dammit."

"Then get the money."

"It's not that easy."

Janey turned away. "God, I can't believe this is happening."

His eyes narrowed. "You're blowing this way out of proportion. It's going to take me longer than I thought to work my way out of my financial bind."

"You should've thought about that when you bought those earrings. Thought about what kind of example you're setting."

"Stop harping on those goddamn earrings!" he lashed back. "And stop judging me. I'll get the money. I promise."

"Unfortunately, a promise is not bankable." She told herself to back off, if for no other reason than to get rid of him. He didn't have the money, and that was that. To continue this conversation would be a waste of time and completely counterproductive.

"I'll let you out," she said, slipping off the stool.

His mouth curled in a smirk. "I'm not Robin. You can't just order me to go to my room."

Janey didn't even bother to respond to that, knowing that she was very close to turning this conversation into a verbal assassination.

"Look, Janey, I'm sorry. It's just that—"

"Get out, Keith," she said in a dull voice. "Just mail me the check."

"I'm not finished. I want to talk about Robin."

Panic welled up inside her. "What about her?"

"Stop being so protective."

"How dare you tell me how to raise my daughter."

"*Our* daughter."

She almost bit a hole in her tongue, trying to hold back a sharp retort.

"Give her a break with Chad. Their relationship is normal and harmless."

Janey's heart thudded to her toes. "Did she put you up to saying that?"

"Not exactly, but she's terribly upset that you don't like him."

"That's between Robin and me."

"Not when she cries on my shoulder about it."

Janey's features tightened. "That's to be expected, when she has a sympathetic ear in you."

"Maybe that's why we should consider joint custody."

Janey held her breath. The ticking of the wall clock, the sounds of nearby traffic—all seemed so far away and unreal.

"Don't even think about it!" she finally managed to choke out. "That's not going to happen."

"Have you ever considered that you might be partly to blame for the mess we're in?"

"You're wasting your breath, Keith."

He went on as if she hadn't said a word. "That if you hadn't gone off half-cocked and started divorce proceedings, we might've worked through our problems and still be a family?"

A mirthless laugh erupted from Janey. "Hey, are you forgetting something? You're the one who had the affair, who broke up our family."

"Hell, Elaine didn't mean anything to me, and you know it. I still love you, haven't ever stopped."

"Oh, please."

Although Keith's face contorted, his voice remained even. "I realize what I lost, and I want you and Robin back."

"I don't want to discuss this anymore," she said in a tired voice. "It's moot. I don't love *you* anymore. That died when you crawled between another woman's sheets."

She had aimed for the jugular and had apparently hit it. His head snapped back as if she'd physically slapped him. Too bad she didn't have the nerve to actually do it.

"Damn you!" he snapped, balling his fist.

Although she wasn't frightened, Janey stepped back. "You can damn me all you like if it makes you feel better, but that's not going to change anything." Janey tipped her chin. "Robin and I don't want you back in our lives."

A sneer replaced the smirk. "I think you'd better consult our daughter on that matter."

"Get out."

"Oh, I'm going, but this isn't the end of it, Janey."

Before she realized what he had in mind, he strode closer, flicked out a finger and ran it down one side of her cheek.

Her head bolted back. "Get your hand off me!"

"I'm warning you," he said in a harsh tone, "you play hardball with me, and you'll lose."

"I'm not the meek and mild woman I was when I was married to you. I'll fight you every step of the way."

"We'll see. But hell, if I can't have you, then I'll settle for Robin." His mouth adopted a cruel line. "Chew on that for a while and see if you can digest it."

Robin sagged against the doorjamb while hot tears saturated her face. She had wanted to cry out loud, to let her parents know that she was there, but the words wouldn't come.

She had no idea how long they had been exchanging verbal blows, but she figured from the gist of the conversation that she had gotten in on the tail end.

Tears had her throat so clogged, she could barely even swallow. When she first reached the side door in the late afternoon, she always called out to her mother. Today had been different. The second she'd opened the door, she heard her dad's voice.

She hadn't meant to eavesdrop, but after her dad said, "Damn you," a blast of dynamite couldn't have sent her slinking up the stairs.

Closing her eyes tightly against the hot sting behind her lashes, Robin gritted her teeth. Why did this have to be happening to her? Why couldn't they be a normal family again? Why couldn't she have her father at home like all her friends did? None of them lived in a single-parent home.

It wasn't fair.

At that moment she hated her parents, for fighting over her like dogs over a bone. Feeling the tears scald her cheeks, she opened her eyes, but she still didn't move. Yet she wanted to. She wanted to run into the store and scream at them to behave, beg them to love each other again.

A whimper escaped her, just as she heard the buzzer on the door. Her dad had left.

Panicked that her mother would see her, she forced her weak legs up the stairs. The second she reached her room, she sat on the bed and grabbed the phone.

When Beverly answered, Robin started sobbing.

"Robin, what's wrong? Did Chad shit-can you?"

"No."

"Then what?"

Robin heaved. "I just wanted you to know that divorce sucks!"

What was *he* doing here?

Even as she asked herself that question, Janey couldn't control her suddenly erratic pulse rate. Since when did the principal show up at a school fund-raiser?

Maybe Dillon just wanted to get his car washed, she told herself, trying to keep things in perspective. After all, it had been raining for several days straight, and everyone's vehicle was a mess.

Around noon the weather had taken a turn for the better. It was now a bright but cool Saturday afternoon, a perfect day for the project, and Janey was so glad she could be part of the fun. Hazel had agreed to hold down the store, enabling her to be here.

She had needed this outing, not so much for herself but for Robin. The breach between them seemed to be widening, and she was desperate to heal it. Her daughter's closemouthed aloofness wasn't entirely to blame, either, though that was certainly a factor. Janey was at fault, too.

That visit from Keith had set her on edge and kept her there. His power to influence Robin had her panic-stricken. In many ways Robin was as mature as a lot of adults, but in other ways she was not. She could be easily swayed. The thought of her choosing to live with Keith was inconceivable.

Yet a niggling voice inside Janey told her that could happen.

"Hey, y'all, look who just drove up," one of the girls shouted.

The sound of her voice shattered Janey's tormented thoughts. She gratefully shifted her attention in the direction of the commotion.

"Mr. Reed! Is that cool or what?"

The twelve girls manning the car wash giggled in response to Beverly Olson's hyper cry; then they all began chattering at once.

Well, at least the kids were excited, Janey told herself, listening to their exuberant exchange. And she was excited, too, only she hated like the devil to admit that.

Christy Olson, one of the three adults in attendance, turned to her and winked. "I don't know about you, but I'm impressed."

"Uh, me too," Janey said, though for a much different reason, she was sure. She watched as Dillon got out of his car and ambled toward the girls. That swaggering walk and killer smile sent a ripple of sexual awareness through Janey's entire body, causing her to clench her hands by her sides while struggling for a decent breath.

Dammit, she had sworn off men!

Ever since that kiss, though, every time Dillon came into mental or physical focus, her body turned pliant with an aching need. She couldn't let on, though, for fear he would devour her, then walk out, leaving her with nothing.

"He genuinely cares," Christy added. "We couldn't have a better man in charge of our kiddos. Don't you agree?"

"Absolutely," Janey said absently.

She couldn't help but notice the puzzled look Christy threw her, but under the circumstances she was doing the best she could.

"Afternoon, ladies," Dillon said, that smile remaining in place as he faced them.

Janey felt his eyes linger on her a bit longer than necessary, or maybe that was simply wishful thinking on her part. God! She had to stop those renegade thoughts. Pressing her lips together, she shifted her gaze.

"The kids are thrilled you're supporting them," Amanda Richards, the other mother, said.

"Wouldn't have it any other way," Dillon drawled. "Besides, my vehicle needs a good scrubbing."

"You heard Mr. Reed, girls." Amanda smiled and made a sweeping gesture toward the wash buckets and paraphernalia. "Let's get busy."

Despite a concentrated effort to ignore how casually sexy he looked, Janey continued to be aware of Dillon with every beat of her heart. She even caught a whiff of his subtle cologne as she started toward the buckets.

"Hey, Mom," Robin called out, "would you get my sunglasses out of my car?"

Janey stopped in her tracks, whirled and made her way toward their automobiles parked in the distance.

She had just retrieved the glasses and slammed the door when she looked up and saw him.

Dillon had followed her.

He had one arm propped on the hood, while his eyes raked over her, missing nothing. She forced a valiant smile.

"So how's it going?"

"It's going," she said, unintentionally wetting her lower lip with her tongue.

A sudden fire leapt into his blue eyes, and her mouth turned terribly dry.

"When am I going to see you again?" he demanded in a thick undertone.

Twenty-One

"Robin, I'm not sure about this."

"Oh, Mom, you worry too much."

Janey frowned up at her daughter, who was dressed in a pair of jeans and a stretchy light blue blouse that hugged her lithe figure to perfection.

Worry? That was mild in comparison with the agony Janey went through every time Robin went out that door. But she refused to smother her child. She wanted Robin to have friends, to have fun, to be popular. On the other side of that coin, Janey continued to expect Robin to hold to the values she'd been taught, not always fall in with the crowd.

Although she trusted her child, she didn't trust many of Robin's friends.

"So where will you be now?"

"At Sally Parrish's house," Robin said, her exasperation obvious, but Janey ignored it.

"I don't much like you going to a house where I don't know the parents. They are going to be home, right?" Janey's gaze and words were pointed.

"Oh, Mom, we've already been through this," Robin wailed. "And you already said I could go."

"I'm not reneging, but—"

"Good, because Ralph's picking me up in about ten minutes."

Janey's eyebrows rose. "Ralph? What about Chad?"

"He's coming to the party, only later."

"Why later?" Janey asked.

Robin lifted her thin shoulders in a shrug. "Something he has to do first. I don't really know. Anyway, Ralph's taking several girls, Beverly included."

"Well, that makes me feel better, anyway."

"So what about you? Do you have any plans?"

A ripple of uneasiness went through Janey. Rarely did Robin enquire about her plans, always seeming too wrapped up in her own busy social life. However, ever since Janey had gone out to dinner with Dillon that one time, Robin had kept closer tabs on her mother.

"Why?" Janey cocked her head, smiling. "You worried about your mother?"

Robin looked awkward. "Nah. Just wondered if you were going out with D—uh, Mr. Reed."

In spite of herself, Janey felt her face turn red, much to her chagrin. Hopefully Robin wouldn't notice. "No, but I'm curious why you would ask that."

Robin shrugged again. "I saw you two talking at the car wash, that's all."

"Oh," Janey said. She hadn't realized Robin had even noticed. Who else had?

"Is that all you have to say?" Robin's tone was a bit put out.

Janey didn't want to lie to her daughter. But she didn't like being put on the spot by her teenager, either. "He asked me out again. Is that what you wanted to know?"

Robin's glazed lips thinned. "Are you going?"

"No."

"Do you want to?"

"Robin, drop it, okay?"

Robin's lower lip rounded out in a pout. "That's the way you talk to me."

"I'm the adult here, remember? Your parent. I'm supposed to be nosy."

"That's not fair."

"Maybe not, but that's the way it is." A horn honked, and Janey looked beyond her daughter's shoulder toward the window. "Your friend is here."

"Cool." Robin leaned over and pecked Janey on the cheek, then dashed for the door.

"Hey," Janey said.

Robin halted, then swung around, an anxious expression on her face.

Janey forced a smile. "Keep in mind that eleven's the magical hour."

"Oh, Mom," Robin wailed again. "Let me stay till twelve. Please."

"No way."

Robin blew out her breath, and Janey could see her mind working, alive like an anthill. She wanted to argue—Janey could see that, too.

"Oh, all right," Robin said, sounding exasperated.

Janey hid a smile. Teenagers! "I love you, kiddo."

"Love you, too," Robin said, dashing out and slamming the door behind her.

Janey parked her car in Gwen's drive, then turned and faced her. "I'm so glad you called and suggested we go to a movie. It was really good."

"I'm glad you came," Gwen responded. "Although you seemed preoccupied."

"Too much on my mind, I guess."

"Want to come in for a nightcap?"

Janey smiled. "Thanks, but no thanks. It's getting late."

"Yeah, it's really late. Hells bells, it's all of ten o'clock."

Janey slapped her playfully on the back of the hand. "Stop making fun of me."

They both laughed.

"Robin's due home by eleven."

"I understand," Gwen said with a chuckle. "Old mother hen needs to be on the nest waiting for her chick."

"Fun, isn't it?"

Thanks to the harsh glare of the streetlights, Janey could see the strange look that Gwen gave her.

"Do I detect a little sarcasm there?"

"God, no," Janey said, mortified.

"It's okay if you feel that way. Damn, you're entitled to have a life apart from Robin's."

"I know, but—"

"But what?"

"I feel guilty."

"That's baloney."

"You're right, of course." Janey rubbed the back of her neck. "It's just that Robin still has illusions of Keith and me getting back together, of us being a family again."

"God forbid," Gwen muttered, then added, "he doesn't give a damn about either of you or he'd cough up his child support."

On the way to the theater, Janey had told Gwen about Keith's latest stunt.

"Oh, I think he cares about Robin, but not enough

to be responsible for her, even though he pretends he wants that responsibility.''

"What he wants is you back,'' Gwen said with her typical bluntness.

Janey made a face.

"So what about Dillon?''

Janey shifted as though she were suddenly on the hot seat. The move didn't escape Gwen.

"Ah, so you *have* heard from him.''

"I didn't say that,'' Janey snapped.

"You don't have to.''

"He came to the car wash.'' Janey's voice held reluctance.

"And?''

"He asked when he could see me again.''

"So see him,'' Gwen said nonchalantly.

Janey raised her eyebrows. "Why the sudden reversal? I didn't think you approved of my seeing Dillon.''

"So I've had a change of heart. At least you're going out.''

"Dillon's not a smart choice. Robin went ballistic that time we went to dinner.''

"She'll get over it.''

Janey shook her head. "I don't know. Besides, being with him in 'that' way is just too weird.''

"Seems to me we've been down this road before. Do you want to see him again? That's the bottom line.''

"Yes, but what's the point? It can never lead to anything.''

"Why not?''

"Oh, Gwen, you're deliberately being obtuse.''

"The hell I am. He's someone for *you*. Get it? Like I said, you're too wrapped up in Robin."

"Well, Dillon's not the answer," Janey declared stubbornly.

Then why couldn't she stop thinking about how he'd looked at her at the car wash, how her heart had gone berserk at his nearness? Even now, she felt heat flood her body at the desire she had seen leaping from the depths of those blue eyes, and heard in the rusty edge of his voice.

He wanted her, and he was making no bones about it.

"I think he is."

"Think he is what?" Janey asked in a breathy tone.

Gwen flashed her another strange look. "The answer. I see no problem if you two got serious."

Janey gasped. "Have you lost your mind? Robin aside, he wants children."

"Has he told you that?"

"No, but he doesn't have to. Remember how devastated he was when Elaine miscarried those two times?"

"Vaguely."

"Trust me, he was."

"It's too bad you started hemorrhaging with Robin and had to have a hysterectomy. Too bad you can't have any more."

"No matter. Even if I could ever trust another man again, I wouldn't want to start over with a baby."

"I hear you."

"Speaking of babies, mine will be home just about the time I get there."

Gwen yanked open the car door. "I can take a hint. I know when I'm being booted out."

Janey grinned. "That's right. Haul ass. And thanks again for calling. We'll talk later."

"You know, you really ought to reconsider. It'd do you good to get laid."

"Gwen!"

"Well, it would. A good roll in the hay would take some of that starch out."

"Get out!"

Gwen laughed. "I'm going. I'm going."

Once she was alone, Janey grabbed her stomach. If only Gwen knew just how much she would like to do just that—to feel Dillon inside her—she would be shocked. Janey's face flamed, and she closed her eyes and took a deep breath.

It was never going to happen. She would make sure of that.

What a great evening.

Dillon hadn't planned to jog in his neighborhood. He didn't like the way his joints took a pounding on the asphalt. It made them sore as hell.

Yet the evening had been simply too beautiful for him to remain indoors. Besides, he was too restless. He needed an outlet for his frustrations and his pent-up energy.

For half a second he'd considered driving to the farm and running on the dirt road that circled it—he'd done that several times lately—but he'd squashed the idea, not feeling *that* energetic.

That was when he'd decided to bite the bullet and hit the streets. Now, as his feet continued their lack-luster love affair with the concrete, he looked at the sky. The sight almost took away what little breath he had left. He would bet there were a zillion stars staring back at him, each one with its own special twinkle.

Not only was the sky perfect, so was the temperature. It was cool, but not too cool. Ideal for being outdoors. Ideal for doing something else—like making love on the floor in front of the fireplace.

With Janey. On top of him.

That image in living color almost stopped him in his tracks. Somehow, he managed to keep his pace without so much as a stumble. Still, he felt the effects: heaviness in his heart and in his loins.

In fact, he wouldn't even look at his crotch. Hell, he didn't have to. It was rod-hard and pushing against his sweats, which luckily were a size too large.

Shit!

He didn't have a lick of sense for letting himself go down that path. She didn't feel the same about him, he reminded himself.

But she felt *something*, he argued back.

He knew heat when he saw it, and he had seen it the other day at the car wash. She wasn't nearly as immune to him as she would have him believe. But if she wouldn't act on those feelings, then he was doomed. Any thoughts of a relationship were doomed.

He wasn't giving up. Sane or not, he wanted to see more of her, wanted to make love to her so badly that he could almost taste her sweet flesh on his lips.

That time he did stumble.

That was when he noticed the commotion up ahead at the house on the end of the block. It was directly across from the neighborhood park. An ambulance and a police car were both in the drive.

Dillon slowed his pace, frowning. What was going on? This was an upscale section that rarely saw a police vehicle, and certainly no crime.

But whatever was taking place wasn't any of his business. With that thought in mind, Dillon was about to up his pace, when a young girl darted out of the house and didn't stop until she reached a park bench and sat down.

His heart almost stopped beating. Robin? Was it Robin Mayfield? Nah, it couldn't be. However, the closer he got to her, the more he thought it *was* her. The streetlights allowed him to see her clearly.

If it wasn't her, it could be her twin. The youngster had her hands crossed over her stomach and was rocking back and forth as though she was in severe pain, while sobbing out loud.

Should he say something? He didn't want to scare her. Should he call her name?

Whoever it was didn't need to be out alone at this time of night. ''Robin?''

At the sound of his voice, the girl's head jerked up and she turned toward him. The stark, ravaged look on her face brought him to a dead stop, fear squeezing his gut unmercifully.

''Robin, my God,'' he whispered, walking over and easing down beside her on the bench. ''What on earth…?''

''I'm dead. I'm dead. I'm dead.''

The dully-spoken litany kept pouring from her lips.

''Trust me, you're not dead.'' If the situation

hadn't been so frightening, he would have smiled. "Talk to me. Maybe I can help."

"Oh, D—" Robin broke off with another sob, her terror-filled eyes raised to him.

"Hey, it's okay. You can call me Dillon when we're alone. Did someone hurt you?" He could barely get those words past his lips, conjuring up in his mind all sorts of things that could have gone on in that house.

"No!" she cried. "But my mom's going to when she finds out."

He tried to curb his panic. "Finds out what?"

"That Ralph drank so much booze that he passed out, and we couldn't rouse him."

"Ralph Palensky?"

She nodded, continuing to rock and moan.

"Where's Chad? Why aren't you with him?"

"He...he never showed up at the party." Her sobs increased.

"So are there any adults in the house?"

"No...sir."

Her teeth were banging together so loudly he could hear them. He placed his arm around her shoulder and drew her against his side, confident the heat of his body, still warm from running, would help calm her. No doubt she was cold, but it was her over-wrought nerves that were the real culprit.

"Were you the one who called 911?"

"Yes, sir."

He didn't know why he'd asked that. It didn't matter, though he thought her being responsible enough to do that might somehow ease Janey's pain.

"Shhh, it's going to be okay."

"No, it isn't!" she cried, pulling away and peering

up at him, her features pinched and drawn. "My mom will never let me out of the house again."

Which might not be a bad idea, he thought, knowing that if Robin were his daughter— He stopped himself, his gut twisting. She wasn't his daughter. He didn't have a daughter, and from the looks of things he never would.

That was when Janey's image popped back into his mind, her belly swollen with his child.

Dillon grimaced and shoved the thought aside. Robin wasn't even aware of it; she was wallowing in her own agony.

"I can't go home," she kept saying.

"Of course you can."

"Poor Ralph." Her sobs started afresh. "What if he dies? What if—"

"He'll make it," Dillon said with far more confidence than he felt. "Anyway, that's not your worry right now. He made his choice."

He stood abruptly.

Robin blinked up at him. "Where...are you going?"

He gently pulled her to her feet.

"Where are *we* going?" she demanded, her voice cracking.

"Home. I'm taking you home."

Robin shook her head and stepped back. "Oh, God, you're going to tell my mom, aren't you."

Dillon placed his hands on her shoulders and peered into her face. "No," he said into the suddenly quiet night. "You are."

Twenty-Two

"You did right by her, Janey."

For a moment Janey was still too numb to respond to Dillon's words of encouragement. She merely stared at him, her eyes glazed with suppressed tears.

"Hey, you have to believe what I said is true," Dillon pressed in a soft, relaxed tone, though his features belied that calm. They were as pinched as hers.

Janey got off the sofa and walked to the fireplace, where the gas logs burned brightly. She stared into that fake flame for the longest time, trying to come to terms with the latest calamity that had befallen her daughter.

How could Robin have gotten herself into such a dangerous situation? She shuddered anew at the thought. How had she herself been caught unawares? That was the question making her crazy. Her daughter was her life, her main responsibility. How could she have dropped the ball so blatantly?

"Janey, look at me."

Like a robot, Janey turned around, though she couldn't quite meet Dillon's probing eyes. Not only was she in a frantic state concerning Robin, but having Dillon in her living room, cloaked in an intimacy brought on by the cozy atmosphere, added another dimension to her anxiety.

She was aware of him with every breath she took. The room seemed to throb with his presence, or was that her pulse throbbing? Yet she was so eternally grateful that he'd stumbled on Robin and brought her home.

"I *am* looking at you," she said in a shaky voice.

"No, you're not."

His gentle bluntness made her smile.

"Ah, that's better."

She crossed her hands over her chest, then said, "Have I offered you something to drink?"

"Twice."

It was that touch of humor quirking his lips that trapped her next breath. That was when their eyes met and held. More flustered and frustrated than ever, Janey jerked her gaze off him and back to the fire.

"I still can't believe what happened," she said, her voice barely audible.

When she'd heard the knock on the door at eleven and had opened it to Dillon and Robin, her heart had taken the first knockout punch.

The second punch had followed shortly, when she'd heard Robin's tearful explanation of what had happened. In fact, Janey had come close to losing it. She would have, if Dillon hadn't been standing by Robin's side as though in full support of her.

After Robin had finished her tale, Janey had told her to go to her room, that they would discuss the matter in more detail later. When Robin obeyed, Janey had been left alone with Dillon, more vulnerable than ever.

"It's over now." Dillon's confident tone broke into her reverie. "Robin's in her room, safe and sound, probably asleep."

Janey expelled a breath. "Thanks to you."

"I think you already said that, more than twice."

That quip unwittingly pushed another small smile through her lips—where it suddenly died. "How could I have been so stupid? That's what gets me."

"Hey, that's the last thing you are. You trusted your daughter, and that's a good thing."

"How can you say that," Janey lashed out, "after what she did?"

"You're getting upset again, and for what?"

"Something horrible could've happened to her."

"Maybe on the park bench, if I hadn't come along. But I doubt even that."

Janey's voice continued to rise. "What about at the party, with no chaperons?"

"Maybe she didn't know Sally's parents weren't going to be there."

"Oh, yes, she did. Come to think about it, I asked her and she never answered me."

"Another of those tiny oversights that come back to bite you later."

"And the drinking," Janey went on in a tormented voice. "That's my main concern. Robin knows not to stay around where that kind of thing's going on."

Dillon gestured toward her, his hands spread. "She's a kid, Janey. Like all of them, she's going to succumb to peer pressure and test the limits."

"That's not the point!"

"What *is* the point, then?" His tone was suddenly as cutting as hers was high. "The way I see it, she got herself into a compromising situation, then got out—but not before calling 911, which shows she acted with a clear head. You ought to be proud of her."

Janey gasped. "Proud?"

"Yes, proud."

Suddenly Janey slapped herself on one side of her head as though trying to knock some sense into it. "I don't know why I'm discussing this with you. You don't understand, can't understand."

"Of course I can't," he said, that old sarcastic bitterness tainting his voice. "Because I've never had a child."

Her eyes turned stark. "I didn't mean—"

"Yes, you did."

Suddenly it was all too much. Janey's emotions couldn't take another blow. Her stomach heaved, her shoulders shook and tears gushed down her cheeks.

"God, Janey, don't," Dillon pleaded in an agonized voice.

Then he lunged to his feet and strode to her, stopping so close that she could feel his breath warm her skin when he spoke again.

"I don't know when to keep my bloody mouth shut."

"It's not your fault," she whispered, her lips accidently grazing his.

That unintentional gesture seemed to freeze them both. Wide-eyed, their gazes held, while Janey's breath constricted and her head reeled.

"Janey, I—"

A vein throbbed in his neck. For a moment she was mesmerized, fighting the urge to touch that tiny pulse with her lips, then stroke it with her tongue.

"God, don't look at me like that or—" He broke off again, then added, "Oh, to hell with it."

As before, his kisses started out featherlight, on her temple, her cheek, her mouth. They barely touched as he murmured, "I didn't mean to upset you more."

"It's all right," she sobbed, circling her arms around his neck until his lips were locked tightly and frantically against hers. Opening her mouth to his thrusting tongue was pure magic, forcing her to cling to him, dissolving under the heat as though she were a wax figure.

Only when his hands moved to the underside of her buttocks and he pulled her against his erection and began to move up and down did sanity return.

My God, her daughter was in the house! If Robin were to awaken and—

"Don't!" she cried, pushing against Dillon's chest. "This is crazy!"

He loosened his hold immediately and stepped back, though he didn't let her go right off. He held her at arm's length and rasped, "I'm not going to apologize *this* time, either."

"I don't want an apology," she whispered, struggling for a decent breath. "What I want is your promise not to touch me again."

His eyes became a deep and tangible invasion. "I'm afraid I can't give you that."

Keith eased his head around to see if anyone was watching. The gods were smiling; no curious eyes were targeting him.

Riding that crest of relief, Keith slid open the file drawer in his desk, leaned over, latched onto the flask, then took a sip of the strong liquid. After it hit his stomach, he stood.

Moments later the burning sensation spread through him, and suddenly all was right with the world. Yet Keith eyed the fancy container with yearning, tempted to take another swig. But he didn't dare. He'd pushed his luck this morning about as far as he could. Besides, he had a prospective client due shortly and he couldn't afford to tip his hand.

A smirk crossed his lips at the unintended pun. However, that gesture was short-lived; he caught a glimpse of himself in the mirror smack-dab in front of his desk.

A goddamn old man.

Shocked and disgusted, he turned away, unable to handle that reflection. For a second he was tempted to jerk the mirror off the wall and smash it to smithereens. What was with him? Why didn't he like his life anymore? Until recently, he'd enjoyed working during the day, then carousing all night, with Sabrina or someone else.

Work had been his main course, sex his dessert.

He'd been content, or so he'd thought. He didn't know when the wind had changed. His discontent showed up first in his work. He reached for the calendar and mentally noted how few cars he'd sold the past month. He'd never been so far in the hole when it came to sales. And it had cost him dearly, especially in ready cash. He had none. Now he was beginning to draw from his savings, which weren't all that substantial to begin with.

Booze?

Was that what his problem was? Why he seemed on a roller coaster that was going only one way: downhill? No, not entirely, not yet, anyway. Oh, he'd indulged too much and too often; he would readily admit that. But the liquor hadn't impaired his sound judgment or his ability to sweet-talk a customer into buying a vehicle.

So why hadn't he sold any?

He no longer gave a shit. That silent declaration was like a sock in the gut; he winced. Although his mental and emotional demise had started several months ago, when he'd begun banging Sabrina on a regular basis and spending money like crazy on her, it was Janey's return that had finished him off.

Damn her. Just who did she think she was, treating him like he was something nasty that had stuck to the bottom of her shoe.

So he'd made a mistake and fucked her best friend. He regretted that more than anyone would ever know. But the way he figured it, that was the proverbial water under the bridge.

Anyway, it hadn't been his fault. Elaine had come on to him, harboring both boredom and guilt because she couldn't have a child. Before he realized what had happened, he'd been sucked in and under.

When he'd seen Janey again after three years, the realization of what he had lost had come crashing down on his head like a ton of bricks. She had changed, and all for the better. She had spark and spunk, two things she hadn't had when they were married. And, she looked smarter and classier; she was now a woman who turned heads when she went anywhere. More mature. Thin, but not too thin. Upthrust breasts...

The list could go on. If only he'd kept his distance, then maybe he wouldn't be in quite as bad shape as he was in now.

However, Robin made that impossible. They shared a living, breathing human who would tie them together forever. All he had to do was come up with a way to get Janey back in his life, in his bed.

And Robin was his best ally.

She wanted them back together as a family, and that was a plus.

But first things first, he reminded himself, that old sick feeling once again gnawing at his gut. He had to sell some cars, get some money so he could square things with the back child support.

If he didn't, his goose would be cooked before he even tried to jump back in the oven. He couldn't allow that. Janey didn't know it, but she still loved him. And there was no other man in her life, which worked in his favor.

The buzzer on his phone sounded and he cursed at the unexpected and annoying interruption. But he didn't dare not pick up; for the most part, the boss was the only one who buzzed him. He latched onto the receiver, a frown on his face.

Minutes later that frown cut deeper into every groove, as he stood in front of his boss's desk and stared at him.

"What?" Keith asked, dumbfounded.

Physically Larry Pinkerton was a runt; mentally he was a giant. And with that latter self-assurance undergirding him, he ran the dealership with an iron fist. It got results, though in Keith's book Pinkerton was a first-class dickhead.

"You heard me, Mayfield." He sat straighter in his chair, propped his elbows on the desk, then went on in his terse voice. "Either you get your shit together or you're out on your ear."

"You can't do that!" Keith exclaimed hotly. "I'm your top salesman."

"Were."

"I'm just going through a tough time right now." He heard the desperation in his voice and hated himself for it. "You've got to cut me some slack."

Larry rose to his full height. At that, he would have reached only to Keith's chest had they been standing side by side. Yet Keith almost flinched at the intimidation this man could manufacture as he glared out of cold, dark eyes—eyes that reminded him of Janey's when she glared at him.

That thought caused a hitch in his breathing.

"I don't have to do Jack shit, Mayfield."

Keith shook his head in order to pull himself together. "Look, I know my sales have been lagging lately, but—"

"There are no 'buts' as far as I'm concerned. Either you produce or you're out. It's your choice. Got it?"

Keith swallowed against the bile that rose in his throat, almost choking him. "Yes," he almost spat.

Larry smiled without humor. "Good. Get back to work."

Keith was about to walk out the door, when Larry spoke again. "If I catch you drinking on the job again, you're out, sales or no sales."

Keith clenched his fists as a resurgence of bile scorched the back of his throat.

Twenty-Three

"**I**'m gone, Mom!"

Janey made her way out of the kitchen into the living room, just as Robin was slinging her purse over her shoulder. Another weekend was upon them, and the drill team was off to a day of training camp. Afterward, Robin was going to her dinner with Keith, from there to a party with Chad, then to Beverly's to spend the night.

Janey had been tempted to tell Robin to leave her dad out of the loop, because he still hadn't paid his child support. When he'd called for Robin, Janey had answered the phone. She had said something to him, but her words had fallen on deaf ears. Hers, however, rang with the sound of more excuses. She almost told him to go to hell.

But she hadn't. Janey didn't want Robin to have to pay for her father's sins, so she'd held her tongue.

Besides, she hadn't wanted to open up that particular can of worms, not on top of everything else. It had been a week since Dillon had brought a frightened and teary-eyed Robin home. During that time, she and Robin had had several heart-to-heart talks. Although Janey still smarted from the horror of the episode, she had cut Robin some slack and hadn't grounded her.

She'd been reluctant to admit it, but Dillon's words kept pounding at her, reminding her that in spite of the gravity of the situation, Robin had acted with a measure of maturity.

Still, Janey shuddered when she thought back on that night, and for reasons other than Robin. The memory of Dillon's hot kisses remained with her.

"Earth to Mom," Robin said, snapping her fingers. "I have to go."

"Be careful, darling." Janey kissed her daughter on the cheek.

"Love you."

Janey hugged her again. "Love you, too. Call me, okay?"

"Sure thing," Robin muttered around a mouthful of granola bar.

Janey stood at the window and watched as Robin climbed into Beverly's car, then disappeared out of sight. She blew out a breath, feeling as if a whirlwind had been through the premises.

That brought a sad smile to her lips. It wouldn't be long until Robin went to college. Janey shuddered to think how quiet and lonely this place would be when her baby left the nest.

Realizing what time it was, Janey brushed aside her maudlin thoughts and rushed into her bedroom to dress. It wasn't long until she had to open the store, and she had several boxes of candy to unpack beforehand.

Too bad she had given Hazel the day off, but the other woman's sister was ailing, so she'd really had no choice. Gwen had offered to help out, but Janey had declined, telling her friend that she could handle the store alone. Unfortunate, but true.

Business hadn't improved all that much, prompting her to dig deeper into her nearly empty pockets to pay for some advertising for Sweet Dreams.

Gwen had tried to follow up on the mall store, calling someone she knew who worked in the offices there. "If she knows anything, she ain't telling," Gwen had related in an irritated tone.

Janey had told her not to worry, to leave well enough alone, that if and when another store opened she would simply have to deal with it. However, Janey hadn't been as blasé about it as she'd conveyed to Gwen. The thought of a chain driving her out of business made her sick to her stomach.

Now, thrusting aside that depressing thought, Janey was halfway down the stairs when the house line rang.

For a second she was tempted not to answer it; then she remembered that her daughter was out and dashed back into her room.

"Hello," she said in an absentminded tone.

"I'm still tasting your lips."

The bottom dropped out of her stomach, and she clutched the receiver so tightly she heard a knuckle pop. She tried to find her voice, but she couldn't; her vocal cords wouldn't cooperate.

"Janey?" Dillon prodded, the warm, husky tone still intact.

"What?" Her voice came out sounding breathless.

"Is Robin around?"

"Er...no," she responded, her knees beginning to tremble. "Why do you ask?"

He chuckled. "I thought maybe I'd put you in a compromising situation where you couldn't say anything."

"Dillon—"

"I warned you I wasn't going to back off."

"Please."

"Please what?"

"Don't do this."

A drumbeat of silence.

"I have to," he said, the humor no longer in evidence. "For my own sanity."

Those words threw her body into chaos, and a throb of heat settled between her thighs.

"I have to see you again."

"Dillon, I—"

"I'm thawing out steaks. I'll expect you for dinner."

"No."

More silence.

"Dammit, Janey—"

"I can't. I won't. You have to understand."

"Don't you think this scares the hell out of me, too?"

"Oh, Dillon," she whispered, clutching the receiver that much harder. "Don't do this to me."

"Then say yes."

"I can't."

Before she burst into tears and made an even bigger fool of herself, she slammed down the phone. Instantly, she wanted to pick it back up and tell him she was sorry, that she—

Janey chopped the rest of that thought off before it could take birth. Yet she didn't move even though it was now past time to open the store. She could have throttled him—literally.

Trembling, she sat down on the edge of the bed and fought for composure. His huskily spoken words,

I can still taste your lips, rattled around in her brain like loose marbles.

She placed her hands over her ears as if she could control them, stop them from rattling. Her ploy failed. The truth was, she *wanted* to go to Dillon's for dinner. She *wanted* to be with him—and not just to eat, either.

She wanted to eat him.

God! Where had that thought come from? Staggering against its implication, Janey jumped up and dashed downstairs, where she grabbed a roll of paper towels and the bottle of glass cleaner. She had to keep busy. That was the antidote to her misery.

Janey stopped long enough to peer with longing out the glass storefront to the empty parking lot. Customers. She needed customers, someone to talk to, something to keep her mind busy, as well as her hands.

Emma. Maybe she would call the old lady to come and visit. Emma would be delighted. But Emma still wasn't feeling well after a bout with the flu. She didn't need to be driving, even to the store. She didn't need to be driving *anywhere*.

Janey had just sprayed the countertop, when the buzzer sounded. After giving the glass a lick and promise with the towel, she looked up and smiled.

The customer was a woman—an attractive woman, at that—with short black hair surrounding a face that was fresh-looking and appealing despite its lack of makeup.

The woman looked familiar, yet she didn't. Janey felt her smile slip somewhat as she tried to pinpoint if and when she'd seen her.

"May I help you?" she finally asked, before the silence became obvious.

The woman smiled; then her brow furrowed. "Actually, yes. I need a gift."

"For someone special?" Janey asked in a warm tone.

"That's right."

"We have a display of just such gifts. Right over there." She pointed. "Why don't you see if anything there will work?"

While the woman looked at the tins and boxes of the more expensive candies, Janey continued to study her from under the sweep of her lashes, that niggling feeling that she knew the lady persisting.

"I'll take this one," the woman said, interrupting Janey's thoughts.

Janey stepped behind the counter and opened the glass cabinet. "Ah, this is a great choice."

"I'm counting on that," the woman responded in a soft but pensive voice. "Do you by chance deliver?"

"We can."

"I'd appreciate that very much."

"No problem."

For the amount she was spending, Janey was willing to do anything to make the sale, which meant, with Robin gone, that she would have to take it herself. No problem.

Janey handed her a card to fill out, only to have the woman shake her head, reach down in her purse and pull out an envelope.

"I've already taken care of that."

Janey nodded, pulled out a notebook and pen, then asked, "So to whom and where does it go?"

"The address is 1515 Lindsay Lane, and the name is Dillon Reed."

For the second time in one day, the bottom dropped out of Janey's stomach as recognition took shape. The restaurant. The night she and Robin had gone to dinner, Dillon had been with this woman.

They had appeared quite chummy. *Obviously they were still chummy.* Oh, God! Hysteria almost bubbled to the surface. It was only through sheer force of will that Janey was able to keep her hand from stopping dead on the paper.

"Is something wrong?"

Surely her reaction hadn't been that apparent. But the woman was staring at her with a tiny frown on her face. "Not at all. I'll take care of it."

"By the way, I'm Patricia Sims."

She extended her hand. Janey had no choice but to take it and smile.

"I've not been in before, though I've intended to."

Janey forced a smile. "I hope you'll make it a habit."

"Oh, I couldn't do that," Patricia said with a laugh. "The pounds would stack up." She paused. "But for gifts, I'll certainly be back."

"That's great," Janey said, giving Patricia her receipt.

Once the woman was gone, Janey slouched against the counter, feeling as if the breath had been sucked out of her lungs.

How dare Dillon!

How dare he call and whisper sweet nothings in her ear while seeing another woman. Damn him! He knew better than to play her for a fool. She had been there, done that. And Dillon knew it. He'd been there himself, suffered through the agonies of betrayal.

Fury fueling her courage, Janey grabbed the phone directory, then the phone, and punched out his number.

When he answered, she didn't bother to identify herself. Instead, she asked, "Is that dinner invitation still open?"

She heard his sharp intake of breath, forcing her to wait a beat for his response.

"That goes without saying."

"Then I'll be there."

Another pause. "What made you change your mind?"

She blinked back tears. "I have something for you."

"Oh, really?" he said, his voice low and thick.

Janey concentrated on her growing anger rather than the lancing pain. "Yes, really."

"I promise you won't be sorry."

No, but you will, she thought, replacing the receiver.

Twenty-Four

He must have been watching for her.

Janey didn't even get the chance to ring the doorbell at 1515 Lindsay Lane before the door opened.

"Hey," he said in a sultry voice that instantly threw her system into chaos. But she wouldn't give in to that feeling, that sexual high that would render her spineless. She had to remain strong and stick to her resolve. No man would play her for a fool again and get away with it.

And Dillon had done just that.

"I have the wine already chilled," he went on, when she didn't respond. He stood aside and waited, while she walked past him.

When she paused in the middle of the living room, her gaze made a preoccupied sweep of the area before settling on the fireplace, which was spitting and hissing with real wood. The fire gave the room a homey feel.

From her previous visit, she remembered the condo being upscale, though it was nothing like the home he'd shared with Elaine. It wasn't nearly as large, either. But then, one person didn't require large.

Maybe there would soon be two, she reminded herself snidely, her fingers tightening around the handle of the large plain sack—a sack he had yet to refer to.

"What are you thinking?"

He was standing behind her, close, too close for comfort. This time she could feel his breath against her neck. And despite her efforts not to react, a shiver shot up her spine.

Swallowing hard, she turned and asked inanely, "About the house?"

"No," he said in a lazy, humorous tone, his gaze sweeping over her, resting on her lips, which she had just moistened with the tip of her tongue.

Her heart leapt, and she thought he was going to kiss her. God help her, regardless of her anger and hurt she wanted him to. But then her sound judgment came to her rescue, and she put some safe distance between them.

Although she figured he'd read her mind, he didn't push, as if the hands-off sign was visible.

"You can relax, you know."

That sultry humor once more colored his voice, adding to her discomfort. He knew exactly what he was doing. She gripped the sack handles even tighter, a reminder as to why she was here.

"Thanks," Janey said, hearing a tinge of sarcasm in her voice.

He gave her an odd look, but amusement still lurked in his eyes. "You might be more comfortable if you took off your jacket."

Was he laughing at her? Fuming inwardly, she let the sack ease out of her hand, then slipped her blazer off her shoulders and handed it to him, making sure she didn't so much as graze his finger. She then watched as he strode to a small desk chair in the corner, where he draped the jacket across the back.

He turned around and asked, "Are you hungry?"

"A little," she lied, having no intention of eating a bite of his food, although it smelled absolutely delicious.

"That's not good enough." He made his way back toward her. "I want you to be real hungry when you sample my steaks."

"I don't remember you being that adept in the kitchen." The words were out of her mouth before she thought. She'd had no intention of bringing up the past. But in her own defense, the past was so much a part of their present that it was impossible to separate the two.

Anyway, she wasn't going to tiptoe around him. Once she accomplished what she'd come to do, she wouldn't have to worry. Private moments like this wouldn't recur.

"I'd like to, you know."

She blinked up at him, first because he interrupted her thoughts, and second because his comment made no sense to her. She tried to read what was behind those smoldering eyes, but he didn't give her a clue. "Like to...what?"

"Pull you down on the floor and make love to you."

Janey's lips parted in a gasp. She wanted to respond, but she couldn't.

"Don't worry," he continued in a thick tone. "I'm not going to—unless you keep looking at me like that."

She felt heat bathe her cheeks, and she quickly

averted her gaze, trying to regain control of her fractured nerves.

"Hey," he whispered.

Of their own volition, Janey's eyes swung back to him. But she still couldn't say anything. She seemed locked in a freeze-frame of her own desires.

Dammit, this hot sexual exchange hadn't been part of her game plan. In fact, she should have had her say by now and already be back home, curled up on her own sofa, a cup of hot tea as her companion.

So what was keeping her here?

"Janey..." Dillon took a step forward.

She took a step backward. "Don't."

No doubt he heard the crispness in her tone. He pulled up short, though the glint never left his eyes. "You want me as much as I want you."

"No," she said again, backing up farther. Her leg bumped against the sack, a move that instantly restored her sanity. Straightening, she reached for it. "I told you I had something for you."

She saw the confusion in his face. Good. She had caught him off guard, which gave her the upper hand for the first time all evening.

"What is it?"

His tone was flat; he was obviously put out by the sudden switch in subject. "Something I think you're going to love."

He frowned.

"More so because it's from someone special."

That glint reappeared in his eyes. "You?"

"Sorry, not me." She watched a muscle jump in his jaw and knew that his patience was wearing thin. So was hers, she conceded, deciding she had lollygagged long enough. "Here, open it." She held the sack out to him.

He took it and, holding it with one hand, reached inside with the other. He let go of the paper and stared at the tin of candy for a second, then looked back at her.

"I don't get it," he said.

"I've already told you—a friend bought it for you."

He blew out an impatient breath. "What friend?"

"As in lady."

"Janey, what's going on here?"

"There's a card inside."

"I'd rather you tell me."

"Patricia Sims. Does that ring a bell?"

"She bought this?" His tone was incredulous.

"That she did."

Dillon's chest constricted and his mouth tightened. She knew he wanted to say something, only he didn't.

"Patricia asked if I—we delivered, and I said I'd be glad to."

Dillon thrust a hand through his thick hair, leaving it mussed. Janey fought the sudden urge to reach up and put it back in place, anything to touch him. God, this was crazy. *She* was crazy.

"Look, I know what you're thinking—"

"You don't have a clue," she shot back, fury changing the texture of her voice, making it quiver again.

"Janey, she's just a friend." His tone had a pleading note in it. "I can't imagine what possessed her to buy me some damn candy out of the blue."

"Oh, I bet if you thought about it long enough, you'd come up with the right answer."

His face drained of color. "Sarcasm doesn't become you."

"Even when it's justified?"

"Look, I'm sorry if you got the wrong impression."

"You don't owe me an apology. You don't owe me a thing."

"You don't believe that or you wouldn't be so upset."

Realizing that he was edging too close to the truth and that tears were threatening, she had to get out of here before things really got ugly. She made a move toward the door.

"I wasn't a monk before you came into my life, Janey. I'm not denying that."

His softly spoken words stopped her cold.

"What I *am* denying," he added to her back, "is that she means something to me. She doesn't. Never has and never will."

Janey swung back around, even though she knew she was playing with fire. She should be halfway home by now. "Actually, I think she's the perfect woman for you."

He rocked back on his heels as if she'd struck him. "Dammit, Janey!"

"No, really, I'm serious. She's young and attractive and seemingly crazy about you. She's the one who should be here with you, enjoying your fine home-cooked meal."

"It's you I want."

His thick but hoarsely spoken words hit her most vulnerable spot. Her breath caught, and her knees almost buckled—but didn't, which allowed her to turn again and all but run for the door.

She never made it. His hand circled her bare upper arm. Even if that gesture hadn't done the trick, his words would have.

"God, Janey, I told you I was sorry even when I've done nothing to apologize for."

His words did little to restore her trust in him. Words were cheap. Her bitter experience had taught her that. Besides, all men were alike. Sex was top priority. Why had she thought Dillon was any different?

Whoa! She couldn't blame all this sexual energy bouncing around them exclusively on him. She wanted what he was more than willing to give.

That was why she had to reprogram her heart and mind.

"What more do you want?" he asked.

"For you to let me go," she said in a broken whisper.

"I can't do that."

Her head remained down, her eyes locked on the hand that hadn't budged. Sensations from those callused fingers pierced her skin like tiny jolts of electricity.

Stopping was a bad idea. No doubt about that. But her fatal mistake was lifting her head to meet his gaze. His eyes were dark and needy. My God, she thought, swaying toward him.

He grabbed her, then pushed her flat against the door, crushing her lips against his.

She moaned under the ravishing assault, drinking from his lips with the same intensity that he was drinking from hers. But it was when his tongue flicked against hers time after time that she thought she couldn't remain upright under the dizziness washing over her.

Flinging her arms around his neck, she clung to him.

"Janey, sweet Janey," he murmured incoherently, as if sensing she'd reached her limit.

She took a deep gulping breath, only to feel his lips blaze a hot trail down her neck to the hollow between her breasts. She realized he had somehow managed to open her blouse and expose her breasts to his greedy eyes and mouth.

"Oh, Dillon," she whimpered, her bones turning to putty under the gentle but unrelenting siege on her body.

Determined to make him as hungry as she was, she touched him between his legs. And lingered. He jerked, his wide, glazed-over eyes settling on her.

"Not here," he ground out in a guttural voice. "In the bed."

The party had been in full swing for several hours. Through the smoke, loud music and chatter, Robin looked for Chad. He had disappeared from her side a while ago, and she hadn't seen him since.

She wasn't surprised, because he was pissed at her, though she didn't know why. And he wouldn't tell her. She suspected it had something to do with the last get-together, which had turned into such a fiasco—the one he hadn't made it to.

However, he'd told her to go, said that he would be there. But after he found out she'd actually gone with Palensky, who had gotten blind, stinking drunk and passed out, Chad had treated her differently, had even been cruel at times with his harsh words and back-stabbing jabs.

On the way to the party, she'd asked him outright what was wrong with him.

"Did you and Palensky get it on at the party?"

She'd been flabbergasted. "Are you crazy? He's never touched me, never even wanted to."

"That's a lie. He told me I was one lucky prick to be dating someone with knockers like yours."

Robin's face turned beet red, but she lashed back, "That's his problem, not mine."

"I'd better not catch you messing around on me," Chad said in a chilling tone, his eyes narrowing on her.

"Don't talk to me like that," she whispered. "It scares me."

"Well, it better, because I mean it." He paused. "If you're not putting out for me, you damn sure better not be putting out for anyone else."

That conversation had strained their relationship, and it hadn't gotten any better. Now, as she continued to seek him through the mass of bodies all crammed in this too-small room, she felt a tap on her shoulder.

"Hey, what's up?"

It was Beverly.

"I'm looking for Chad. Have you seen him?"

"Yeah, the limp dick's over there guzzling beer and ogling Ava Runnel's boobs."

Her friend's voice was filled with venom. Shocked, Robin's gaze followed Beverly's pointed finger. Her blood turned to ice in her veins.

Chad's face was so close to the girl's that he might as well have been kissing her. Without giving it a second thought, Robin shoved her way through the other kids, Beverly right behind her.

"Leave him be, Robin."

"No. He's mine, and I won't share him."

By the time she made it to Chad, he was nuzzling Ava's neck. "Stop that!" Robin cried in an agonized tone.

Chad merely looked at her, then shrugged. "Two can play this game."

"I told you, I haven't done anything. Obviously I can't say the same for you."

Suddenly Chad was looming over her. "Watch your mouth, bitch."

"Chad, please," she whispered. "Don't talk to me like that."

"I'll do anything I damn well please."

"Chad!"

He raised his hand, and Robin cringed.

Twenty-Five

The playground of his imagination had been fertile all right, but nothing could have prepared him for the real thing.

Naked. On her back. In his bed. He couldn't ask for more.

Dillon had dreamed about this moment, but he had begun to think it would never come to fruition. Now, clothes discarded in a pile on the floor, they were together, his hands and mouth all over her body, where they belonged.

"Oh, Dillon!" Janey cried against his lips, digging her fingers into the hard flesh of his shoulders, holding him as if she would never let him go.

That was fine with him. He didn't want to let her go, either. Suddenly, as the magnitude of that thought washed through him his body seemed to shut down.

Had he lost his mind? She would never marry him.

But that tormenting thought was for another time. Now was the time to concentrate on her and how every bone, every muscle in his body, was stretched to the breaking point with need.

"Dillon," Janey whispered, staring up at him out of questioning, uncertain eyes, as if she'd felt his tense hesitation.

"It's okay," he whispered back. "In fact, it's perfect. *You're perfect.*"

And she was. Her body was a delight, her breasts full and firm, her nipples rosebud pink and just the right size, feeling like soft pebbles under his tongue. There was a roundness to her stomach from giving birth that took the edge off her slenderness, adding a graceful maturity.

Simply looking at her aroused him. "I want you so much it's killing me," he said, his voice strained.

"And I want you."

He explored her moist, swollen lips once again, more aroused than he'd ever been with any other woman, even Elaine. Maybe this was the right time in his life, after all. Maybe *she* was the right *woman*.

Tiny sounds erupting from deep within her refocused his attention; he moved his lips to her breasts, then down her tummy and lower. Groans rumbled in his throat as he nudged her legs apart to reach the warmth hidden there.

His finger invaded her wetness.

Janey's eyes widened, and her gasps became intermittent and mixed with moans. Loving those sounds that were exclusively hers, he eased his finger in and out until he felt her climax.

"Please," she whimpered, her body arching upward.

"Please what?"

His intention was not to make her beg. After all, he was torturing himself even more by not taking her that instant. He was so hot and hard that he was in physical pain from holding himself in check. But he wanted to savor this moment, touching her, feeling her, *tasting* her.

That was when he replaced his finger with his tongue.

When it pierced, then delved into that warmth, Janey cried out, once more lifting her hips off the bed.

Taking advantage, he moved over her, then bent down and recaptured her lips in a hot, reckless kiss.

"Now, Dillon!"

He surged forward and up, embedding himself high in her.

"Oh!" she cried.

He began to move frantically, while their voices and eyes smoldered in unison with an intensity that only heat against heat could generate.

They came at the same time, but it was her scream of pure ecstasy that would linger in his mind always.

He finally collapsed against her, settling his lips next to her ear. "Next time it'll be your turn on top."

Janey awakened with a start. What time was it? Her eyes drifted to the clock on the table beside her. Midnight.

Oh, dear, what had she done? She closed her eyes again, her breath stalled in her throat. She had done what she'd promised herself she wouldn't do. She'd made love to Dillon—countless times in just a matter of hours.

Her heart clamoring, she glanced beside her, her gaze resting on him.

Keep your cool. Don't fall off the edge. Take some deep breaths and you'll be just fine. Who was she kidding? She would never be fine again. But she wouldn't cry. She wouldn't subject herself or him to such an immature cop-out.

Stealing another glance at him, a more lingering one, Janey thought how peaceful he appeared, sleeping like a baby. But he didn't look like a baby—anything but. He looked like the man's man he was. His body was muscled and hard-toned, no spare flesh anywhere. She ought to know, she reminded herself, she had touched every square inch of it. Even now, her gaze dropped to the sheet that barely covered his lower half.

All she had to do was reach out and touch....

Janey balled her fingers to keep from doing just that, sucking in her breath and holding it. But oh, was she ever tempted; she would shamelessly admit that.

Still, she didn't turn away. She continued to soak up the sight of him as if she were a sponge. A dark stubble covered his face with bristles that not so long ago had chafed her skin. Suddenly her cheeks felt as if they were on fire.

Awesome! Robin's favorite word jumped to the forefront of her mind. Sex between them had been that and more. He was not only a greedy lover—hot and demanding—but a gentle and considerate one, determined to see to it that she was fulfilled.

Awesome! That word wouldn't stop ringing like a loud bell inside her head. While sex had been good with Keith, it couldn't compare with the wild, scorching lovemaking she'd shared with Dillon.

What she'd experienced with him had been nothing less than sensational. And she'd had no qualms about letting him know that, she thought now, recalling her repetitive cries and moans of pleasure.

So what did this all mean? Was she just a sex-starved divorcée seeking instant and short-lived gratification? No. She could declare that with a clear conscience. What had gone on between them in this bed had been much more than that. He had touched her on a new level—a level that Keith had never come close to reaching—and she reveled in it.

In fact, in the latter years of her marriage, she'd even begun to think she'd lost interest in sex, that some hormonal change had taken place in her body. Keith had no longer been able to turn her on, to elicit anything more than a perfunctory response.

Well, nothing was wrong with her. Dillon had proved that. Her hormones were alive and well, thank you. Her gaze wandered back to that forbidden area of his body, and she was tempted once again to ease back the sheet and bury her face....

Without warning she had become a wanton and needy woman. And Dillon Reed, of all people, had done that to her. *Bizarre. Crazy. Off the wall.* All those expressions were right on target. Yet it had happened. He had waltzed back into her life and done what she'd sworn no man would ever do again: stoked her emotional fires.

That thought brought her back to her original question. What did this all mean? That was the biggie, the overwhelming question, the one she couldn't answer with the same clear conscience.

And where did they go from here? A repeat performance? Was that what she wanted, only on a steady basis? The titillating thought made her cheeks sting.

Surprisingly, or rather miraculously, she realized now that Dillon's invasion of her body and emotions had somewhat lessened the sense of anger and betrayal left in the wake of Keith's unfaithfulness. But then, she'd known for a long time that she should stop wallowing in self-pity and bitterness, and move on with her life.

Was now the time?

The thought of not seeing Dillon again on an intimate basis was unthinkable. Yet there was Robin. *Robin!* Oh, God, what would her reaction be to what had gone on?

Robin would never have to know. After all, Janey's life was no concern of her daughter's. But her daughter was dearer to her than her next heartbeat, and Robin was dead set on her parents getting back together.

Dillon didn't fit in the picture at all.

She must have vented her agony out loud, for Dillon's eyes suddenly popped open. When he saw her, a lazy grin broke across his lips.

"Hey."

Instinctively she reached for the sheet and covered her nakedness.

He chuckled. "Don't you think it's a little late to worry about modesty?"

His words and lazy drawl shot her senses into sexual overdrive, a frightening phenomenon. But she didn't let on. Instead, she clutched the sheet that much tighter, silently agreeing that the gesture was ridiculous. But in the ways that counted, he was still a stranger. And, her instincts warned her not to let him know exactly how he and his body had affected her.

At this point, she was much too vulnerable and still had so much to work through. She wanted no commitments from him, long-term or otherwise, because she didn't intend to give him any.

Voilà! The answer to one of her questions.

"Janey?"

The husky sound of her name on his lips sent another shaft of longing through her. She averted her head before he could see her reaction.

"You aren't thinking about going ballistic on me, are you?"

She swung back around to find Dillon's grin had spread. How could she get mad at him, especially when he was looking at her with a mixture of vulnerability and mischief?

That was when it dawned on her that he wasn't entirely comfortable with this new and different level of their relationship, either—which helped to even things out a bit.

"No, at least, not right this minute."

Her honesty was obviously a relief. His grin returned, along with a glint in his eye.

"Don't even think about it," she warned, though there was a distinct catch in her voice that she couldn't prevent. The warning was as much for herself as for him, as she fought the urge to fling herself back into his arms.

That would never do.

Dillon chuckled, a warm, intimate kind of laugh that cut to the heart of her. "I can just see those wheels turning inside your head."

She jutted her chin, though she knew there was a hint of a smile on her lips. "You wish."

He laughed outright. Then his face became serious. "I want to make love to you again."

"Dillon..."

"You want that, too, I know."

Of course she did. But she wasn't going to.

Granted, their lovemaking had been dynamite, even all-consuming. That kind of heady stuff was addictive. Who in their right mind wouldn't want more? But she had to weigh the overall consequences of her shameless abandonment, later in the privacy of her own mind. At the moment, restraint was in order.

"Are you on the pill?"

That quietly spoken question robbed her of her next breath, not to mention coherent speech. "I—"

"Since we obviously didn't use anything," he continued, "we could've made a baby."

Oh, God. "Dillon, there's something—"

The ringing of a phone brought her thoughts and voice to an abrupt halt. At first she couldn't figure out where the sound was coming from—certainly not from Dillon's phone on the nightstand beside her.

"What the hell?" Dillon muttered, his eyes also scanning the room.

Janey realized then that it was her cellular. After scrambling to reach it inside her slacks, which were puddled on the floor, she lifted it to her ear.

"Hello," she said in dread.

Moments later, the tiny phone slipped from her hand.

"Janey, what's wrong?"

Somehow she forced her stark white lips to move. "Robin's in the emergency room."

Twenty-Six

Janey wanted to throw up. But her stomach was clenched in such a tight knot that even if she took the time to hang her head over the toilet, nothing would happen.

During the race to the ER, she felt Dillon's eyes on her every chance he got to take them off the road. At that time of the night, his lack of concentration didn't put them in danger because there was no traffic. But she didn't respond to him. She was too caught up in her own feelings of fear and misery.

Janey still couldn't believe the call. After she'd told Dillon that Robin was in the hospital, he'd bounded out of bed and immediately jumped into his clothes. She had done the same.

"What happened?" he'd asked, his tone all business.

"I'm...not sure." Her voice had been barely audible.

"What did they say?" Dillon pressed.

"That she'd been injured, but not seriously." She began to tremble all over.

"God, Janey, don't." His tone was filled with suppressed agony as his narrowed eyes tried to trap hers.

She knew what he was thinking; he wanted to hold

her. And she wanted him to, in the worst way. But she knew that wasn't possible. She blamed herself.

Lately Robin hadn't been her top priority. Dillon had. Her anxieties had already borne fruit. What had she been thinking of?

They'd had only one evening of incredible sex, and she was a mess. But who wouldn't have been? The bombshell that Dillon had dropped in her lap right before the call surged back to the forefront of her mind.

We could've made a baby.

Her stomach took another turbulent tumble. She placed her arm across it and pressed. The awe she'd heard in his voice had pierced her heart, reminding her just how much he still grieved over not having any children of his own.

If only Fate had allowed her to tell him the truth, then she wouldn't be saddled with that extra baggage now. But for the moment, she couldn't worry any more about Dillon. Robin took precedence over everything and everyone else.

Oh, please, dear God, she prayed, *let my daughter be all right.* She couldn't bear it if anything happened to her child, especially when she felt it was her fault. If only she'd paid closer attention to Robin, she wouldn't be on her way to the hospital. That episode with the other party should have been warning enough.

Janey remained immobile, fear an invisible malignancy that threatened to devour her.

"I know you don't believe me," Dillon said with calm assurance, "but she's going to be all right. I can feel it in my bones."

"How can you say that?" she asked in a quivering voice, folding her hands tightly in her lap.

"I know you're upset, and you should be, but—"

"Stop it! I don't want to hear it. It's all my fault."

"That's pure hogwash."

She glared at him. "No, it's not! If I'd been paying more attention to her, instead of—" Tears got in the way of her words, and she couldn't go on.

"Me. Is that what you were going to say?"

"Yes."

He didn't respond right off, which made for a long and uncomfortable silence. But she didn't care. All that was important was getting to her daughter.

"I don't mind you using me as a punching bag, Janey. I'm tough, I can take it."

"Not now, Dillon, please. I—"

"No, hear me out. Just don't beat up on yourself. You're a good mother. I don't want you to forget that."

"Right," she choked out bitterly. "That's why I'm on my way to the ER in the dead of night."

As if he realized there was no consoling her at this point, he didn't say anything else. After looking at him for a second, Janey couldn't tell if he was angry or not, but that didn't matter.

They didn't speak again until he brought his vehicle to a stop in front of the ER entrance. "We're here," he said, his hand jerking up the door handle.

Now that they had arrived, paralysis seemed to have taken over her body, making it difficult to function.

"Janey?"

She faced him with what she knew were tear-stained cheeks and panic-stricken eyes.

"It's going to be all right. I'm not leaving you to face this alone."

In light of what had gone before, his words should not have been comforting. His *presence* should not have been comforting. She should be facing this crisis alone, like every other single mother.

But she was glad he was here. Suddenly she wanted to lean on him, let his big, capable body absorb all her pain, make it go away.

"Let's go," he prodded gently. "Robin needs you."

Her daughter's name was the catalyst that shoved her body in gear. In seconds she had bounded out of the vehicle and through the hospital doors, Dillon right beside her.

"Are you Mrs. Mayfield?" a nurse asked.

Janey nodded, her throat too tight to speak.

"Your daughter's in the first room. The doctor just went in."

"Is she—" Further words once again stuck in Janey's throat, just as Dillon's arm clamped around her shoulders.

For a moment, she sagged against him; then, reclaiming control of her emotions, she charged toward the room. That was when she saw several of Robin's friends huddled together.

"Hi, Mrs. Mayfield," Beverly said, her uneasiness obvious.

The others didn't say a word. They just stared at her out of unreadable eyes.

Janey gave them the briefest of nods, before dashing into the room.

"Mom!" Robin cried when she saw her mom.

Janey pulled up short and gasped. Robin's upper

lip was split, and swollen to twice its normal size. Already signs of discoloration were showing.

"Oh, honey," she whispered, crossing to her daughter and reaching for her.

Robin sobbed against her shoulder, while Janey stared at the doctor, then Dillon, who had propped himself against the far wall, his features shadowed.

"Shhh," Janey said, pulling back and easing Robin's hair out of her face. "I'm here now."

Robin swiped at her eyes with the back of her hand. "Why isn't Daddy with you?" She glanced at Dillon.

Janey cringed inwardly against the tangible vibes of hostility and resentment bouncing off her daughter.

"Janey, do you want me to leave?" Dillon asked in a tight voice.

God, what a mess. Before she could answer, however, Robin spoke again. "Mom, are you...mad at me?"

"Oh, honey," Janey said again. "Of course I'm not mad at you. I'm just thankful you're not hurt worse."

"Mrs. Mayfield, I'm Dr. Ryan."

"Uh, sorry, Doctor," Janey said, reaching for his outstretched hand. After they shook, she gestured toward Dillon, who stepped forward. "This is Dillon Reed."

They shook hands, too; then Dr. Ryan faced Janey again. "I'm about to stitch that lip up."

"Whatever it takes," Janey whispered in an unsteady voice, feeling her stomach roll.

Robin fixed her gaze on the doctor. "Will...will it hurt?"

"Very little," he said in a soothing tone. "Turn this way for me."

Janey moved back, only to nearly step on Dillon, who was right behind her. He steadied her with a hand, then moved aside, creating a small space between them. Though she turned her head when the doctor reached for a long needle, she sensed that Dillon was watching every move Dr. Ryan made.

Her stomach and her nerves couldn't take it. The thought of that needle piercing her baby's skin made her crazy. But the thought that someone had done that to her daughter...

The thought sent a cold, numbing chill through her. How had this happened? Robin's friends. They could tell her. All she had to do was step out the door and ask them. However, she wanted to hear the truth from her daughter, not from her cronies.

Thinking of the kids holding vigil made her realize that Chad hadn't been among the group. Why? Shuddering, Janey wrapped her arms around herself, feeling that numbing chill again.

"All finished," the doctor said at length.

Janey swung around and returned to Robin's side, grabbing her around the shoulders. "Are you okay?"

Robin nodded and looked at her out of slightly glazed eyes. Janey clutched her daughter tighter as she glanced at the doctor.

"She's going to be fine," Dr. Ryan told her. "I froze her up pretty good, but when that wears off she'll experience some discomfort. I'm sending some mild pain pills home with her to use as needed."

"Thank you, Doctor," Janey murmured.

He turned at the door and smiled—a smile that

included them all. "You're welcome." Then, to Robin he said, "Take care, young lady, you hear?"

"Yes, sir," Robin managed to eke out around her unnaturally large lips.

Once they were alone, silence beat in the room like a far-off drum. Dillon's posture was tense with expectancy, as was hers. She knew Robin needed to be taken home and put to bed, but not until they had a talk.

"I'm waiting, Robin, to hear what happened."

Robin shifted her gaze and seemed to grit her teeth, which set off an alarm inside Janey.

"It was an accident," Robin said at last.

"An accident? How?"

"I slipped at the party."

"Robin, look at me."

"Mom!"

"Robin, look at me," Janey repeated, her voice brooking no argument.

Dillon chose that moment to move closer to the table. Janey knew he sensed Robin was fibbing. After all, he dealt with this sort of thing on a daily basis.

"Mom, I told you what happened," Robin said in a slightly belligerent tone.

Her concern mounting, Janey gazed at Dillon, whose features were now visibly taut, before turning back to her daughter. "Then give me the details," she said with as much patience as she could muster.

Robin's eyes shifted toward the door, just as it opened and Beverly's head poked around it. "Er...is it all right if I...we come in?"

"Yes, why don't you do that?" Janey exclaimed. "Maybe *you* all can tell me exactly how this happened."

The others seemed to rally around Beverly, whose gaze zeroed in on Robin. "You mean you haven't—" She broke off abruptly, her eyes widening.

"No, Beverly, she hasn't," Janey said tersely.

"All right, guys, let's hear it." The sound of Dillon's low, gruff voice yanked the youngsters' heads up like puppets on strings.

Still, no one said a word.

"Beverly, do you know the details?" Dillon asked.

Although she should be the one doing the grilling, Janey was thankful she didn't have to. Anyway, it didn't matter. If Dillon could get to the truth, then so be it. The result was all she cared about.

"Uh…" Beverly stalled, glancing at Robin.

"Look at me, Beverly," Janey ordered. "Or Mr. Reed."

Though her face was tissue-paper white, Beverly stared at Janey, though she still remained silent.

"It's okay, Bev," Robin said. "You're off the hook."

"Then let's hear it." Janey's voice was weary.

Robin's chin worked as she tried to hold back tears. "Chad hit me, Mom."

Twenty-Seven

"**Y**ou're dead on your feet."

Janey stared at Dillon, who stood by the fireplace. His words were barely penetrating. They had just arrived back at her house, and he had insisted on seeing that she and Robin were settled before he left. He hadn't even let her go by his place to get her vehicle, promising it would be returned.

She hadn't argued. He was right; she was simply too exhausted, both mentally and physically. She actually felt as though someone had taken a sharp knife and hollowed her out.

Under those circumstances, it was actually comforting to be told what to do. Tomorrow, in the light of day, when she could put the traumas of this evening in better perspective, she would probably wish she'd handled the situation differently, that she'd told Dillon to stop interfering because she was in charge.

Ha, some joke that was.

Her life seemed to be careening out of control, and she couldn't do a damn thing to stop it. Now, however, Dillon's presence was strengthening and calming, and she wasn't about to look a gift horse in the mouth.

She didn't want to, either. For more reasons than

one, she didn't want to let him go. Refusing to dwell on that disturbing admission, Janey cast it aside.

Robin.

At the moment her daughter should be the only person who filled her mind.

"Actually, I'm numb," she finally said, feeling Dillon's intense gaze and finding herself wanting to squirm under it.

"Do you think she's asleep by now?" He motioned his head in the direction of Robin's room.

"She certainly needs to be, but I seriously doubt she is. She asked if she could call her daddy."

"That's to be expected," Dillon said, a troubled look further darkening his already grave features.

"Maybe so," Janey countered bitterly, "but I don't like it."

"Do you think he'll come over?"

"He'd better not. He's the last person I want to see."

"You know he'll be upset."

"If he's not drunk," Janey said, shuddering.

"I probably should've left, especially after what Robin said, but wild horses couldn't have driven me away."

"Don't take what she said personally. She really likes you. It's just that—"

"She's jealous," Dillon interrupted, finishing the sentence for her.

"And determined."

"But things will work out," he assured her huskily.

Janey ran an unsteady hand through her hair. "I wish I could be so sure of that."

Dillon's features softened somewhat. "I know how you must be feeling. Robin's—"

"No, you don't," she said more sharply than she had intended, which was becoming a habit when Robin was discussed. "Look—"

"Stop apologizing. And you're right, I don't know. If that were my daughter—" He broke off, took a breath, then went on in a harsh tone, "I know what I'd like to do, only it's not repeatable."

"At least she's going to heal," Janey whispered. "At least he didn't hit her somewhere else, where it would've done more damage." She shivered visibly, and her eyes filled with hot tears.

"Hey, stop tormenting yourself," Dillon pleaded, crossing the room and sitting on the sofa beside her. He reached for her hand and clasped it in his callused one. Yet his touch was soothing, not sexual, which once again proved that under that facade of Marine-tough masculinity was a sensitive, gentle man.

"It's all my fault," Janey responded dully.

"No, it's not." His tone was emphatic.

Janey extracted her fingers and got to her feet, suddenly feeling that if she didn't move she would scream. Maybe if she peeked in on her daughter she would feel better. Later, she told herself. After all, Chad was no longer a threat.

Or was he?

"What's wrong?" Dillon demanded, as though he'd picked up on the shock waves continuing to wash through her body.

"Chad. He's what's wrong."

"I told you, I'm going to take care of him." Dillon's tone was deadly now. So were his eyes.

If she hadn't despised that boy and what he'd done

to her daughter, she could almost feel sorry for him. Dillon would prove a dangerous enemy.

"I know you did, but I still have to deal with Robin and her feelings for him."

"Surely she no longer cares." Dillon frowned. "I wouldn't think she'd ever want to see him again."

"You'd think that, all right. But I'm not banking on it."

"Well, when I get through with Chad, he won't hurt her again. You can damn sure bank on *that*."

She had no doubt he would give Chad his best effort. But she knew her daughter and her stubbornness. Janey prayed that this episode had been a life-altering one. But when promise rings were in the offing, there were strong ties.

"You trust me to deal with this, don't you?"

Apparently he'd taken her silence the wrong way. "That's not the question."

And it wasn't. After Robin had told them what Chad had done, Janey had grabbed her chest, feeling as though she were suffocating. By the time she found her voice, the other kids had slunk out of the room.

"My God, Robin!" she had cried. "How..." She couldn't go on. There were no words to express her fury, her fear, her disappointment.

"Mom..." Robin began to sob.

Janey had placed loving arms around her, and both had cried.

That was when Dillon had taken over. "Come on, I'll drive you home."

The ride to the house had been made in total silence. Robin had sat curled up in the back seat, her eyes closed. Janey had sat beside Dillon, reed straight. Once they reached the apartment, Robin had made her way toward her room. Janey had let her go, knowing that tomorrow would be the day of reckoning for them both.

"Janey, stop torturing yourself," Dillon said now, jerking her back to the present.

"I was just reliving the hospital scene." Her chin quivered but she refused to break down, at least in front of him. Later, in the darkness of her room, she could let the tears loose. "I still can't believe this has happened, that my daughter has fallen prey to—" She stopped abruptly.

"To what?" Dillon urged, an edge to his tone.

She swallowed. "Nothing."

"Nothing, hell," he muttered. "Did Keith ever hit you?"

She swallowed again, this time with more difficulty. "No, but he shoved me a couple of times."

There. She'd said it for the first time. Out loud. She'd never shared that humiliating fact with another living soul. Until now. Until Dillon. And she had no idea why. But then, Dillon had a way of making her behave totally out of character.

"That sonofabitch!" Dillon's features contorted again. "It wouldn't do for me to get my hands on him or Chad about now."

"I don't expect you to fight my battles, Dillon." Her tone was soft, but the rebuke was there nonetheless.

His mouth tightened. "I know, dammit, but—"

"I think you'd better go. I don't know how much longer I can remain upright."

His gaze softened. "I'm sorry if I've caused you more grief. I—"

She met his direct stare, and his words seemed to just dry up in his throat, along with all the air in the room. Janey fought for a decent breath, while myriad emotions stampeded through her.

She knew what he was thinking. And heaven help her, she was thinking the same thing. She wanted him to hold her, to kiss her, even to make love to her, to make her hurt and pain go away. But that wasn't the answer. Dillon wasn't the answer. There was no longer room in her life for any man.

This nonsense with him had to end. Her loyalties could no longer be divided. Tonight had made that clearer than ever.

"Thanks for everything," she whispered, withdrawing her eyes.

"Don't do that." His lips twisted, as if he could read her mind and see the writing on the wall. "You don't owe me anything." He paused. "I'll call you."

She didn't say anything. She didn't even move until she heard the door close downstairs. Long after he was gone, she locked the bolts, checked on Robin—who was now sound asleep—then walked into her room and fell across the bed.

Sleep was not in the cards. While her body cried for relief, her mind remained on the warpath. She couldn't even cry. Her tears seemed to have dried up under the heavy burden she bore.

She had made love to the man whose wife had severed her marriage, and her daughter had been assaulted by her boyfriend.

She was living her nightmares.

"Oh, God," Janey whimpered, rolling onto her back and staring at the dark ceiling.

She shouldn't even be thinking about Dillon and

the smoldering passion they had shared. Her thoughts should be centered on what she would say to her daughter come morning.

But for some reason, she couldn't separate the two. Guilt. That was what was making her crazy. Robin hadn't wanted her to be with Dillon, had even resented it. It wasn't Dillon personally, she knew. Robin would resent any man who she saw as a threat to her mother and father getting back together.

The tears finally came, and Janey gave in to them, hoping they would help cleanse her soul. But the pain remained, especially when her thoughts returned to Dillon.

Was that partly the reason she was so exhausted?

Of course it was, she admitted, placing her hands to her cheeks, feeling the heat from them scorch her palms. One couldn't indulge in that type of sexual marathon and not experience lasting side effects.

Janey's hands fell to her sides, but the heat didn't abate, nor did her torrid thoughts. Why on earth would Elaine have wanted to sleep around on Dillon, especially with Keith?

As far as lovers went, there was no comparison. Keith was definitely not in Dillon's league. Dillon had done things—delicious things—to her body that Keith would not have dared.

So why had she let Dillon have carte blanche? He hadn't asked. He'd simply seized the moment, taking her on the sexual ride of her life.

Penis power.

She had been told there was nothing like it. She believed that now. Suddenly she lurched up in the bed, wild-eyed. Where had those high-voltage thoughts come from?

What had triggered them? She didn't know. But she couldn't take any more, not when she didn't intend to let Dillon have another go at her body.

Feeling the need for a purifying shower, Janey dashed into the bathroom and shed her clothing. But while the hot water relieved her body, it did very little for her heart.

It still smarted.

Pam Burnette sobbed quietly, while her husband Burt sat helplessly by and patted her back.

"I hated like hell to have to do this," Dillon said, "for all the reasons you can guess."

"I still can't believe it," Burt said in a rusty-sounding voice.

Dillon had arrived at the Burnette household a short while ago, giving them time to return from church and have dinner. He had noticed that Chad was not around. For the moment, he was thankful. He'd wanted to talk to the boy's parents alone.

Now, after the fact, Dillon felt like a heel, not because he'd told them—that had to be done—but because he'd known how they would react. Denial had followed horror.

They were in some mixture of the two states now. He couldn't say that he blamed them, either. He'd fought the same battle himself, having known the kid since he was born, for chrissake.

Now that he looked back on things, he realized that he should have taken Chad's dark side more seriously. But even if he had, he never would have thought Chad capable of physical violence.

"I'm like Burt," Pam was saying around her sobs. "I can't believe my son would ever hit a girl."

She was an attractive woman, with blond hair and blue eyes. Sort of dingy, Dillon had always thought, but that didn't make her a bad mother. Burt, on the other hand, had it all together, an investment banker who was sharp as a tack.

How had *they* missed the signs?

"Well, he did," Dillon said flatly. It was a fact he'd already stated several times since sitting down at the kitchen table.

"Had he been drinking?" Burt asked.

"Yes," Dillon said, mincing no words.

Burt rubbed his lined forehead. "Do you know the details?"

"Only what some of the kids said, which isn't much. Robin and Chad were apparently exchanging verbal bullets when Chad hauled off and hit her."

Even speaking those words made Dillon cringe. It also made him want to get his hands on Chad.

Pam began sobbing again.

"Ah, honey, don't." Burt patted his wife's arm. "That's not going to solve anything."

"He needs counseling," Dillon said with authority.

Pam's head came up. "But what will my friends—"

"Screw your friends," Dillon snapped. "It's your son you need to worry about. You have to nip this in the bud."

"I think we can take care of that ourselves," Burt said, circling his wife's shoulder with his arm as if closing ranks and preparing for battle.

Dillon released a sigh. "Don't gang up against me, Burt. It won't work. Besides, you have to know I only want what's best for Chad."

Burt's eyes narrowed. "I know, but we have to handle this in our own way."

"That's right, Dillon," Pam added in a broken voice.

"And since it didn't happen on school property, there's nothing you can really do about it."

Dillon stood. "No, Burt, but for your son's good and yours as a parent, you'd best act on this. Now."

Burt stood, as well, extending his hand, but he didn't meet Dillon's eyes. Dillon sighed inwardly, wanting to shake them both out of their denial and into action.

"Thanks for coming," Burt said in an uneasy tone.

Dillon made a face. "Yeah, right."

He was out the door and nearly to his vehicle, when Chad drove into the drive. Fate had indeed smiled on Dillon. This was the opportunity he'd longed for, though for a second he feared the boy might shove the car in Reverse and back out.

"Uh, hi, Mr. Reed," Chad said, after finally climbing out of his four-wheel-drive.

Dillon noticed that the boy's face was a sickly-looking green. He didn't know if that was from a hangover or from seeing his principal. Dillon suspected a little of both.

"How's it going?" Chad asked, his walk a bit awkward as he came around the vehicle.

"Cut the crap, Chad."

Chad straightened as if hit, and his eyes turned apprehensive. "I didn't mean—"

"You're apologizing to the wrong person." Dillon was close now, but Chad didn't so much as move a muscle. "It's Robin who deserves that."

"Did...did you tell my parents?"

"What do you think?"

Chad's face turned greener, but when he spoke his tone had a sullen edge to it. "I was drunk."

Dillon's nostrils flared. "And you think that excuses your behavior? Not in this lifetime."

Chad stepped back.

Dillon closed the distance and bore down on him. "And I'll tell you something else, you little creep. If you ever lay a hand on Robin or any other girl again, I'll personally beat your ass. And that's a promise!"

Twenty-Eight

"**Y**our breakfast is ready."

"I'm not hungry," Robin responded in a muffled tone, her head buried under the covers.

"I want you to eat, anyway." Janey waited, knowing why Robin would rather remain in bed. Of course her daughter didn't want to face the consequences of the choices she had made. But no way was Janey going to sweep last night's horrible episode under the rug.

"I'm waiting."

Robin eased the sheet down so only her eyes were showing. "Do I have to?"

"Yes."

"I know you're pissed—"

"Don't use that word," Janey snapped.

"Sorry," Robin muttered again, then tossed back the covers and dangled her feet over the side of the bed.

Janey's breath caught. Her daughter looked as if she'd been in a kick-boxing match and lost. The cheek on the side of the split lip was now black, where last night it had been a purplish blue. Robin was a mess. Thank God the doctor had said no plastic surgery would be necessary, that the cut would heal and wouldn't be noticeable.

"I look terrible, don't I," Robin said.

"I've seen you look better." Janey kept her voice light, though she ached to jump in the car, drive to Chad's and give him as good as he'd given.

The idea that someone had done this to her child was totally and completely unacceptable. And she intended to do everything in her power to see that it didn't happen again.

"How can I ever face my friends," Robin wailed, having gotten up and raced to the mirror, "with my face looking like this?"

"Your friends will like you no matter what."

Robin threw Janey a look, then shifted her gaze like a skittish colt.

A moment of silence followed.

"Honey, you can relax." Janey held on to her light tone. "I'm not mad at you."

"But you're disappointed," Robin said in an anxious tone, walking back to the bed and sitting down.

"I won't deny that. And you certainly have a lot of explaining to do. So get yourself together, and we'll talk."

Janey was on her second cup of coffee, when Robin finally walked into the kitchen, dressed in a lightweight sweat outfit. Her hair was still damp from the shower, and she smelled like a bouquet of fresh flowers.

"First off," Janey said, rising, "I want a hug."

Robin practically ran into her arms. After holding her tightly for a long moment, doing her best to keep back the tears, Janey pushed Robin to arm's length. "Now I want you to eat. Your oatmeal's ready, and so is your toast."

"Thanks, Mom."

Janey had a tough time watching Robin try to eat around the protruding, thick upper lip, but her daughter managed to get down half the soft buttery toast and all the oatmeal.

"Feel better?" Janey asked, when Robin pushed the bowl away and reached for her cup of hot chocolate.

"Much. I was starving."

Janey hid a smile. "That's nothing new."

Another silence fell between them while Robin squirmed visibly in her chair as if she were suddenly on a hot seat. Well, she was, Janey thought, but it was Robin's own fault.

"It goes without saying that I love you."

"Mom, he didn't mean to do it."

Janey's heart sank to her toes. Oh, dear Lord, she couldn't believe—she didn't want to believe—that Robin had said those words.

"Surely you don't mean that," Janey declared in a stunned whisper.

"The booze made him do it. Chad's not himself when he's drinking."

As if that excuses his behavior. Janey was aghast but tried not to let it show. She couldn't push the panic button; she had to remain rational, so as to try to talk some sense into her daughter's head. She had known this "come to Jesus meeting" wouldn't be pleasant, but she had never expected it to take such a disturbing turn.

"Oh, honey, honey," Janey said, reaching across the table and grabbing Robin's hands. "That's not what loving someone is all about, and you know that.

Drinking or not, Chad should never lay a hand on you except in a caring way."

"Mom, you just don't understand. It's my fault. I shouldn't have accused him of flirting."

"Dear God, Robin, that's no reason to haul off and slug you."

"It wasn't that dramatic."

"If only you could hear yourself." This time Janey did begin to panic. She was losing ground, and losing it fast.

Robin's entire body seemed to stiffen. "Chad loves me. He didn't mean to hurt me."

"But he did hurt you, honey," Janey pointed out in the calmest, gentlest voice she could muster. What she wanted to do was scream at her daughter to wake up and hear what she was saying, that her defense of Chad made no sense whatsoever.

"I'll be all right." Mutiny hardened Robin's tone.

Janey steeled herself against that response, determined not to let her guard down for one second and to take the necessary measures to convince her daughter that Chad was not right for her.

"Can't you see what he's doing? That's his way of controlling you, which is a very dangerous precedent to set. I've tried to instill in you a sense of independence and self-worth. No woman, young or old, deserves to be treated in such a manner. And you know that."

"I happen to like Chad the way he is. I'm where all my friends would love to be. I've told you a thousand times, they're green with envy that Chad chose me over all of them."

Those words took another chunk out of Janey's heart. Still, she didn't have the luxury of giving up, of sitting there and wallowing in self-doubt and self-pity, asking herself where she had gone wrong, how she had failed as a mother.

"Besides, everyone deserves a second chance," Robin said into the heavy silence.

"Not everyone, Robin. Not Chad."

"Not Dad, either, huh?"

Robin's bitterness was so up front and in Janey's face that Janey actually flinched. "This is not about your dad."

"It's the same thing."

Janey's calm slipped. "No, it isn't. It's about what Chad did to you."

"I thought forgiveness was a big thing with you." Robin's voice broke. "At least, that's what you've always taught me. Only you haven't lived up to that. You don't have forgiveness in your heart."

"It doesn't matter what's in my heart. It's what's in yours that counts."

"If you had forgiven Dad after his affair, we would still be a family."

"What?" If she hadn't been sitting down, Janey would have fallen down. *Shocked* was too mild a word to describe how she felt as she gave her daughter an incredulous stare.

"You heard what I said," Robin murmured, tears in her eyes.

"How did—" Janey choked on the rest of the sentence, feeling as if someone were holding her hands against her will and pulling out her fingernails one at a time.

"The last time Dad was here, I came home and heard you two talking—or rather, fighting."

"Oh, Robin, honey, I'm so sorry you had to find out like that."

Robin shrugged. "It's no big deal."

"There's so much you don't understand."

"Oh, Mom, I'm not a child. You could've told me."

"I didn't think you were ready to hear the truth about your dad."

That look of mutiny crossed Robin's features again. "I forgave him."

Janey struggled to talk around the pain pounding at her. "I'm glad you feel that way."

"Do you know who the other woman was?"

"Is that important?" Janey asked in a strained voice.

"I'd just like to know."

Janey's hesitation was short-lived. If Robin was old enough to ask, then she deserved the truth, or at least a portion of it.

"It was Elaine, Dillon's wife."

Robin showed no emotion, though Janey made it a point to delve into those usually expressive eyes.

"I kinda thought it might be her."

"Robin, look—"

"Don't you think it's kind of weird for you and Dillon to be getting it on?"

"Robin!" Janey was horrified and couldn't stop it from showing.

"Well, aren't you? Getting it on, I mean?"

"What we're doing," Janey said between clenched teeth, "is none of your business."

Robin thinned her mouth, then winced at the obvious pain the gesture triggered.

"I thought you liked Dillon," Janey continued in a more conciliatory tone.

"He's all right," Robin replied in an offhand manner.

It was all Janey could do not to remind her daughter how cool she had once thought Dillon was. But Janey refrained, realizing how precarious a turn this conversation had taken.

"But I want you and Daddy to get back together. He wants that, too."

"It won't work."

"Why not?" Robin demanded bluntly.

"Because I don't love him anymore. And in your heart you know that. But that—your dad, me, Dillon—is not what this conversation's about. It's about how you're going to deal with Chad." Janey paused. "I won't have him touching you in any way that's not respectful."

"Are you saying I can still see him?" Robin's tone held shock.

Of course, you can't, Janey wanted to lash out. But she didn't. If Janey were to forbid Robin to see Chad, that would only make the girl that much more determined, which meant she would have to sneak around. Janey couldn't bear that thought.

"No. I'm saying it's your decision, that I trust you to make the right one."

"Oh, Mom," Robin cried, "why do you always have to be so holier-than-thou?"

"Because I'm your mother and I love you."

"Well, I'm not going to give Chad up," Robin said, lifting her head and jutting her chin.

Another chunk fell off Janey's heart, but she didn't let her agony show. Instead, she looked at her daughter with love spilling from her eyes. "I told you, I trust you. I know you'll do what's right."

Damn, but he hated talking into those machines.

Now, however, that seemed to be a way of life. Dillon frowned as he put the receiver back on the cradle. He had hoped to talk to Patricia personally, to thank her for the candy, though he was pissed that she'd pulled such a stunt.

She hadn't known he had the hots for Janey, of course. Still, she shouldn't have taken such liberty, knowing how he felt—or rather, didn't feel—about her.

"Ah, to hell with it," Dillon muttered, grabbing his hat and walking out the door. He had more important things on his agenda.

Thirty minutes later he was at the farm, having a conversation with his brother-in-law. "How'd you do it?"

Mike grinned. "Things seem to be going my way lately. What can I say?"

Dillon matched his stride to Mike's as they left the barn and headed toward the house. Mike had just told Dillon that he'd found another prize mare for sale at a reasonable price.

"You don't have to say anything except how much she's going to cost me."

Mike cut him a glance. "I didn't say cheap. I said reasonable, so keep that in mind."

"Just tell me."

He did, and Dillon pulled up short. "Man, I don't have that kind of money."

"Can you get it?"

Dillon mulled over the question as they reached

the house and went inside. Allie was in the kitchen, taking fresh bread out of the oven. The wonderful aroma permeated the house.

"My, my, I swear my eyes are playing tricks on me again." Allie tempered her sarcasm with a smile.

"Go ahead, make me feel like a bigger heel than I already do."

"Okay," Allie countered glibly.

Mike kissed his wife on the cheek. "Truce, you two. How 'bout it?"

Dillon kissed his sister on the other cheek, then hugged her. Afterward, he pushed her away and scrutinized her. "You're looking better, even if those dark circles aren't gone from under your eyes."

"Thanks."

"You *are* feeling better, right?"

Because he hadn't been as attentive to Allie as he should have been, his conscience pricked him. Hell, all he could think about these days was school and Janey, and not necessarily in that order. It had even been several days since he'd been to the farm, which was a rarity for him.

"You're off the hook again," Allie was saying, her face wrinkled in a smile. "I still have my moments, but overall, I'm better." She cast her husband a quick look.

"So what did the tests show?" Dillon pressed, wondering if they were keeping something from him.

"I'm going to live at least another few years," Allie quipped.

Dillon glared at her. "Dammit, I'm serious."

"Hey, me too." Allie laughed. "I'm okay, really. So get your shorts out of a wad and sit down. The bread's done."

Dillon did as he was told, more relieved than he could say that Allie was okay.

"So can you get the money?" Mike asked, pulling out a chair and joining him at the table.

Dillon blew out a breath. "I'll have to do some figuring and some finagling, that's for sure."

"Well, put the pencil to the paper and let me know."

Allie chose that moment to give them each a slice of bread and cup of coffee. She joined them and watched as they munched in silence.

"Where's yours?" Dillon asked, his mouth full.

"I'm watching my weight."

Dillon snorted. "As if you need to."

Allie ignored him, changing the subject. "I'm ready to have the barbecue."

Dillon stopped chewing for a moment. "Are you sure?"

"Yep. In fact, I've already started inviting people. Can I count on you and Janey?"

Just the mention of her name caused his loins to tighten. He shifted uncomfortably. "I can't speak for her."

"Want me to give her a call?"

Relief shot through him. "Would you?"

"Sure." Allie gave him an odd look. "Is something going on that I ought to know about?"

In spite of himself, Dillon felt color rush into his face. Allie's lips twitched, and she patted his hand. "Don't worry, I'll take care of it. And you."

Twenty-Nine

Did she have rocks for brains?

She must have, Janey told herself, or she wouldn't be at this shindig. But when Allie had called her midweek and invited her, she'd been caught so off guard that she hadn't been able to come up with an excuse. Later she'd thought of a million reasons not to go and had been about to decline.

Then Dillon had called.

"Hey," he'd said in that low, sexy voice of his.

"You rat."

He laughed, a warm, deep chuckle that set her every nerve on fire. Still, she said in a terse tone, "Don't you dare sugarcoat this. Why didn't you just ask me yourself?"

"Would you have said yes?"

"No."

He chuckled again. "That's why, when Allie volunteered to call, I gave her the green light."

"This is crazy."

"I'm crazy about you."

That unexpected confession, spoken in that same sexy tone, made her head spin and raw heat settle between her thighs. She clutched the receiver as though it were a lifeline. She wished he wouldn't say things like that to her.

Since their evening of seemingly endless lovemaking, she hadn't aired her feelings in daylight. They remained tucked away in a corner of her heart.

"I know that wasn't what you wanted to hear."

Janey fingered her hair. "No, it wasn't."

"Even if it's true."

"Dillon, it's just about sex." God, she couldn't believe she'd said that.

"You really think that's all we're about?" he asked hoarsely.

"I asked for that, and I'm sorry."

"You should be, dammit."

"Still, under the circumstances, I don't think the barbecue's—"

"Don't say it. It'll be good for you to have a frivolous day of fun. I know things have been pretty tough for you lately." He paused. "And I'll be good. I promise."

A sigh erupted. "In another lifetime, maybe."

"Seriously, I wanted to call sooner but I figured you needed the space. So how did your chat with Robin go?"

"Not good." This time she paused. "Have you spoken to Chad?"

"You bet I did. His parents, too."

"And?" Janey held her breath.

"You won't have to worry about him physically hurting Robin ever again." Dillon's tone had turned hard and cold as granite.

"Oh, God, Dillon, I can't thank you enough." Her voice cracked.

"Don't. It's going to be okay. Robin's a good girl. If she hasn't seen the light, she soon will."

"That's what I'm praying for."

There was a short silence, then Dillon asked, "Is five o'clock okay with you? Oh, and if you want to, bring Robin."

"She already has plans, but I'll pass the word along. And thanks."

"Dammit, stop thanking me."

"All right. I'll be ready."

Now, as Janey forced her mind back to the present, her eyes drifted to the sky. Not a cloud in sight on this chilly but lovely Saturday afternoon. Perfect weather for an outing.

Apparently the other guests thought so, as well. The grounds were teeming with couples and lots of kids, all laughing, talking and indulging in everything from beer to wine to soft drinks. There was even a small platform where a band belted out a country and western tune.

And the smell of barbecue was enticing, though she wasn't particularly hungry. Maybe because her heart was lodged in her throat and food couldn't get past it.

Dillon was to blame. If only he would stop giving her those smoldering looks. But the instant he'd appeared at her front door, the tension had begun to mount and hadn't let up.

At first she had thought he was going to grab her and kiss her. But he hadn't. She didn't know if she was terribly disappointed or terribly glad. If her errant thoughts were any judge, she would have to say it was the former. *Rein it in,* she blasted herself silently. Why couldn't she just let it go? Why couldn't she just let *him* go?

"You're looking deep in thought."

Janey's head shot up, and when it did, she met his eyes head-on with collision force.

"God, Janey," he muttered darkly, "it's all I can do to keep my hands off you as it is."

She averted her gaze, knowing her face was splotched with color. She hoped no one else had heard him.

"Instead of barbecue," he went on in that same raspy voice, "I'd like to eat *you*."

She swung back around and stared at him, her mouth open and her heart hammering.

"Hey, everybody, listen up!"

Mike's strong voice hailed from the platform, where the band was now silent.

"Wonder what's up?" Dillon muttered, focusing his attention on his brother-in-law.

Janey didn't have a clue, either, but she could have run and hugged him for interrupting their conversation. It had gotten far too heavy to suit her.

"Allie and I have an announcement to make," Mike called out.

"Come on," Dillon said, clasping her elbow, "let's move closer. Something's definitely up."

"You don't have any idea what this is all about?" Janey asked, her steps matching his.

"Nope."

"Well, I guess we're about to find out."

Allie had stepped up beside Mike, and both were smiling like two cats who'd been slurping rich cream out of a fancy bowl.

"Dear friends," Mike said, "we're pregnant. Actually, Allie's going to have the baby, but—"

The remainder of his words were lost amid catcalls, loud laughter, whistles and clapping hands.

"Well, how about them apples?" Dillon responded in a slightly dazed voice, a slow grin spreading across his face. "Now I know why she's been feeling under the weather." He peered down at Janey. "This calls for a big hug from big brother. Want to come?"

"No, you go ahead. I'll offer my congrats later."

Janey watched as he pushed his way through the guests, grabbed Allie and hugged her, then slapped Mike on the shoulder. It was when he turned back toward her that she saw the hint of darkness in his eyes.

She clutched at her chest as if to stave off the sudden pain.

He wished he was the one having a baby.

"I guess you can say this is one time I got caught with my drawers down." Dillon set two heaping plates of food on the small picnic table under a huge oak before sitting across from her.

Janey smiled, which made his eyes linger a bit longer than usual on her provocative coral lips—lips that he wanted to crush under his.

As if she could read his mind, she cleared her throat and lowered her eyes to the food. She almost gasped aloud at the quantity. Dillon had piled the plate full of chicken, ribs, sausages, beans and potato salad.

"Surely you don't expect me to eat all this?" she asked, a frown marring her perfect skin.

"I do."

"Right."

He grinned, picking up his fork and digging in. "I'm waiting on you like one hog waits on another."

Janey shook her head, then reached for her fork. Even that small gesture fascinated him, but then, everything she did turned his fancy. Dressed in a pair of jeans and a long-sleeved gold T-shirt that hugged her curves, she delivered a knockout punch to his gut every time she moved.

And though she wore a bra, she might as well not have; her nipples were still visible, though he wasn't sure she was aware of that. He damn sure was, and it made him ache to suck them.

Sweat dotted his upper lip. He had to get control of himself or he would be slinging her down on the ground and ripping her clothes off.

He reached for his napkin.

Janey's brows rose. "I can't believe you're perspiring."

"If you knew what I was thinking, you'd believe it." Then, realizing what he'd blurted out, he held up his hand. "Sorry, that was out of line."

"That it was," she said, glaring at him.

He attacked his food once again, and didn't let up until his plate was nearly empty. She gave him an incredulous stare. "I don't know where you're putting all that."

He touched his flat stomach. "I'm a growing boy."

She merely shook her head again, and they munched in silence for a while. It was Janey who finally spoke, her voice impersonal. "How are things at the school?"

"Smooth as silk."

She looked exasperated. "I'm serious."

"I know. So far, we haven't had any more malicious break-ins, but I'm not holding my breath."

"I'm assuming the guilty party's still on the loose."

"That's a good way of putting it, though I think that little creep Hal Aimsworth who hit on Robin is behind it all. Your break-in, too."

"As far as I know, he hasn't approached Robin again. That's one thing to be grateful for."

"I don't think you have to worry about that. I'll kick his narrow ass out of school if I catch him anywhere near her. And don't thank me, either."

Janey toyed with her empty cola cup. Finally she said, "Speaking of Robin, you've been so protective of her. I just hope you won't take offense at her attitude toward you."

"Hey, I've got tougher skin than that. Besides, I know where it came from. She's just jealous. She's still not open to you having another man in your life."

"But like I told her, in her heart she knows Keith and I will never get back together."

"Well, her mind's still in there fighting."

"That's one of the reasons I should never have come back here."

"Don't say that."

Their eyes met, and hot desire held them together. He didn't know how much more of this togetherness he could take, and not touch her. And whether she wanted to admit it or not, she felt the same. It was written all over her—in her eyes, in the tenseness of her body.

Why didn't she just give in to her feelings and let him love her? *Love?* Had he lost his mind? He didn't love her. He just wanted to *make love* to her. There was a big difference, and he'd best keep that in mind.

For him, love and marriage went hand in hand, and, though he sure wanted a child of his own, he wasn't ready for that.

"If you dare say what you're thinking, I'll kill you dead."

He had to laugh. "Kill me dead, huh?"

"You know what I meant," she snapped.

"So what do you think about my sister having a baby? Pretty amazing, wouldn't you say?"

"I think it's pretty great."

"Me too."

"Are you sure?"

He felt himself tense, then asked bluntly, "Do you think I'm envious?"

"No, I think you're proud," she said softly, "but I also think it brings back your own pain and loss."

"You're right, it does," he admitted in a bleak tone, then shrugged. "However, I'd cut my tongue out before I'd let her know that."

Another silence followed his words, during which she shifted her gaze from him.

"Janey?"

"What?" She looked back at him, her eyes wide.

"Have you by chance missed a period?" he asked in a rusty voice.

Her face drained of color. "It's too soon. But you sure know which buttons to push and when to push them."

"I didn't mean to start World War Three."

"Well, then don't ask me things like that."

"Sorry."

Dillon suddenly became aware that several women had sat at the table behind them. He wouldn't have thought a thing about that, as the place was still jumping with music, laughter and loud talking, if he hadn't heard his name. Obviously they didn't realize he was sitting right there.

He froze.

"What's wrong?" Janey asked.

He leaned forward and whispered, "One of those ladies behind me just mentioned my name."

Janey's eyebrows rose, and she stared beyond his shoulders. Both listened.

"Isn't that just awful?" It was the same woman speaking.

"What are y'all talking about?" another chimed in.

"It's *who*—Dillon Reed and Janey Mayfield."

Dillon's blood curdled at the same time that Janey's hand flew to her mouth.

"What about them?" a third woman asked.

"Surely you haven't forgotten that his wife had an affair with her husband."

"So? Big deal. That happens all the time."

"You're right," the first woman said. "Only now the two of them are an item."

"That's disgusting, for God's sake."

"Amen to that."

Dillon couldn't stomach any more. He didn't even have to look at Janey to know her reaction. She was devastated, and he didn't blame her.

On legs that felt like stone posts, Dillon stood. "Come on," he said in a curt tone. "Let's get the hell out of here."

They walked away together, ignoring the startled gasps behind them.

Thirty

"Are you about to open?"

It was Gwen on the phone.

"Yep. In fact, I was just walking out."

"Call me when you get in the shop."

"That's all right," Janey said, sitting back down on her bed. "I have a minute."

"Well, I hadn't heard from you in a while, and I was getting worried."

"Things have been wild. I won't deny that."

"Wild how?" Gwen asked.

Janey told her about the visit to the ER and the episode with Chad.

"Why, that piece of scum," Gwen spat. "How dare he lay a hand on that child?"

"I can't tell you what I've been going through," Janey responded, the old sick feeling invading her stomach.

"Why didn't you call me from the hospital?"

"I wasn't alone, thank goodness."

"Oh."

"Don't 'oh' me. Dillon was with me."

"Ahhh."

"You're treading on dangerous ground, my friend."

Gwen laughed. "Actually, I'm delighted he was with you—for whatever reason."

"You've made your point," Janey said on a warning note, though her voice held a hint of humor.

Gwen laughed again. "Okay. For now, I'll cut you some slack." Then her tone turned serious. "Back to Robin, how did you handle the aftermath?"

"With kid gloves," Janey said, taking a trembling breath.

"So you didn't demand she keep her distance?"

"No. That's what I wanted to do, only I didn't."

"Smart lady. If you forbid her to see the jerk, then she might do it just to spite you."

"That was my reasoning, though Robin's not prone to that kind of behavior—or at least she never has been. But I have to say that when it comes to that boy, she's not thinking clearly."

"I can imagine how Dillon took this."

"He spoke to Chad's parents first, then Chad."

"Man, would I have loved to be a fly on the wall and heard those conversations."

Janey rubbed her neck. "Me too. And I really don't know the details, either. Dillon just told me I didn't have to worry about Chad hurting Robin again."

"I'm sure that's right. I wouldn't want to be on Dillon's bad side."

"I still can't believe it happened—that my daughter was actually abused by her boyfriend. It seems like a horrible nightmare."

"It happens all the time. But I'm like you, it's not supposed to hit that close to home."

"I pray I handled it the right way," Janey said,

her trembling increasing. "But I don't know. I agonize over it day and night."

"You trust her, don't you?"

"Yes."

"Then you did the right thing. The only way you can make her leave Chad alone is to lock her in her room."

"Believe me, I thought about that."

"As a mother, I'm sure you did."

"But that's not the answer, and I know it."

"Robin'll come through." Gwen's tone was reassuring. "You wait and see. She'll can his ass."

"I'll keep you posted. And I didn't mean to dump on you like this."

"Hey, dump on me anytime. I'm pissed that you haven't already called."

"Well, like I said, it's been hectic."

"What about your ex? Did he get in on it?"

"After we got home from the ER, Robin called Keith—but I haven't talked to him. Though I need to. He's still behind on his child support."

"That bastard. What's he doing with all his money? I thought he was the stud salesman of the dealership."

"He's always made good money, I know that. What he's doing with it, I haven't a clue."

"Taking him to court might be your only alternative. He needs to be taught a lesson."

"I would, if it weren't for Robin. Right now, she's too vulnerable to handle anything else. And so am I."

Gwen was quiet for a moment.

Janey didn't know what set off the warning bell inside her. Perhaps it was the fact that Gwen didn't have a quick comeback, that she was suddenly too quiet.

"Now it's your turn," Janey forced herself to say.

"To do what?" Gwen asked innocently.

"To tell me why you called. It wasn't just to say hi."

"How do you know?" Gwen's tone was blustering now.

"Come on, 'fess up."

Another silence.

"The rumor's true," Gwen said flatly. "That candy store's coming to the mall." Her breathing was harsh. "I hated like hell to tell you."

"Oh, no," Janey wailed, feeling more overwhelmed than ever.

"You said you wanted to know," Gwen countered on an anxious note.

"Of course I did. But still, it's the pits."

"Look, you're going to survive. I just know it. You give personal service, and that counts for a lot."

"Unfortunately, not money," Janey said in a forlorn voice.

"Now, you listen here, Janey Mayfield, you're not a quitter. You never have been. And I'm not about to let you throw in the towel now."

Janey stiffened her resolve. "You're right, I can't. The shop's my livelihood, and Robin's. I'll just have to look at it as one more fight to win."

"That's it. Give 'em hell. Go on the attack."

Janey laughed. Gwen's no-nonsense approach to life never failed to help her put things, good or bad, in perspective. "I'll keep that in mind. But for now, I'd better get my tush downstairs and open up."

"Go. I'll give you a holler soon. Meanwhile, keep your chin up."

Moments later, Janey turned the sign to Open, wondering with a pang how much longer she would be doing that. *Stop it!* she told herself. She'd meant what she'd said to Gwen. She wasn't going to just give up. Instead, she would come up with a plan to combat the chain. Until then, she would keep an up-beat attitude.

But it was difficult. Everything seemed to be closing in on her, and she felt powerless. After Gwen's phone call, her burdens suddenly seemed too heavy to bear.

Yet she had so much for which to be thankful. Robin's lip was healing nicely, and so far she hadn't mentioned wanting to see Chad outside school.

Janey was nowhere near ready to declare victory, though. It was much too soon. It was about time for Robin to mention her plans for the weekend, following the football game.

Janey almost panicked when she thought about Robin asking to go out with Chad. Despite Dillon's assurance that Chad would never harm her daughter again, she didn't trust Chad. She never had and never would, especially with her precious child. No longer a child, she reminded herself. Robin was a young adult who had a mind of her own, and she was stubborn beyond her years.

The end-all split had to be Robin's idea, not her mom's. Janey had told herself that from the get-go, and she hadn't changed her mind. But it was hard to keep her mouth shut, hard to realize that her daughter was grown and had to live with her choices and the consequences of those choices.

Would she survive Robin's senior year? The way things were going, she wasn't sure.

Janey sighed wearily as she arranged a fresh bouquet of flowers that she'd picked up at the grocery. She was desperate for anything that would lift her flagging spirits.

Dillon also weighed heavily on her heart and mind. She was worried not only about her daughter's well-being, but about him. That mind-boggling incident at the barbecue had really upset him. Actually, he'd been livid, although he hadn't said as much.

But she'd known. He had remained silent and standoffish the entire trip to her house. She hadn't wanted to discuss it, either, too mortified herself. Still, his attitude had made her feel worse, as if *she'd* done something wrong.

Later, after he'd left and she'd crawled into bed, his attitude had really started to rankle. He seemed to think he'd been the only one with something to lose. After all, she had to deal with the public, too. To hell with him and his mood swings, she told herself. That was another reason why they weren't good together, why she should end their relationship once and for all.

All she had to do was tell him that she couldn't have children, and he would end it himself. When she closed the store, perhaps she would do just that.

Suddenly the buzzer sounded. Janey looked up with a start. "Why, Emma, darling!" she cried. "I'm so glad to see you."

He would rather have a root canal than do what he was about to do, but he didn't feel as if he had any choice. Still, when he pulled up in Patricia's driveway, Dillon remained in his vehicle for a moment, mustering up the courage to get out and ring the doorbell.

She was waiting. In response to the voice message he'd left, she had called and asked if he would come over. She'd insisted on fixing dinner for him, though he'd tried his best to talk her out of it. His pleas had fallen on deaf ears. It was all right, he told himself. He owed her that much. Besides, she was a friend, and he wanted her to remain so.

"Hey, come on in," Patricia called from the doorway.

Crushing a sigh, he got out and strode inside. He'd been to her home many times, a heretofore pleasant experience, as it was cozy and decorated in the best of taste. This evening was different, however. He was here on a mission.

Once he was seated, she handed him a chilled glass of wine. "Your favorite," she said with a smile, though he could see the shadows lurking in her eyes.

God, he felt like a heel, but it couldn't be helped. "Something sure smells good," he said, breathing deeply, hoping to ease the tension.

"Gumbo. I know how much you like it."

He sat his glass on the coffee table and faced her.

"I know what you're going to say, but can't it wait?"

Caught off guard by her words, he opened his mouth, then shut it. Hell, he wished he cared about her instead of Janey. But he didn't, and that was that.

"Yeah, it can wait," he said in a low but gentle voice. "If that's what you want."

Patricia lowered her eyes. "Of course it's not what I want, not really. But then, you know that."

"It's over, Pat," he blurted out, despite her request. Emotional games weren't his forte, though he was already playing one with Janey. That was more than enough.

"It's another woman, isn't it."

"Is it that obvious?" he asked wearily.

"I've heard rumors. It's the lady who owns Sweet Dreams, isn't it?"

"Yes. And I'm sure you know the rest of the story, too."

"I'm sorry."

"Shit," he muttered, his gut clenching. "I'm sorry, too, for more reasons than one."

She waved a hand. "I knew it before I heard the rumors, if that makes you feel any better. A woman's instinct."

"You're a good woman, Pat, and you deserve the best."

She stood. "Under the circumstances, maybe you shouldn't stay for dinner." She extended her hand. "But no hard feelings. I enjoyed the ride while it lasted."

He ignored her hand, leaned over and kissed her on the cheek. "Take care of yourself."

"You too. And good luck."

"Thanks," he said wryly, then walked out.

Once he was in his vehicle, he cursed loudly.

Hunter was a small town. What more was there to say?

Thirty-One

Her moans rent the air as she rode him hard, her head pitched back, while his hands gripped her hips, keeping her atop him....

Cursing, Dillon jumped off the sofa and tossed his empty can in the nearest wastebasket. No matter how hard he tried, he couldn't erase that image from his mind. For some insane reason, it had haunted him all day long.

Well, he could forget that image becoming reality. After the way he'd behaved following that episode at the barbecue, he would be lucky if she gave him the time of day again.

He had picked up the phone a half-dozen times to call and tell her he was sorry, though he figured she wasn't interested in hearing anything he had to say.

But not seeing her was driving him crazy. He had it bad. He didn't know if it was love that made him ache in his heart and in his loins, or just pure lust. At this point, he didn't care. He just wanted to see Janey, smell her, touch her.

He groaned again, then strode into the kitchen, where he opened the refrigerator and grabbed another beer. He'd already had one beer too many.

But what the hell, Dillon told himself. It was the weekend, and he was alone. Besides, he rarely indulged in any kind of alcoholic beverage. But once in a blue moon he craved a good cold beer, and tonight was one of those times. He wasn't on school time, meaning he didn't have to march to the administration's drummer—or anyone else's, for that matter. He could do what he pleased.

Who gave a rip, anyway? Janey sure didn't.

His conscience suddenly pricked him. His sister cared. But she was caught up in her immediate family—Mike and the soon-to-be baby. Big brother was just a dangling participle on the perimeter of their life, not really a part of it.

Ah, hell, he should stop feeling sorry for himself and hit the sack, even though it was only nine o'clock. But he was dog tired. He'd spent all day at the farm, mending fences, cleaning out the barn, doing sundry other things that had needed his attention. Mike had worked alongside him, until Allie had had a bout of nausea and he'd gone to stay with her.

Dillon had considered returning to town, but then Mike had phoned a short time ago and said he'd called the vet to come out and look at Dandi. The mare hadn't been up to par lately; Mike had pointed that out right after Dillon had arrived that morning.

The horse's appetite had been off, and she'd been lethargic for several days—which didn't mean anything was necessarily wrong, Dillon had assured himself.

Still, he was concerned. Dandi was one horse he couldn't afford to lose, even though he'd been able to borrow the money to buy that other mare for breeding purposes. With two prized mares in his stables, he could be well on his way to making money.

That aside, Dandi was his prized horseflesh, and

he couldn't bear the thought of anything happening to her.

He couldn't bear the thought of not ever touching Janey again, either.

Another curse tore through him just as the phone rang.

"Yeah," he said into the receiver.

As expected, it was Mike. "The vet's here."

"I'm on my way."

The fact that she knew exactly where she was going didn't help any. She had made two wrong turns, which should have told her something. She ought to turn around and go back home.

However, Janey ignored that niggling in the back of her mind and kept on going. At the moment she had tunnel vision. Her thoughts, her mind, were zeroed in on Dillon.

Once she had closed the shop and eaten a frozen dinner, she had been as restless as could be. Robin was with Keith, which meant she wouldn't be returning home until tomorrow. Gwen had a date, and Janey had been delighted about that, as her friend rarely found someone she enjoyed going out with.

Still, being alone had sucked, big time.

She could have spent the evening with Emma. The old lady would have loved that; her plight had not changed one iota. After Emma had left the store today with her little sack of candy, Janey had cried. She would give anything if she had the means to help Emma. But she didn't. She was barely making ends meet herself, especially since Keith still hadn't met his obligations.

If something didn't happen soon, maybe she

would have to consider Gwen's suggestion and threaten him, something she abhorred doing. If she had her way, she would never have any contact with her ex-husband again. But Robin made that impossible. Still, it went against her grain to beg for anything, even for her daughter's sake.

Now, as she put thoughts of Keith aside and concentrated on getting to her destination, Janey tried to quiet the butterflies in her stomach by taking several deep breaths in a row.

That helped. However, when she finally saw the road leading to the cabin, the butterflies went on another rampage.

He probably wasn't here, she had told herself shortly after she'd set out on this harebrained venture. She'd gone to his house in town, and when that hadn't proved fruitful she'd taken a chance on finding him at the farm.

After all, what did she have to lose? Nothing. Instead, she had everything to gain. Hot, physical attraction was the only solid factor they had going for them. The other side of their relationship had too many holes in it ever to work.

Their past. Robin's jealousy. Janey's inability to have another child. Those were the biggies that made a future impossible.

A future.

She almost laughed. Where had that come from? Neither one of them had ever mentioned that word.

Sizzling attraction. Thus far, that and that alone was what had drawn them together and what had kept them together.

After tonight, that would no longer be the case.

Taking another deep breath, Janey pulled to a stop

and stepped out of her car into the darkness. The sound of critters that belonged only to the night brushed her ears as she made her way onto the porch.

The wind also added to the noise, making the set of chimes hanging nearby tinkle to its own pleasant melody.

She knocked several times. When she got no response, her disappointment mounted. She shouldn't have been surprised. He was probably out on the town with Patricia Sims. After that barbecue, it was logical that he'd want to be seen with someone else, to quell the rumors.

That thought pinched. She hated to admit it, but it did. The thought of him touching another woman with the same intensity and passion with which he'd touched her made her ill.

"Janey."

The unexpectedness of Dillon's gruff voice from behind sent chills up her spine. She swung around and swallowed. "Er, I was beginning to think you weren't here." She heard herself speaking as though she were out of breath.

The glow from the dim porch light allowed her to see his expression. It was a mixture of shock and anxiety.

"Is something wrong?" he asked, bounding up the steps.

Instinctively, she stepped back, even though she knew he wouldn't touch her. "No."

"Then why—?"

"Why am I here?" she interrupted.

"It doesn't matter." His eyes delved. "I'm just glad that you are."

From where she was standing, which was not all

that close, she could feel the heat coming off him. Her heart lurched. "I...I felt we needed to talk."

"You're right, we do."

"Is this a bad time?" She didn't know why she asked that, why she even cared, since she'd come to speak her piece. But when he appeared both worried and weary, she found herself sidetracked.

"Is your sister all right?"

A fleeting smile crossed his lips. "She's just pregnant. What more can I say?"

"So where were you?"

He sighed, as if impatient with her insistence. "Does it really matter?"

"I guess not."

"I was in the barn," he finally admitted. "The vet just left. My horse Dandi's under the weather."

"I'm sorry."

"Yeah, me too."

"Look, maybe I should go."

He moved closer, causing her to panic. This was not the way this meeting was supposed to go. She wasn't supposed to get all hot and bothered when he came near her. Her reaction was ridiculous.

"I don't want you to go."

Feeling as though she had suddenly walked into a pool of quicksand that was slowly but surely sucking her under, she licked her lips and tried to speak.

"Don't."

She blinked up at him. "Don't what?"

"Do that to your lips."

"Why?"

"Because it makes me hard."

She sucked in her breath. "Dillon..."

"Dillon, what?"

"That's not why I came here."

"But that's what you want."

"No, it isn't."

"Yes, it is. That's what we both want. That's what we want every time we get near one another."

"You're...you're not being fair," she said in a wheezing voice, as if she were having a sudden asthma attack.

"What's not fair is depriving ourselves of each other."

He took her hand and placed it on his zipper.

Janey gasped, the strength and heat of his erection pushing against her palm, scorching it. It was then that he reached out and cupped her between the thighs.

"Oh," she whimpered, her eyes rolling back in her head as he began to rub her there, creating a friction that would have buckled her knees had her hand not clung to the bulge beneath his jeans.

"This is crazy," he muttered. "Let's go inside."

Minutes later they were naked on his bed, with his hands and mouth all over her. It had happened so fast, so furiously, so desperately, that she was still reeling from the unexpected turn of events.

But it was too late to go back now. It seemed that the minute he'd stood in front of her, the die had been cast.

Now he tongued her ear, then trailed his hot tongue down one side of her throat onto her breasts, where he drew patterns on each one. When both were wet all over, he settled on one nipple and sucked.

Janey moaned, thrusting her hands in his hair, while emotion after emotion rolled over her like thick, hot waves. She'd never before felt this way.

His mouth, teeth and tongue were wreaking havoc in every crevice of her body, melting her, making her ache with an age-old need that only having him inside her could assuage.

"Oh, Dillon!" she cried, as he moved to the other nipple, paying it the same homage.

Only when she ran her hand down his hard stomach and surrounded his shaft did he turn loose, then stare at her out of dazed eyes. "Oh, God," he rasped, "I can't take much of that."

Boldly, she circled his lips with her tongue. When she did, she felt him harden that much more. "You want me to stop?"

"No," he rasped again.

Two fingers were now toying with the smooth end of his penis, at the opening. A drop of moisture came off on one finger; she knew he couldn't contain himself much longer.

She was more than ready herself. The apex of her thighs throbbed and pulsated with the need for him, even as she continued her sweet assault on his body.

"God, Janey, you're killing me!"

His hoarse cry seemed to come from the depths of his being, especially now that she had repositioned herself and was bending over him. With his still-dazed eyes tracking her every move, she replaced her finger with her mouth, easing down on that hard flesh.

"Ohhh!" he cried.

Realizing that he had reached his limit, she took pity on him and lifted her head. That was when he went on the attack. His hands went directly to her hot spot, and while his eyes held hers, he slipped two fingers simultaneously into her wetness, then eased them out, then in again.

"You're more than ready," he whispered.

She moaned and thrashed about under his thick voice and insistent fingers. Nothing mattered now except their gratification. The world could come to an end, and she wouldn't care as long as he gave her what she wanted—his body.

"Remember, it's your turn."

She didn't know what he was talking about, but it didn't matter, as he chose that moment to thrust into her.

Wide-eyed, she met his hot lips in a kiss so deep and desperate with longing that her mind went blank. Nothing mattered except their bodies joined as one.

It was only when he rolled over and took her with him that it dawned on her. It was her turn to be on top.

"Dillon!" she cried, feeling him stroke her breasts, then return his hands to her hips, moving her in rhythm with him.

Her eyes seeking his, she moved slowly, then faster, until the explosion came. She pitched her head back and cried out.

"Oh, baby, yes!"

His cry matched hers at the exact moment that she felt his hot seed spill into her.

Then his arms encircled her as her drenched body collapsed on his, and she nestled her head in the dampness of his neck.

His arms tightened around her, as if he would never let her go. She prayed he wouldn't.

Thirty-Two

She didn't have an excuse.

And she wasn't about to bother to manufacture one. Although she hadn't consciously sought him out to this end, she hadn't tried to stop him from making love to her, either.

How did one go about ending a relationship when the heart continually overruled the head? She could have fixed the problem long ago and wouldn't be in this predicament, she reminded herself, if she could have answered that question. But that "if" factor seemed to dog her continually.

The truth was, she didn't want to stop making love to Dillon. Despite the difficulty in admitting that, it was so. She couldn't deny the truth any longer. But that didn't mean she wanted or expected a lasting relationship with him.

That was not to be, for all the reasons her heart refused to accept.

"Are you awake?"

Startled, Janey turned her head and found Dillon leaning on a crooked elbow, peering down at her. A lamp with a low-wattage bulb had burned the entire time they had made love, enabling her to see the myriad expressions that had crossed his face during that tumultuous time. She could see some of those same mirrored expressions now.

"I was never asleep," she said in an unsteady voice.

A thick eyebrow quirked. "Oh, really?"

"What's that supposed to mean?"

"I could've sworn I heard you snoring."

Janey's mouth gaped. Had she fallen asleep? More important, did she snore? That thought was appalling.

It was then that she recognized the glint in Dillon's eye for what it was. She punched him lightly in the stomach. "You're putting me on, you rat. I don't snore."

He grinned. "I had you going there for a minute, though, you have to admit."

"I don't have to admit anything," she said churlishly.

He chuckled, that warm chuckle that never failed to melt her insides. As though he picked up on her body's vibes, a glint of another kind leapt into his eyes.

"Janey." Her name came out sounding like a caress.

Her body went into double meltdown, but she wouldn't give in to her carnal needs, not again. They needed to talk. They *had* to talk.

"I loved being inside you," he said in a strained voice, a hand wandering over the flat smoothness of her stomach before venturing lower.

She wanted to stop him; she truly did. But when that hand cupped her mound and two fingers slid into her warmth and began to move, she whimpered as she gave in to the hot desire stabbing her.

When it was over, she stared at him through dazed eyes. "Why?"

"Why what?" he asked in a low, indulgent tone.

"You didn't..."

"It doesn't matter. I love to watch you come."

Her face flamed, and she opened her mouth, but nothing came out.

He chuckled again. "I can't believe you can still turn red after what we've done to each other's bodies."

"That's the first time..." Her voice played out again, and she licked her lips.

He groaned, dipped his head and kissed her long and hard. When he pulled back, he was breathing far too fast. "You mean you've never been finger-fucked?"

"Dillon, please." Her eyes were pleading, especially as his fingers were tugging on a nipple.

"I'm glad that bastard never had that pleasure. I like being the first."

"Please," she pleaded again, on fire.

His eyes probed. "Please what?"

"Don't...talk like that."

"Why? Does it turn you on?"

"Yes!" she cried.

"Good."

Then, while still staring at her, he gently parted her legs and dropped his head between them. When his tongue hit its mark, her hips bolted upright and she clutched at him wildly.

"Hold on," he rasped, shifting positions and entering her with a hard thrust.

Minutes later, both breathing hard and exhausted, they lay wrapped in each other's arms.

"Dillon," she began, after she could find enough strength to speak.

"Let's sleep."

"No."

He semi-roused and met her gaze. "You aren't sleepy?"

"No."

"Wanna make love again, then?"

"I'm serious, Dillon."

"Oh, baby, so am I."

"Dillon, we have to talk."

He sighed. "If you say so."

She paused, suddenly unable—or maybe *unwilling* was the right word—to voice her torrid thoughts.

"Why can't you just let things happen?" Dillon asked, pulling her closer against him.

She felt his bristly chin graze her forehead before it rested gently on the top of her head.

"Why can't you just let *us* happen?" he went on, before she could speak.

"I'd say that's exactly what we've been doing."

"But that doesn't work for you, does it."

"It's not that simple."

"I know," he said, sighing again. "There's Robin."

"And other things."

"I'm listening."

"Do you think we're sick?" That question shocked even her. She hadn't meant to ask that, so where had it come from? But now that she'd asked it, it seemed right. In fact, she needed the answer—good, bad, or indifferent.

He pulled back, a scowl further darkening his features. "What kind of question is that?"

She gulped. "You know."

"The hell I do."

"Think about it."

"What?" He sounded impatient. No, he sounded put out.

"Us. You and me, making love."

"That's all I do think about."

"That's not what I meant, and you know it. You're being deliberately obtuse."

"And you're being deliberately paranoid."

"I think I have reason," she said in a small voice.

"It's those goddamn gossipy old women who are responsible for all this."

"Partly, I'll admit. You heard what they said."

"Yeah, I heard what they said." His tone was harsh.

"And it cut deep, too, didn't it?"

"Hell, yes. People talking about us was one of my worst nightmares. But as you can see, I lived through it and so did you."

"Still…"

"Ah, hell, honey, I say screw 'em. Who cares what they think? All I'm concerned about is you and Robin."

"She knows about the affair."

A gurgling sound came from his throat as he once again put some distance between them.

"She knows everything?" he asked.

"She overheard Keith and me talking."

"How'd she take it?"

"Bottom line? She thinks I ought to forgive Keith and take him back."

He spat an expletive.

"But that's not going to happen."

"What *is* going to happen? With us, I mean? You have to know that I'm not going to leave you alone unless you tell me to. Even then, I'm not sure I can do it."

"You have to."

He cursed again. "Leaving Robin out of the equation for now, give me one valid reason why."

"Dillon..."

"You know, we didn't use any protection this time, either."

Tell him! her mind screamed. Tell him you can't see him anymore—and why. But the words wouldn't come; her heart kept her silent.

"So you must've thought about the possibility of a child, of your having another one."

Suddenly Janey scrambled out of his arms and sat, trembling, on the side of the bed.

"God, Janey, is the thought that distasteful to you?"

She heard the pain in his voice and hated herself for putting it there. But nothing she could say or do would change things or make them any better.

"No," she finally said, turning and facing him. "It's just that I—"

A loud knock on the front door froze her mid-sentence.

"Shit!" This time Dillon scrambled upright, then off the bed, and slipped into his jeans. "I'll be right back."

Once he'd left the room, Janey's trembling increased. She covered herself with the blanket while tears clogged her throat and eyes.

"Janey."

At the sound of his voice, she swung around and

caught her breath. He looked like someone had knocked him upside the head.

"What's wrong?" she asked, thick-tongued.

"My mare just died."

He was in a funk that he couldn't seem to shake.

But then, what did he expect? He'd been dealt a big blow. The thought of losing Dandi had never entered his mind. He'd known the horse had been ailing, something he had thought he'd covered by having the doctor examine her.

"Damn, Dillon, I thought she was fine," the veterinarian, Bob Brenner, had told him after Mike had called him back.

"I thought she was, too, or I never would've left her," Dillon muttered in a choked voice.

"Well, I didn't leave her," Mike said, "and I couldn't stop it. So don't beat up on yourself."

But even now, several days after the fact, Dillon was still beating up on himself.

At least Janey had been there to comfort him, though when he'd returned to the house he'd half expected her to be gone. When he'd walked in, she'd been dressed and standing in the living room.

Without saying a word, she had opened her arms. He'd gone straight into them and sobbed like a baby.

"I'm so sorry," she whispered, clutching his shoulders tightly.

He hadn't responded verbally. There hadn't been anything to say. He'd just let her hold him until he'd gotten a grip on his emotions.

"Now you've seen me at my worst," he said, pulling back, feeling as if he'd been gutted.

"At least I know you're human."

''Was that ever in question?''

''No,'' she said thickly.

''Janey, don't go.''

She moved out of his arms. ''I have to.''

''Robin's not home.''

She hesitated for one second, but that was all he needed. He jerked her back into his arms and kissed her hard.

''Dillon, please, don't do this,'' she whispered, when he lifted his lips.

''I have to. I need you too much.''

She had grabbed his hand then and led him back into the bedroom.

But they hadn't made love. She'd merely held him until dawn. Then she'd gotten up and left. He hadn't seen her since, though that had only been three days ago. However, he'd walked her to the car and told her that he would see her Friday night after the game. She hadn't argued.

Now, as he thought about both Janey and his mare, he got to his feet. He'd been at school for over an hour and hadn't accomplished anything. He'd been too busy feeling sorry for himself.

What was done was done. Dandi was gone, and he would have to accept that. Still, it had sent his plans back to the Dark Ages. He'd counted heavily on Dandi to get the breeding operation started. And while he had the other mare, one alone wasn't enough. Besides, this new piece of horseflesh was nowhere near Dandi's caliber.

Dillon was a mess, financially and emotionally. Financially, he would recover. He would make sure of that. Emotionally was a different matter altogether. He'd done what he'd said he wouldn't do.

He'd fallen head over heels in love with Janey—
and didn't know how to tell her.

Unable to deal with that mind-boggling realization, he got up and walked out of his office and into
the hall during the change of periods. The first student he saw and recognized was Robin. She was
walking away from her locker.

"Good morning," he said, falling in step beside
her.

She stopped, looked around, then turned back to
him, her features pinched. "I wish you'd stay away
from my mom."

Thirty-Three

She owed him the truth.

The fact that she hadn't told him continued to weigh heavily on her mind. The other evening, when she'd gone to his ranch with every intention of doing just that, she had missed a golden opportunity.

But after what happened to his horse, no way could she have told him anything else that would upset him. Even though he had never mentioned the word *love* in any context, she knew he cared deeply about her.

Or was it only sex that continued to motivate him?

No, she was convinced not. He could have sex with lots of women, Patricia heading the list. Yet he couldn't seem to stay away from Janey, regardless of the baggage she carried.

Keith was the largest piece of that baggage, a piece she could never drop. At various points in her life, he would pop in and out. The best she could hope for was eventual peace and harmony between them.

She had already made great strides toward that, she realized now, as she drove home from the football game. And Dillon was the reason. Since he had come into her life, she'd mellowed, which actually surprised her. That she could admit it surprised her more.

But she enjoyed his company, not to mention his bed. Just thinking about the latter made her go limp. When he touched her, she seemed to lose all her inhibitions, continuing to let him explore her body at will, to make love to her in ways she'd never imagined. And vice versa. She had done things to him that she'd only conjured up in the secret parts of her mind.

Shameful remorse? Was that the emotion she should be feeling, especially in light of her wanton behavior at the farm? Were those ladies who had ridiculed and condemned her relationship with Dillon right in doing so, contrary to what Dillon said?

And what about Robin?

Janey would die if that kind of gossip reached her daughter's ears. And the shop, she couldn't forget about that. With the chain coming to town, she couldn't afford to alienate anyone. She needed all the business she could get, and then some.

But Robin and business aside, how did *she* feel about the situation in the deepest recesses of her heart? Janey released a deep sigh. Apparently she wasn't ready to let him go, or she would have found a way to tell him the truth. Where there was a will, there was a way.

So what about her will tonight? Was it strong enough? He was going to meet her shortly at the house, offering another opportunity. Could she spill the truth and watch him walk out of her life for good?

Although that thought made her sick for reasons she refused to delve into, she knew she had no choice. For his sake. He deserved a woman who

could give him children. He was so good with them
and wanted them so badly.

She couldn't help but notice that evening at the
football game how he laughed and talked with various kids, regardless of their race or station in life. It
was obvious by the look on each student's face that
they adored him and held him in awe. Yet he ruled
them and the school with a Marine fist, and they
knew they could only push him so far.

Before Janey had become involved with Dillon,
Robin, too, had adored him.

Another sigh forced its way through Janey's lips,
just as she turned the corner onto her street. Later,
she didn't know why she hadn't noticed the car
parked against the curb, but she hadn't. Apparently
she'd been so preoccupied with her own problems
that the world around her hadn't existed.

Until she saw her ex-husband leaning against the
side door.

Fury whipped through her. What was he doing
here? If it was to give her money, then she would
forgive him. If not...

Still, he had no business just showing up unannounced, as though he would be welcome. He was
good at that. He'd always been too arrogant for his
own good.

Controlling her anger as best she could, Janey got
out of the car and walked onto the porch. He straightened. That was when she smelled the liquor. It
seemed to ooze out of his pores.

Her stomach revolted, and she kept her distance.

"What are you doing here?" she demanded.

He smirked. "Hello to you, too."

"Keith, I'm not in the mood."

"Honey, when were you ever in the mood?"

"What do you want?" she asked through clenched teeth.

He cocked his head. "What if I said I had money?"

"Do you?"

"No."

"Dammit, what kind of game do you think you're playing?"

"Don't you think our daughter looked super tonight?"

She gave him an incredulous look. "You really don't expect me to believe you came here to talk about Robin."

"Look, could we go inside?"

"I don't think that's a good idea."

"Well, I do. I want to talk about Robin and Chad."

Janey steeled herself against the fear that charged through her. "What is it?" she barely managed to ask.

"Let me in and I'll tell you."

Shaking, Janey did as he asked, though she refused to go upstairs. Instead, she opened the door to the shop and switched on the back lights. Keith followed her inside.

Whirling, she faced him, fear keeping its stranglehold on her. "Now, what about Robin and Chad?"

"She wanted me to talk to you."

"Oh, dear God," Janey choked, white-faced. "She hadn't mentioned him lately, and I thought—"

"That she didn't care about him? Get real."

"No, you get real!" Janey lashed back. "And try

to act like a responsible parent and not take her side on this.''

"If that's what she wants, then I'm all for it."

"Even after he hit her?" She felt disdain, and her gaze roamed over him. "How could you?"

Keith shrugged. "He won't do it again."

"If he doesn't, it won't be because of anything you did."

"How do you know?"

"Well, did you talk to Chad?"

"No, I didn't."

She almost choked on her disgust. "Well, Dillon did. And that's the only reason Chad will keep his hands to himself."

Keith's features twisted. "Robin told me you two were an item."

"That subject's off-limits."

"Oh, I just bet it is," he countered in a nasty tone. "How can you criticize *me?*"

"What?" she shrieked. "You were both married."

"Is fucking him your way of getting back at me?"

Her eyes flared. "How dare you," she seethed.

One giant stride closed the distance between them, and he loomed over her. She jerked back, his foul breath almost knocking her down. "Get away from me!"

He grabbed her arm and yanked her hard against his chest. "You stay the hell away from him. You hear me? You belong to me!"

"Get your hands off her."

Had Dillon crashed through a glass door like gangbusters, it would not have been more explosive than the cold, hard sound of his voice.

Janey froze. Keith cursed. Then both swung around and faced Dillon.

"Do it!" he commanded again.

Janey felt Keith's fingers relax. That was when she wrenched her arm out of his grasp and stepped out of the way. But Keith was no longer paying attention to her. His entire focus was on Dillon.

The intense hate that filled the silence was almost tangible.

"Go fuck yourself, Reed, and leave my wife alone."

"I suggest you walk out of here while you still can," Dillon said in that same calm, cold tone. "Because if you open your foul mouth one more time, I'm going to put my fist in it."

Keith took a step toward Dillon. "Go f—"

Janey didn't see it coming, though she shouldn't have been surprised. Lightning fast, Dillon's fist shot out and collided with Keith's mouth, knocking him flat on his back.

Janey gasped, her eyes wide with horror.

After shaking his head as if to clear it, Keith was slow in getting up. "Why you...you bastard!" he spat past the blood dripping from his upper lip.

"If I were you, I wouldn't say another word." Dillon's voice rang out, as lethal as a pistol's bullet.

"Do what he says," Janey said to Keith in a strained whisper.

Keith crossed to the door, all the while swiping at his lip with a handkerchief. Once there, he pivoted. "I'll be back, Janey. Count on it."

After he slammed the door behind him, Janey sank wearily against the counter, shaking so hard she feared her bones might shatter. God, what if Robin had walked in on that episode? Just the thought almost short-circuited what little mind she had left.

"Janey, I'm—"

She held up her hand. "Don't say anything, Dillon."

"What does that mean?"

"I want you to leave, as well."

She hadn't meant to say that, or at least, she hadn't planned on it. However, once the words were out of her mouth, she realized she meant them.

He jammed his hands in the pockets of his slacks and leaned his head to one side, his mouth thin. "Do you mind telling me why?"

"For starters, that macho stunt you just pulled."

"Excuse me?"

She heard that deadly note in his tone, but she didn't care. So she'd made him mad by seeming ungrateful for his help. That was his problem, not hers.

"I could've handled Keith."

"Really."

She ignored his sarcasm. "Yes, really."

"That's not the way it appeared from where I stood."

Janey jutted her chin. "I don't approve of your caveman tactics."

"Even when that son of a bitch was out of control?"

"I told you, I could've handled the situation," she declared staunchly.

"How about telling me what this is really all about."

"What if Robin had walked in?"

"She didn't, so that's moot."

"Look—"

"Do you want him back? Is that why you objected to my defending you?"

"No!" she cried, mortified. "You know better than that."

"The hell I do."

"It's as simple as I said it was. I don't like violence."

"Sometimes it's necessary, and in this case I thought it was."

"You were wrong."

"I'm not going to apologize."

She stiffened. "That's your call."

"Yeah, right."

For the second time in one evening, the door was almost knocked off its hinges. She didn't know how long she stood there before she heard it open again.

"Mom?"

Thirty-Four

The two uniformed officers, Riley and Temple, stood on the other side of Dillon's desk. Dillon was staring back at them, his face livid.

"At least we have a clue this time," Riley said, readjusting his pistol holster around his girth.

"Finding that baseball cap is the break we've been waiting for," Temple put in. "Plus, we're going to beef up the patrol around the grounds."

"I'm getting damn tired of my school being held hostage by some little creeps," Dillon spat.

The school had been broken into again during the night. This time it was the home economics lab, where the destruction was widespread.

Dillon had had it. He wanted the culprits caught. His patience had run out.

"What about those two boys you've had your eye on?" Temple asked. "The ones you suspect of being gang members?"

"My gut still says they're definitely spearheading all this vandalism, but I have no concrete proof."

"Been behaving like model students, huh?" Riley commented with sarcasm.

Dillon stood. "Pretty much near it, but then, my assistant and I watch them closer than a dog watches a june bug."

"Well, tell the teachers to be on the alert for any-thing suspicious, anything out of the ordinary that anyone says or does."

"I've already taken care of that. The faculty and staff have been briefed."

"We're gone for now," Temple said. "We'll let you know as soon as we've checked out the cap."

Dillon walked them to the door. "That's got to be the smoking gun that puts an end to all this non-sense."

"Let's hope," Riley said, following his partner out the door.

Dillon turned and went back to his desk, though he didn't sit. He was too agitated. He wished he were at the farm, on Dandi.

But Dandi was gone. He grimaced, thinking how much he missed his horse. But life had to go on—though at the moment not according to his plan.

There had been too many bumps in the road to suit him. He was damn tired of clinging to the steer-ing wheel so he wouldn't run off the road.

So far, he hadn't done that well, either. He seemed to spend most of his time in the ditch.

At the moment, the school break-ins weren't his only pressing problem. He hated being on the outs with Janey. Perhaps she'd been right that physical violence the other night wasn't the answer, that he should have kept his hands to himself and his mouth shut.

But dammit, she hadn't been in control, despite what she'd said. Keith was a bully, especially when he was under the influence.

Dillon hadn't been so much concerned that Keith would strike her, but rather that he would kiss her.

The thought of either had made his blood boil, and he'd acted on pure adrenaline, gratifying his own needs. Selfish stunt? Probably. An antic he should have been above. Still, he didn't regret clobbering the bastard. Keith had deserved that and more. In fact, for all these years Dillon had secretly ached to bring bodily harm to the man who had slept with his wife.

He'd finally gotten that chance. But for some inexplicable reason, the victory had been a hollow one. Getting even with Keith was no longer important to him. He no longer cared, except where it concerned Janey.

After seeing Keith, he realized that he was truly free from the chains of the past, that if Keith hadn't been giving Janey a hard time, Dillon could easily have ignored him.

That was why he had to see her and make things right between them. Hell, if they were going to be at odds, let it be over something important, not a scumbag like her ex-husband. Keith wasn't worth it.

Still, Dillon didn't know quite how to handle the volatile situation. He knew Janey cared about him. He also knew she enjoyed the incredibly hot sex that seemed to be the focus of their relationship. As far as anything beyond that went, he had his doubts.

He winced against that thought. He wanted there to be more between them, something much more than sex. What? Love? Marriage? Home? Family?

Yes, to all, he realized, feeling a tightness in his chest. He wanted to love her forever, and he wanted everything else that went along with that deep and abiding love, including the responsibility of Robin.

He almost choked on that silent admission, especially after his encounter with Robin in the hall. It was a given that he wasn't high on her list.

Before he could begin to deal with Robin and her jealousy, though, he had to patch things up with Janey. By day's end, he would have a plan. Meanwhile, he had work to do.

Dillon buzzed his secretary. "Mildred, I need a few moments of your time. Bring the board meeting agenda with you, please."

Jancy scrutinized her daughter, whom she thought appeared a little more peaked than usual. Was Robin coming down with the flu that was going around town? No. Janey answered her own question without hesitation. She very much feared that it was Chad who had put that look on her daughter's face.

And while she abhorred mentioning him, she didn't have any choice. She had hoped that Keith wasn't telling the truth, that he'd simply been trying to rile her when he'd told her that Robin and Chad were back together. But even for Keith, that would have been a big stretch of the truth, one that could have come back to haunt him. So Janey doubted he would take his lying that far.

Regardless, she had to know. Keeping tabs on her daughter was a must, whether it was pleasant or not.

"Are you still seeing Chad?" she asked pointedly but in a guarded tone.

Robin threw her a petulant look. "Do you want the truth, Mom?"

Janey was taken aback. "You know better than to even ask that. Of course I want the truth. We've always been honest with each other, haven't we?"

"Yes," Robin declared tightly.

"So?"

"So...sort of."

Janey wanted to die right there on the spot. But she couldn't. She had to hold herself together. She had to be strong. At the moment, she was the only stable influence in her daughter's life.

After that encounter with Keith, she knew that he would never be able to offer Robin anything except surface love. With the bottle as his companion, he was capable of little else.

"What does 'sort of' mean?"

"We're just talking."

"I thought by now you would've seen his true colors." Janey kept her voice light.

Robin toyed with her hair, then returned Janey's scrutinizing stare. "I haven't gone out with him."

"You know, I'm cutting you much more slack than I ever thought I could. My good sense tells me I shouldn't let you out of the house until you reach menopause."

"Mom!"

"I mean that."

"I guess Mr. Reed tattled."

"Actually, it was your dad. He saw you with Chad."

"That's okay, then."

"Why would you think Dillon had told me?"

"He watches me like a hawk, that's why."

"Maybe it's for your own good," Janey said mildly, becoming more troubled by the minute.

"I doubt that," Robin said tersely.

Robin had turned and was fiddling with her backpack. "Look at me," Janey said.

Robin sighed, then swung around.

"What did that last statement mean?"

"I don't want to talk about it," Robin said. "I don't want to talk about him."

The way she said "him" sent dread through Janey. However, she didn't show it. She kept her emotions under wraps. "But *I* do," she stressed.

"Oh, Mom," Robin wailed, "I have to go."

"Not until you answer me."

"Will you write me a note if I'm late?"

Janey didn't bother to respond to that. "Robin, I'm losing my patience—and fast, too."

"Oh, what the heck," she retorted. "He'll probably tell you, anyway. He came up to me in the hall and I—" Robin's voice faltered.

"And you what?"

"I told him to leave you alone." Her head was tossed back in defiance, but her lower lip was quivering, as if she might burst into tears at any minute.

Oh, dear Lord, Janey thought, humiliated. What on earth had he thought? She could imagine. Feeling as if something heavy was sitting on her heart and crushing the life out of it, she blew out a breath.

She didn't dare berate Robin, however; the balance was simply too delicate. Yet she had so hoped... Never mind what *she* had hoped. It was Robin whose needs were the most important, not hers. She had to stop losing sight of that.

"Oh, honey, it's okay." Janey crossed to her daughter and pulled her close. "I thought you liked Dillon," she said, stepping back and forcing a smile. "That you thought he was cool."

"He's okay, but I don't want him taking Dad's place. I'm not giving up on us being a family again."

Janey released a deep sigh and her daughter at the

same time. "We'll talk about all this later. Right now, you skedaddle." She kissed Robin on the cheek. "I love you."

"Me too," Robin muttered, scurrying out the door.

Janey immediately sagged against the wall, feeling as if all the air had been let out of her body. But she didn't have time to ruminate over her personal problems. For the moment, she would have to bury her heartache. She had to get ready and open up the store.

Every day, every dollar, counted.

"Come back soon, Mrs. Thornton."

The middle-aged woman gave Janey a warm smile. "You know I will. After all, you're the only one who stocks my kind of candy."

But maybe not for long, Janey thought with a sinking feeling.

As if Eva had read that thought, she leaned over and gave Janey a hug. "Don't you worry about that old chain store opening in the mall. The customers that were loyal to Lois will stay loyal to you."

Janey smiled. "You have no idea how much I needed to hear that. It's like music to my ears."

"Well, believe it. You'll see. Now, I've gotta run."

Once Eva was out the door, Janey went back to the counter, then stared at the clock. Ten minutes until closing time. She totaled up for the day and found that she'd made much more than she'd anticipated. The past few days, business had shown a marked improvement.

If only that other store weren't opening, she could

really get excited. But the soon-to-be competition loomed large, and she couldn't ignore it.

Sighing, she got up, locked the door and turned the sign around. That was when she saw Dillon's vehicle whip into the parking lot.

While her pulse leapt, she also felt trepidation. She hadn't seen him since he'd knocked Keith down, and they'd parted on less than amicable terms.

Even though she realized she'd overreacted and hadn't given him a fair shake, she hadn't contacted him. She had told herself it was better this way, that they had no future, so if he never sought her out again, that would be all right.

Now she knew how much she'd deceived herself. She ached to run to him and throw herself in his arms, which was ridiculous. But he looked so big, so strong, so capable that she couldn't imagine him no longer being in her life.

However, she'd best get used to it. The fact that she'd continued to withhold the truth from him all but doomed their relationship.

The sooner she accepted the inevitable, the sooner her heart could start to mend.

How many more times could that important organ be broken before it became irreparable?

The buzzer claimed her attention.

"Are you still mad at me?" he asked without pre-amble, striding through the door, that engaging, sheepish grin on his face.

The scent of him was so powerful that she had to fight off the urge to fling herself at him. "I should be."

"Ah, so I'm out of the doghouse?"

"I didn't say that."

His features sobered. "You don't have any idea how badly I want to kiss you, do you?"

Her senses clamored. "Dillon..."

Suddenly the phone rang, shattering the spell that had fallen over the room. Reaching for the receiver, she heard Dillon curse under his breath.

"Hello," she said.

A few seconds later, her eyes widened in horror. "Don't move, Emma. I'll be right there."

"What's wrong?" Dillon demanded, when she replaced the receiver.

"My eighty-five-year-old friend fell, and she's alone."

Dillon reached for the phone again. "I'll call 911, then I'll take you over there."

Thirty-Five

"**D**oes your mom know?"

Robin gave her friend Beverly a fleeting look before turning and watching another carload of kids pull into the spot next to them. Following drill team practice, they had stopped for fruit slushies at one of the local drive-in restaurants.

"I'm not going to let you off the hook, so you might as well 'fess up."

Robin settled her eyes back on Beverly, then shrugged. "Yeah, she knows."

"Is she pissed?"

"Highly," Robin said, down in the mouth. "But she hasn't grounded me."

"Boy, you're lucky."

"She hasn't ragged me about it, either."

Beverly looked shocked. "Damn, you're more than lucky. Why, my mom would be nipping my butt every step I took."

"My mom trusts me to do what's right."

Beverly sucked from her straw, then said, "My mom doesn't. She thinks I'm dim-witted."

Robin shot her friend a look. "She does not."

"Well, she still wouldn't react like your mom. So what's going on between you and Chad?"

Robin turned pensive. "I'm not seeing him outside of school."

"So your mom *can* trust you."

"What if he hit me again?" Robin shivered. "That thought gives me the willies."

"Hit the SOB back." Beverly grinned, suddenly lightening the mood.

"Sometimes I'd like to, believe me," Robin admitted with a sarcastic smile.

"Are you still in love with him?"

"Right now, I'm confused about Chad and everything else."

"Life sucks, I know."

"Chad still wants me to take the promise ring."

"But only if you put out." Beverly's reply was a flat statement.

"You got it."

Beverly took a sip of her drink. "So how do you feel about that?"

"Like I said, mixed up. And afraid of my mom."

"She wouldn't have to know."

"Oh, but she would, even if I didn't tell her."

"That's what you get for being so close to her, for confiding in her. I wouldn't dare tell mine half the stuff you do."

"What can I say, except my mom's always been pretty cool."

"Yeah, she is that. I'm envious, actually."

Robin drank some of her slushie, then sighed. "Don't be. At least your mom and dad are still together."

"Why is that so friggin' important to you?"

Robin gave her an incredulous look. "How would

you like it if your parents split? Put that shoe on and wear it for a while and see how it feels."

"You're right. I'd hate it."

"So do I," Robin muttered.

"You think it'll ever happen? Them remarrying, I mean?"

"It's doubtful, especially since my mom's—" Robin broke off abruptly when she realized what she was about to divulge. Jeez, she didn't want anyone to know her mom was dating her principal. In fact, she was mortified at the thought, afraid of all the heckling she would get as a result.

It had boggled her mind to learn her dad had had an affair with Elaine, Dillon's wife. And now her mom and Dillon were an item. She knew her friends would think that was perverted. That was why she'd told Dillon to leave her mom alone.

But how did she feel deep down?

"I'm waiting."

Robin shook her head, having almost forgotten that she wasn't alone. "Uh, for what?"

"You to finish your sentence."

"It was nothing."

"Oh, come on," Beverly countered. "I know better."

"You promise you won't breathe a word to anyone else, especially your mom?"

"I promise."

Robin confided in her then. When she had finished, Beverly's eyes were as round as saucers.

"Awesome!"

"You think so?" Robin asked, taken aback.

"He's awesome. He could eat crackers in my bed any day."

Robin felt her face color. "So you think he and my mom might be getting it on?"

"Is the sky blue?"

"The last time I checked," Robin said drolly.

"My point."

"Somehow, I can't imagine her in bed with anyone but my dad," said Robin.

"So what happens if they actually got together for real and forever?" Beverly asked. "Could you handle that?"

"I don't know. That thought is something I don't want to deal with."

"It *is* weird, I have to admit."

You don't know the half of it, girlfriend. Robin wanted to tell Beverly the rest of the story, about her dad and Elaine, only she didn't have the stomach for that. The only way she could discuss that was if Beverly heard about it through gossip. She shuddered inwardly at the thought.

"But still, it's plenty cool," Beverly threw into the silence.

"Chad doesn't even know," Robin said, more to herself than to her friend.

"Speaking of Chad again, what are you going to do about him? Are you going to accept his ring?"

"I'm not sure. I told you, I don't know. I'm too screwed up in the head."

Beverly giggled. "Speaking of screwed, aren't you the least bit curious as to what it would be like to screw him? God, he's a stud. Can you imagine how big *it* would be?"

"Beverly!"

Beverly snorted. "Don't act so prissy. You know you've considered doing it with him."

"Well..."

"Hey, you're blushing," Beverly pointed out laughing. "I can't believe that."

"Go jump in the lake."

Beverly laughed outright. "Like I said, life sucks."

"On that note," Robin said, "we'd best get our rears home. Mom'll be wondering where I am. I'm supposed to have dinner with my dad."

Beverly cranked her engine, then waited for the carhop to come get the tray. Once that was gone, she still didn't move. Instead, she gave Robin an intense look. "You ought to give your mom and Mr. Reed a break, you know."

"That's easy for you to say."

"Right, but I know you want your mom to be happy."

"Of course I do," Robin said impatiently.

"Well, maybe she doesn't want to go back to your dad. Duh? Have you ever thought about that?"

"Yes," Robin snapped.

"Then give her a break, okay? Look how much slack she's cut you on Chad."

Robin threw her a sulky glance. "All right already. I'll give it some thought. Are you satisfied?"

Beverly backed the car out. "For the moment."

"Thanks for listening."

"When I fall in lust, which I hope is soon," Beverly responded, "you'll get to return the favor."

Robin laughed, and it felt good.

Dillon stared at the phone. He wanted to pick it up and call Janey for more reasons than one, he thought, his eyes straying to the letter on the table by his bed. However, it was too early. Since it was Saturday, he figured Robin might be sleeping in, and he didn't want to disturb her.

Aside from sharing the contents of the letter, he wanted to tell Janey he'd definitely found a way to help the old lady. Poor Emma. Like Janey, he'd fallen in love with Emma.

On the way to her house, Janey had told him about Emma's plight, which had jerked heavily on his heartstrings. Then, when he'd seen where and how she lived, he had understood even more why Janey was so concerned.

The dwelling had been spotless, but poverty was evident. Also evident was the fact that Emma shouldn't have been left alone.

Dillon and Janey had beaten the ambulance there, which had been both good and bad.

"Oh, my God, Dillon, what should we do?" Janey had demanded in a panic-stricken voice upon reaching Emma and squatting beside her.

"Nothing, honey. It's not safe to move her, even her head. Something may be broken."

"I knew this was going to happen," Janey wailed, tears flooding her eyes. "But she's so darn stubborn, she wouldn't listen or let anyone help her."

"She doesn't have anyone who cares?" Dillon asked.

"No. Oh, she has a niece somewhere, but the woman doesn't give a hoot because Emma doesn't have anything to give her in return."

Dillon muttered an expletive.

"I've talked to Aunt Lois, who loves Emma as much as I do, about helping her financially, only neither of us is really able."

"Would she have taken it?" Dillon asked gently.

"I wouldn't have given her a choice. At first I thought she could sell her house and go into an assisted living facility. Now I know that's not possible." Janey looked around. "She couldn't get enough for this shack to pay six months' upkeep."

"Well, let me see what I can do. I have a buddy who owns one of the local nursing homes. Maybe that's the answer."

"Are you sure you want to get involved? I mean—"

"Hey, if you're involved," he said with gentle seriousness, "I want to be involved."

A tear spilled onto Janey's cheek as their eyes met for what felt like a long time. "I don't know what to say," she finally whispered.

"You don't have to say anything."

Moments later the paramedics had arrived, and Emma had been transported to the hospital, where she'd remained for several days now. She had suffered a stroke, which so far had left her paralyzed on the right side. But the doctor had said that might only be temporary. Dillon sure as hell hoped so, because Janey was awfully torn up about her friend. And he couldn't stand to see Janey upset about anything.

But at least something good had come from the tragedy. While they were waiting in the ER for the doctor to examine Emma, Dillon had gotten a chance to apologize, which was the reason he'd gone to see Janey in the first place.

"You were right," he said. "I acted like an ass."

"Actually, I'm glad you decked him."

"You are?" he asked, slack-jawed.

"I'm surprised I said that, too, actually. At first I

wasn't happy. But now that I've had time to think about it, Keith was definitely out of line and out of control.''

''Yeah, but I still should've used more restraint.''

''Probably.'' Janey's mouth flirted with a smile. ''But he had it coming. I just wish I could've been the one who knocked him on his rear.''

Dillon's lips twitched. ''Me too. That would've been true justice.''

''It must have made you feel better.''

''It did, but only for the moment. After you got so angry, things suddenly seemed to fall into place. I realized getting back at Keith was no longer important, that I didn't give a shit anymore.''

Their eyes met again, and he felt himself grow hard as a piece of iron. He hoped her eyes wouldn't dip any lower, or she would see his reaction.

Then the doctor walked in and saved his kazoo.

''Emma's going to pull through,'' he told them.

Now, as he dressed in jeans and a sweatshirt and thought back on that conversation, Dillon felt energized. He knew Janey cared for him—even loved him, he hoped, if he hadn't misinterpreted that look in her eye. And he didn't think he had, though he hadn't had time alone with her. She'd insisted on spending the night with Emma, after making plans for Robin to stay with a friend.

Dillon stared at the phone again, then decided once more not to bother her. However, he *would* bother his sister. Allie would know how to handle the letter.

Grabbing it and a cup of coffee, he headed out the door, whistling all the way to his vehicle, clinging to the letter and the thought that Janey just might love him.

He stopped abruptly, a cold feeling washing through him. What if she didn't? What if he was fooling himself?

He wasn't. Relief replaced the ice in his veins. He even felt confident he could win Robin over, and convince Janey to marry him.

A piece of cake.

Thirty-Six

"How's my pregnant sister?"

Allie made a face and rubbed her extended tummy. "Sicker than anyone ought to be, that's for sure."

Dillon chuckled; then, when Allie glared at him, he sobered, though a twinkle remained in his eye.

"I ought to clobber you," Allie wailed. "Being with child sucks."

Dillon's right eyebrow kicked up. "You don't mean that."

"I do after I've just gotten through puking up my toenails."

"Aw, sis," Dillon said in a sympathetic tone, crossing to her and giving her a great big hug.

Allie gestured toward a kitchen chair. "Have a seat. I'll get us some coffee and hot bread."

"No, you have a seat, and I'll get the goods."

"Fine with me," Allie said, sitting down, her breathing slightly labored. "You know where everything is."

Dillon was glad he'd come to see Allie. It was the weekend, and he looked forward to attending to the mega chores around the farm that needed his attention.

Mike was already hard at work. As soon as Dillon

finished here, he planned on joining his brother-in-law.

Lately though, his neglect of Allie seemed to play on his mind more than usual. That was why he'd decided to stop by the house first. He missed his sister and vowed to make more of an effort to spend quality time with her.

After the baby came, he wouldn't have any choice. He knew Allie would expect him to be a "hands on" uncle. And he wanted to, even though it still smarted that he didn't have any children of his own.

But he had high hopes that would soon change. If things worked out the way he hoped, then he and Janey...

"You're awfully quiet all of a sudden, brother dear."

"I'm busy doing a woman's work," he flung back over his shoulder, grinning.

"You oughta be used to that by now," Allie responded, answering his grin.

Shortly he was back at the table with cups and hot bread in hand. "Reckon you'll still make bread after the baby comes?" he asked.

Allie gave him a put-out look, though her lips twitched. "Why wouldn't I? I'm having a baby, not a mental breakdown."

"True, but—"

She laughed, reached out and patted his hand. "It's going to be okay. My...our life's not going to change that much."

"Wanna bet?"

Allie grinned. "You're probably right. I'm living in a dream world."

"You'll love every minute of being a mother. You'll be perfect."

"So what about you?" Allie asked, changing the subject.

"What about me?" Dillon's tone was innocent.

"Stop it. You're a man on a mission. Don't ask me how I know. I just do."

"You're right."

"It has to do with one of two things—the farm or Janey."

Finding that he couldn't quite discuss Janey yet, Dillon chose the former. "Well, Mike has his eye on a couple of other mares that might be for sale at a reasonable price. In fact, we're going to take a look at them this afternoon."

"Losing Dandi really cut deep, didn't it."

"In more ways than one. She was my prize breeder, and without her, becoming competitive in this business is going to be tough."

"You'll do it. You've always done what your heart's into. And it's definitely into this farm."

"The other mare I recently purchased isn't half bad, so we'll see."

"Now, about Janey? How are things going there?"

"So so."

Allie toyed with her piece of bread. "You can do better than that."

Dillon didn't answer right off. Instead, he took a bite of his bread and washed it down with a swig of coffee. Then he averted his gaze, his features pensive.

"Hey, brother, I'm not going anywhere. I've got all day if you do."

He faced her again, reaching in his back pocket and pulling out an envelope. He handed it to her.

"What's this?"

"Read it. It's self-explanatory."

He watched with arms folded across his chest, trying to gauge her reaction. When she finished, Allie gave him a jubilant smile. "A superintendent's job. Wow, this is great!"

"I thought so, too, at first. Now, though, I have mixed emotions."

"Why? Are you crazy? This is what you've wanted for a long time. It's a much bigger school, and they've *asked* you to apply, not the other way around. I see all pluses and no minuses."

Allie was right. He'd received an unexpected and golden opportunity to climb the ladder in his profession. He would be making more money, which would go a long way in solving his problem with the farm.

"How can you even hesitate?" Allie asked, breaking into his thoughts.

"Did you notice where the position is?" His question was pointed.

"So it's a hundred miles away."

"That's a lot when you have everything you want here."

Allie cocked her head. "We're talking about more than the farm, right?"

"Right."

"Ah, Janey. That's why you're not jumping for joy."

"I love her, Allie."

"How does she feel about you?"

"I don't know."

"Oh dear."

"Don't say it like that." Dillon got up and walked to the window, suddenly feeling like a caged tiger with coiled insides.

"I didn't mean it the way it sounded. But surely you have some idea."

"I know she cares, but she's gun-shy, like me."

"That's no reason not to go for the gold, if you know what I mean."

"I know what you mean, and I'm willing. Lord knows how much I want a family, how much I've always wanted one."

"Have you told Janey that?"

"Not directly, but I've hinted like hell." He paused, slouching against the counter. "There's Robin to consider. She's the biggie."

"How does she feel about you?"

He grimaced. "Not good." He told Allie what Robin had said to him in the hallway.

"Oh dear," she said again.

"It's no secret she wants her parents back together."

"She sees you as a threat," Allie declared.

"Oh yeah."

"Do you think it'll happen?"

"Nope, but even the thought cuts to the quick. And it's what the kid thinks that counts."

"Janey and Robin are pretty tight, I would imagine."

"For sure. And there's the candy shop. We can't forget about that."

"That's Janey's livelihood." Allie's tone was pensive. "She's not going to want to leave it, though she's about to have some stiff competition."

Dillon's eyes widened, questioningly.

"You didn't know?"

"Know what?"

"There's a chain store coming to the mall."

"Damn!"

"I'm surprised she hasn't said anything to you about it."

"I guess that tidbit got lost in the shuffle."

"Guess so."

"Still, if Janey loves me, it can work," Dillon insisted, his tone borderline belligerent.

"I agree with you there. So what are you going to do?"

Dillon rubbed his jaw. "Go saddle a horse and ride until I can unjumble my thoughts. Then we'll see."

Allie gave him the thumbs-up sign. "I'll be holding a good thought."

"Thanks, sis," he said despite his suddenly tight throat.

Janey was at loose ends.

It was Saturday evening, and Robin was spending the night with Beverly. They were going to a play with Beverly's parents. At least tonight she didn't have to worry about Robin and whose company her daughter was keeping.

Janey had tried calling Gwen to see if she wanted to have dinner and go to a movie, but her friend hadn't been home, either. What she'd really wanted to do was call Dillon. She had considered it earlier in the day, on the pretense of asking if he'd talked to his friend about Emma.

However, she'd had a busy day, both at the shop and away from it. The drill team had had a bake sale, and she and Robin had worked their two-hour slot. Back at the store, it had taken both her and Hazel to handle the spurt of late-afternoon customers, which had lifted her spirits considerably. But then she would think about the soon-to-be competition and turn green.

Still, she wasn't about to let it get her down. Compared to the traumas she'd already survived, this was nothing. She would survive it, too.

What she might *not* survive was her affair with Dillon.

No matter. She ached to see him, make love to him. When was this addiction going to end? she wondered. Maybe never. That thought panicked her. If they had no future, which they didn't, then what was the point?

The sudden sound of someone knocking on the side door stole her attention. Frowning, Janey made her way downstairs. If it was Keith and he'd been drinking, she would call the law. She refused to take any more nonsense from him.

"Who's there?"

"Dillon."

Her stomach bottomed out as she opened the door.

"I was hoping you'd be home," he said huskily.

"I was hoping you'd come." Her voice was husky, as well.

He grabbed her and gave her a long, hot kiss. Weak-kneed, she clung to him for a few seconds.

Thrusting her out to arm's length, he asked, "Can we go upstairs?"

"Uh, sure."

Once they were in her living quarters, they faced

each other, their eyes saying what their voices did not.

"First, I wanted to let you know I was able to help Emma."

"Oh, Dillon, that's great news."

"There's a lot of government mumbo jumbo involved, but if she's willing, she'll have a nice place to live where she won't be alone."

"If I can just convince her of that."

"I don't think she really has a choice."

"You're right." Janey kissed him again. "Now, what's the second thing you have on your mind?"

"I've been offered a superintendent's job," he said bluntly.

Her heart faltered. "Here?"

"No, in Rivercrest, which is a little over a hundred miles away."

"I know," she said, trying to keep her scattered emotions from showing.

"It's a great opportunity."

"So are you going to take it?" she asked, running her tongue over her bottom lip.

His gaze heated up. "Depends."

"On what?"

"You."

"Me?" she whispered.

"I love you, Janey."

That raw and unexpected confession made her dizzy. "And...I love you."

The heat in his eyes turned into a blazing fire. "Then marry me and go with me."

"Oh, Dillon, if only it were that simple."

"Why isn't it?"

"I think you know the answer to that."

"Robin," he said in a shaky tone.

"She's at the top of the list, certainly. And there's the shop—" Janey's jaw snapped shut. She suddenly felt unable to cope with the warring factions inside her. Her mouth was dry; her head ached.

"Look, I know Robin has a problem with us, but in time surely she'd come around. Besides, this job wouldn't begin until next year, which means she would've graduated."

"It's not all Robin."

"You could open another candy store there if you wanted to work."

She heard the desperate undertone in his voice, but her own insecurities overrode them. "There's something about me you don't know."

"I don't care. All I know is that I love you and don't want to live another day without you."

"Dillon, it's—"

"Just say yes," he responded, closing the distance between them.

She held up her hand. "No, don't touch me."

He pulled up short, his eyes darkening. "Has Robin won?"

"What are you talking about?"

"Are you and Keith…?"

"God, no."

"Then if you love me, why can't you make a commitment to me?"

"I just can't make a decision of this magnitude right now, especially not in a knee-jerk fashion."

He frowned. "So what are you saying?"

"Just that it's too much, too soon."

"You knew this was coming, Janey."

"Maybe so. Still, I'm not ready. I can't be

pushed.'' She stared at him with pleading eyes. ''I *won't* be pushed.''

''And that's what you think I'm doing?''

''Yes. I need time and space.''

''Then I guess that sums it up.'' His tone was harsh.

Janey blinked. ''Meaning?''

A silence filled the room for several heartbeats.

''You've apparently made your decision. I won't bother you anymore. That way, you'll have all the time and space you need.''

Before she could speak past the huge lump in her throat, Dillon was bounding down the stairs.

Thirty-Seven

"**M**om, I'm talking to you!"

Janey gave a start. "Sorry, darling, I was thinking."

"That's all you've been doing lately. You've been so preoccupied."

"I know."

Robin picked up her purse and backpack. "You're worried about money, aren't you."

"Money and other things," Janey admitted, mustering a light tone while shoving a strand of hair behind her ear.

Robin frowned as she slung her pack onto her shoulders. "It's me and Chad, isn't it."

"Partly."

"You worry too much."

"Do I?"

"Yes." Robin's tone was tight.

Janey swallowed a sigh, determined not to pursue the subject. She simply wasn't up to another verbal sparring match with her daughter first thing this morning.

As it was, she had barely been able to get out of bed and function, her heart and her body were so weighed down with pain and despair.

She'd done her best to hide her morbid feelings

from her daughter, but apparently she hadn't been all that successful. Some things were easier to hide than others.

Losing Dillon had been such a shock to her system that she doubted she would ever recover. She'd just *thought* she'd suffered with Keith. At that time, Robin had been her salvation. Now, even Robin couldn't overcome the heartache that dogged her day and night.

"Mom, is the store doing all that bad?"

"No, but it's not doing all that well, either, though lately we've had some decent days. But you know we're about to have mega competition."

"I heard."

Janey forced herself to smile. "Look, don't you worry. It'll all work out."

"Has Dad paid you?"

Janey was taken aback, having tried to shield Robin from her dad's low-down tactics. "I didn't know you knew."

"Of course I knew," Robin said impatiently. "I'm not a child, even though you think I am."

Janey's smile was real this time.

"Anyhow," Robin went on, "I heard him talking to someone about it on the phone. I think he was trying to borrow the money."

"I can't imagine what he does with his money," Janey mused out loud.

Robin didn't reply for a second, then said in a rushed tone, "If only you'd go back to Daddy—"

"Oh, honey…"

"It's Dillon, isn't it." Robin's voice was slightly unsteady. "He's the reason."

"No, he's not the reason. Actually, I'm...not seeing him anymore."

Robin's eyes widened. "You're not?"

"No." Janey could hardly get that word past her stiff lips. His name struck a nerve. All she wanted to do was cry, something she'd been doing every night, long after the house was quiet. Those soul-wrenching tears had saved her life, kept her functioning.

"Why?"

Robin's simple question forced her back to the moment. "It's too complicated to explain."

"I bet," Robin said huffily.

Suddenly a horn honked.

"There's Beverly. Have a good day, and I love you."

"Me too," Robin called back, making tracks toward the door.

Janey eyed the sofa with longing, wanting to sit down and wallow in her self-pity. But she couldn't afford that luxury.

Broken heart or not, she had to go on.

"Hey, wait up."

Robin swung around and watched as Chad strolled leisurely toward her. When he reached her side, she said, "Good morning."

He didn't respond in kind. Instead, he scowled down at her. "I said, wait up."

"I know what you said." Her tone was testy. For some reason, she wasn't in the mood to put up with *his* mood. She couldn't get her mother off her mind. She hated seeing Mom unhappy and moping around like a sick puppy.

Suddenly Robin felt herself smile. She'd acted just like that when she'd first met Chad. Now...

"What the hell's wrong with you?"

"I was thinking," Robin said, glancing up at him. That scowl remained on his features.

Suddenly he stopped, grabbed her arm and jerked her to a standstill. "Dammit, when are you going to learn to do like you're told?"

"Turn me loose."

Chad gave her a mocking smile. "And if I don't?"

"Stop acting like a jerk!"

His hold tightened, as did his lips. "You'd better remember who you're talking to."

"I don't like it when you treat me this way." Robin heard the quiver in her voice and hated it.

In fact, in that moment she hated *him*.

Her breath caught. What had she just admitted? Was it true? Or was she just over-reacting? After all, his meaty hand had her arm in a viselike grip. He was hurting her, something he had promised never to do again.

"When are we going out?" he asked, his tone rough.

"Let me go and I'll answer you." Robin was gazing about to see if any of her friends were watching what was going on between them.

But no one seemed to be paying any attention, which was a relief. All she needed was for Dillon to walk by. He would for sure tell her mother. Though since Mom and Dillon were no longer an item, maybe he wouldn't.

Why did everything have to be so darn complicated? She wanted her mother to be happy, but she wanted to be happy, too. Her conscience suddenly pricked her, at the thought that she might be to blame for Mom and Dillon's split. She couldn't imagine why that bothered her.

"You haven't answered me," Chad said, interrupting her thoughts. "When's that bitch of a mother of yours going to let us go out alone?"

"Don't call my mom a bitch," Robin lashed back.

"Well, that's what she is."

"Chad—"

"Look, I'm tired of you stringing me along. If you don't want to put out, then just say so. I'm tired of waiting for you to spread your legs."

Robin felt high color rise in her face. "I wish you wouldn't say things like that."

"Why not? It's the truth."

"Still—"

"Aw, hell, stop stalling. Like I've told you, there's plenty of girls who are more than willing to accommodate me."

"Then maybe you should find one."

His features turned menacing. "Don't threaten me, baby. That's a big mistake."

"I'm not threatening you. I'm serious."

He snorted. "Yeah, right. You wouldn't know what to do without me."

"Maybe not," Robin admitted, looking him directly in the eye. "But I'm willing to find out."

"You're full of shit," he spat.

"Actually, what I'm full of is you and your crummy attitude. I don't want to see you again, Chad. It's over."

"It's not over until I say it is."

With her heart lodged in her throat, Robin turned to walk away.

"If you take another step, you're right, baby, you can kiss me goodbye."

Robin kept on walking.

Janey sat straight up in bed, her gown drenched. What had happened? Then it hit her. She'd been dreaming about Dillon—vivid, erotic dreams, dreams that had her entire body in flames.

His mouth had been on her everywhere—her lips, her neck, her breasts, between her legs....

She lunged out of bed, only to feel her head reel. She grabbed the bedpost and held on until the room righted itself.

That was when she heard the soft sobs. She froze and listened. *Robin.* Without hesitation, Janey dashed down the hall and paused outside her daughter's door, her own heart hammering so loudly she could barely hear the continued sobs.

Should she intrude? Or should she let Robin have her privacy?

Unwittingly, Janey's fingers curled around the knob, and she turned it. Her child was hurting, and she couldn't stand that. If there was any way she could ease that hurt, then she had to try.

Robin was sprawled across the bed on her stomach, her face buried in the pillow. A lamp burned softly on the chest of drawers.

"Honey, what's wrong?" Janey whispered, placing a tentative hand on Robin's shoulder. She felt Robin's muscles tighten, but her daughter didn't reject her touch.

Instead, she rolled over and stared into Janey's eyes. "Mom—" Her voice cracked.

"I'm here, darling. Are you sick?"

"No."

Janey smoothed the damp hair off Robin's face. "Want to talk about it?"

Robin's mouth worked, while more tears poured from her eyes. "I...I broke up with Chad."

Praise the Lord! Janey wanted to shout, but, of course, she didn't. She didn't show any reaction whatsoever, for fear of spooking Robin and forcing her to clam up.

"He just kept pushing and pushing until I'd had it." Robin sniffled, then hiccuped.

Janey reached for a tissue and gently dabbed at Robin's cheeks. "Now you're having second thoughts about what you did, right?"

"I don't know," Robin wailed, bringing on another onslaught of tears.

"Shh. You'll make yourself sick."

"I...know you're glad."

"I only want what's best for you," Janey said. "You know that."

"He's...a big bully."

Janey hid her smile. "I won't argue that."

"And I'm not sorry, really." Robin's tone turned fierce. "Except—" She stopped and drew a shuddering breath.

"Except what?" Janey pressed gently.

"I'll...I'll be a nobody now."

"Oh, honey, that's not true. You have a lot to offer. Chad's the one who's not deserving of you, not the other way around. Why, you watch and see if you don't get hit on as soon as word gets around."

"Oh, Mom!" Robin cried, throwing herself into Janey's arms.

Janey's tears mingled with her daughter's. Then

she pulled back and stared into Robin's eyes. "I'm so proud of you."

"I don't know why, after what I did."

"You didn't do anything."

"If only I hadn't told Dillon to leave you alone, then maybe you'd still be together. I've heard you crying every night."

"Oh, honey, my not seeing Dillon isn't your fault. And I won't have you think that."

"Maybe if I talked to him..."

Janey's heart was so full she could hardly speak. "Listen to me. There are a lot of reasons why Dillon and I aren't together."

"But maybe you should be. Maybe you're no longer supposed to be with Dad, just like I'm not supposed to be with Chad." Robin sniffled again. "I didn't understand that until Chad pushed me too hard. Is that what happened with Dad?"

"More or less. When he was unfaithful to me, I could never get past that. Apparently he was unhappy and I didn't know it."

"I know that must've been a terrible time for you. I'm so sorry."

With a new batch of tears blurring her vision, Janey grabbed Robin again and squeezed her.

"Mom! You're crushing me."

Laughing, Janey let her go. "Oh, honey, I'm so proud of you, more than you'll ever know. But you're growing up, and that makes me sad."

Robin picked at the sheet for several seconds. "Do you still care about Dillon? I mean—"

"I know what you mean."

"Look, I wouldn't be upset if you made up with him."

Janey was both stunned and elated by her daughter's comment. And speechless, too. But her daughter's approval had come too late. She had lost Dillon.

She kissed Robin on the nose. "Maybe you shouldn't worry about that either, okay? Instead, how 'bout getting some sleep? Six o'clock comes early."

"You're telling me."

Janey stood, then pulled the covers up to Robin's neck. She kissed her daughter on the cheek and whispered, "I love you."

"I love you, too, Mom."

Janey smiled through her tears. "Tomorrow's another day. We'll see what that brings for both of us."

Thirty-Eight

Dillon stared at the blank wall in front of him. He really should put something in that space, he told himself. However, that wasn't the only empty space he had to fill.

His life was now a void.

With each passing day he missed Janey more. Every time he saw Robin on campus, which was often, his gut twisted into a tighter knot. He hadn't realized until now how much she favored her mother.

He ached to hold Janey, touch her, *taste* her. That was not to be, thanks to his hard head and his macho pride.

Dillon had damned himself more times than he cared to admit for his lack of self-control, wishing he could recall his words and do things differently.

Life had a way of not offering second chances, at least for some people. But when Janey had more or less thrown his love and his proposal back in his face, he'd been devastated. He had convinced himself that if she loved him, anything was possible.

Wrong. At least, not to her way of thinking. Still, he'd acted with his heart instead of his head, and now he was sorry. But sorry was like a limp dick; it wouldn't cut it.

He hadn't tried to contact her directly, but he'd

hoped he would run into her at the nursing facility where Emma now resided. So far he'd missed her, though he knew that Janey went every day to see Emma.

The old lady, while not quite recovered yet from that stroke, was, at least, well taken care of. Emma had quickly become a favorite of his friend who owned the facility.

Dillon's gaze suddenly strayed to the letter on his desk. He couldn't believe he'd turned down the superintendent's offer, especially under the current circumstances.

Allie had had a fit.

"Have you lost your mind?"

"Probably," he'd said.

"But why? Since you and Janey split, I figured you'd grab the chance to start over."

"Me too, but it didn't happen. I just couldn't leave, not if—"

"There's a chance you might patch things up between you."

"Right, though I don't think there's much hope of that."

"Oh, Dillon," Allie moaned, "sometimes I'd like to shake you."

No more than he would like to shake himself, he thought now. What was wrong with him that he couldn't sustain a relationship? What was he lacking?

If anything, he loved Janey too much.

He dropped his head in his hands, more miserable than he'd ever been in his life. Yet good things were happening to him.

In addition to Emma's good fortune, two kids had

been caught for breaking and entering, both at the school and at Janey's store. Aimsworth and his crony Jarvis had been the culprits, just as he'd thought. The ball cap had indeed been the smoking gun.

Things at the farm were also looking up. The mare he'd bought right before Dandi died was shaping up nicely. Mike had made arrangements to breed her. Also, they were still negotiating to buy at least one of the mares they had looked at last week. Another buddy at the bank believed in what Dillon was doing and had agreed to lend him whatever he needed.

But somehow the full effect of these fortunate events was kept at bay by that void inside him. If only...

Suddenly, Dillon heard a noise, as if a car had blown a tire on the street—only the sound was too close for that.

He lunged to his feet, just as Mildred appeared in his open door.

"Oh, my God, Mr. Reed, someone has a gun in the gym!"

Janey stared at her ex-husband and felt nothing but extreme sadness for what had been. But the bitterness that she'd nurtured all those years was gone. She could finally look at Keith and feel nothing, something she hadn't thought would ever happen. She didn't even wish him ill. In fact, she hoped he found peace in his life, if not happiness.

Falling in love with Dillon had been the cure-all for her heart. Even though that love would never come to fruition, she didn't regret one moment she'd had with him.

But while she had gotten over the first love in her

life, which was Keith, she doubted she would ever get over the second. She would love Dillon forever, despite the fact that it was over between them.

Fighting back the urge to cry, she faced Keith, who was staring at her as if trying to figure out what was going on inside her head. She had phoned him to come by before she opened the store.

She knew her call had surprised him, especially after the way they had last parted.

"I appreciate your coming by so early," she told him, smiling briefly.

His stare deepened, as if he realized she hadn't smiled at him in ages.

"No problem. If it's about the money, I have it."

Her mouth dropped. "You do?"

He handed her a check for the full amount.

"Thanks. Our daughter's extracurricular activities are very costly."

"I'm sorry about the delay." He paused. "And I'm also sorry for acting like an asshole the other night. I deserved that shiner Dillon gave me."

Janey's eyes widened. "I didn't think I'd ever hear you say that."

"Trust me, I didn't think I'd ever say it, either. But I realize just how far over the edge I'd gone. My actions even disgusted me."

They were silent for a moment.

"Look, Janey, I don't know why you called. Maybe it was just about the money, but if it wasn't, then—"

"It's truly over, Keith. Between us, I mean." She spoke in a low, soft voice. "I'm not ever coming back to you. I wanted you to know that once and for all so you could get on with your life." She paused again. "That was really why I called, to tell you that."

He seemed to wilt right in front of her, but when he spoke his voice was steady. "I've known that, but I just refused to accept it."

"Even if we'd been willing to try, it would never have worked. There's just too much water under the bridge."

Keith blew out his breath. "I don't know so much about that, but I guess it doesn't matter now." His features were grim. "I was just hoping that Robin would win you over."

Janey gave him another smile. "Well, it wasn't from lack of trying, believe me. But you'd be proud of just how mature our daughter's become. She and I had a heart-to-heart talk, and she's quite a young lady."

"Thanks to you. Since I've been nursing the bottle, I certainly haven't been the father I should've been."

"Does that mean you're reforming?"

"I'm going to try." His face brightened. "If I did stop drinking, would that get me back in the ballpark?"

"No."

"It's Dillon, isn't it."

A tinge of that old resentment entered his voice, but she ignored it. "Yes," she said simply.

He shook his head, disbelief etched on his face. "Who would've thought it? First me and Elaine, now you and Dillon."

Unfortunately, there is no me and Dillon, she wanted to cry. However, her personal life was no concern of his. Only when something pertained to Robin did they ever need to converse.

"I hope you find what you want in life, Keith. Despite what's happened, I wish you the best."

"The best was you."

"Don't. I told you, it's over, and you need to accept that."

"You don't leave me much choice."

He walked to the door, where he turned and looked her up and down. "Hope things work out for you."

With that he was gone.

If her insides hadn't been in such a tangled mess over Dillon, she would have celebrated. She had come to terms with the past, and that had been a major hurdle in her life. Now if she could only come to terms with the present.

Pushing aside those feelings of despair, Janey switched on the lights and opened the shop, just as Hazel drove up. After pleasantries were exchanged, both she and her helper went to work in the back, unpacking new shipments of candy.

She had just opened the first carton when the buzzer sounded.

"Starting early," Hazel said with a grin. "That's a sign we'll have a *good* day."

"Keep your fingers crossed," Janey responded, hurrying to the front.

"Hey, Mary Beth. It's good to see you."

The mother of another drill team member didn't come in often, but when she did, she always bought mega bucks worth of candy. This was definitely going to be a good day if Mary Beth held true to form.

"So how are things going?" she asked Janey, eying some chocolates.

"I have no complaints."

"Me, either, except it's run, run, run for Sheila. I swear those kids are in more stuff and need more stuff than ever, especially with the drill team."

"I know what you mean," Janey responded. "But it's so important to them to be a part of that."

"Tell me about it," Mary Beth said, down in the mouth. "By the way—"

The phone chose that moment to ring, which cut Mary Beth off. No great loss, Janey thought, reaching for it. The woman would talk the horns off a billy goat and back on again.

It was Robin calling to say that she had cramps and needed her medicine from home. Though slightly irritated at having to leave the shop, Janey didn't have much choice. Robin was known to throw up if she didn't take her medication almost immediately.

"That was my daughter. I'm going to have to leave and run to the school."

Mary Beth rolled her eyes. "See what I mean?"

"Exactly." Janey grabbed her purse. "But we wouldn't have it any other way." She paused. "Sorry I have to skip out on you like this, but if you're in a hurry, Hazel will take care of you. If not, I'll be back in a jiffy."

Once Hazel was in the front and she had the medicine in her purse, Janey headed out the door. Since Robin was just finishing her health class, in the gym classroom, Janey wouldn't have to fight the student traffic in the main building, which would cut down on time.

Usually the drive to the school only took ten minutes or so. Today it seemed as if every slowpoke in town got in front of her. From now on, she was going to see that Robin kept some medicine in the nurse's office for such emergencies.

When she parked at the gym entrance and found Robin, the class had apparently just been dismissed, but Robin and several others were still inside.

"Oh, hi, Mom," Robin said, getting up, then reaching for her book, which was still open on the table. "I hope you didn't mind doing this, but I'm in a world of hurt."

She looked it, too, Janey thought, taking in her daughter's pale and pinched features. She looked like she ought to be home in bed rather than at school.

"Are you sure you're up to staying the rest of the day?" Janey asked, helping Robin stuff her work in her backpack.

"I'll be fine as soon as I take something."

It was in that moment that Janey heard the first scream, followed by a shrill shout. "He's got a gun!"

"Mom, did you hear that?" Robin asked, her eyes wide with shock.

Janey's eyes had already turned toward the hall where the cries had originated. Seconds later, Chad rushed into the health classroom, slammed the door behind him, then leaned against it and pointed a gun.

At Robin.

"Oh, God," Janey whimpered, groping for her daughter, who had shifted closer to her side.

"Mom!"

Robin's shaky use of her name voiced the fear that was spreading through Janey like a lethal virus.

"Chad, have you lost your mind?" one of the

other students demanded into the stunned silence. "Put that stupid gun down."

"Shut up!" Chad said. "All of you just sit down and shut the fuck up!"

No one needed any second invitation, especially Janey. Without hesitation, but without taking her eyes off her daughter's ex-boyfriend, whose eyes were wide and manic, she clutched at Robin's arm, and together they sank into the two nearest chairs.

"Please, Chad," Janey pleaded. "Put that gun down before you hurt yourself or someone else." She had to do something, anything, that might defuse the terrifying situation. But if she couldn't, if there was even the remotest chance he might actually use that gun on Robin, then she was prepared to lunge in front of her daughter and take the bullet. This sick boy was not going to deprive her of her child. "Let your friends go," she added. "I'll stay here with you."

"Just shut up, you bitch!" he lashed back at Janey.

She flinched at the crude word at the same time that she felt Robin's arm slide around her shoulders. "If it hadn't been for you, Robin and I would still be together."

"That's a lie!" Robin cried.

"Hush, Robin." Janey placed a hand on her daughter's knee and squeezed it.

"You're all going to do what I say, when I say it," Chad declared. "Understood? I'm in charge here."

"All right," Janey said, forcing her voice to remain low and level. "We'll do whatever you say, especially if you lower that gun."

"I told you to shut up! This is payback time for you and your fickle daughter there. So I suggest you be nice to me." He walked away from the door and made his way toward Janey and Robin, the gun bobbing up and down in his hand.

"Stop talking to my mother like that, you big jerk!" Robin cried in a shrill tone, attempting to rise to her feet.

"No," Janey whispered, digging her fingers into her daughter's arm and yanking her down, fear boiling up the back of her throat and almost strangling her. "Sit down. Don't antagonize him."

"Yeah, you'd best listen to your mom," Chad sneered. "Like a good little girl."

God, what a nightmare, Janey told herself, relaxing her grip on Robin, but not turning her totally loose. She had to touch her daughter, rationalizing that somehow that made Robin safer.

How had this happened? she asked herself, surveying the scene in front of her. It almost seemed like she was playing out a dream. However, when she stared at the boy with the gun, she knew it was no dream. Brutal reality was staring her in the face.

In the distance, she could hear a commotion outside. Turning her head slightly, she peered out the nearest window, taking in the police, who were already visible. Other people were also beginning to gather on the grounds, among them frantic parents, the media, the entire faculty and staff, though all were well behind an area that had already been cordoned off. No one was being allowed anywhere near the gym.

"Mom, Chad's lost it," Robin said in a hushed tone, her voice strained to the max.

"Shhh, don't—"

It was in that moment that the door opened and Dillon strode in, closing it behind him.

Janey managed to put her hand to her mouth in time to mute her strangled cry as Chad swung around and aimed the gun straight at Dillon. No, no, no. Why did Dillon have to make such a bold move? The two people she loved most in life were now in dire jeopardy, and she was powerless to help them.

"Chad, son, give me the gun."

"I'm not your son!" His nostrils flared, and his eyes narrowed to slits.

"I can help you," Dillon went on as if Chad hadn't spoken. "We can resolve this so no one gets hurt."

"It's too late! So back off, you hear?"

Dillon ignored him and took a step closer. "That's not going to happen, Chad."

Janey sucked in her breath and watched, not daring to breathe. If Chad hurt Dillon...

"I'll shoot you, Mr. Reed. I swear to God I will."

Dillon kept on walking. "Then do it, because I'm not stopping until that gun is in my hand."

Chad backed up, his eyes taking on a frantic glint. "You...better stop." The gun began shaking as hard as his voice.

Suddenly Dillon's hand shot out and grabbed Chad's wrist. That was when gunfire erupted and Dillon staggered back.

"Oh, God, no!" Janey cried.

Thirty-Nine

Janey carefully opened the door of Robin's room.

After the policeman had questioned each person that Chad had held at gunpoint, recording their rendition of the happenings, Janey and Robin had been allowed to go home.

Once there, Robin had shed her clothes, taken a shower, then fallen into bed, while Janey had walked the floor, still too emotionally traumatized to function even halfway normally.

The idea that Robin and Dillon could've been killed was too overwhelming for her mind to accept.

He hadn't meant to hurt anyone, Chad had sobbed after the fact, especially not Mr. Reed, who had always tried to help him.

While Janey sympathized with both Chad and his parents, she couldn't be entirely forgiving. Yet she realized he was a disturbed young man and hoped he received the care he needed. She did feel sorry for his parents, however.

Janey couldn't imagine anything more awful than to have to deal with the aftermath of such a horrendous episode. Thank God she and Robin had a special bond that hopefully precluded anything so horrible ever happening.

As she eased the door open farther, Janey was

taken aback. She had expected Robin to be sound asleep, exhausted after the event. Instead, her daughter's eyes were wide open.

"Hi, Mom," Robin said in a muffled tone.

Janey smiled as she made her way deeper into the room, where shadows played across the walls as daylight fast faded into darkness. "I thought for sure you'd be out like a light."

Robin scooted over in the bed, making room for Janey to sit beside her. "I couldn't sleep."

Janey lifted Robin's left hand to her lips, her mouth working. "Oh, honey, I'm not surprised. Maybe if I got you some Tylenol, it would help."

"It's just that I keep seeing Dillon—" Robin's voice broke.

"Me too," Janey whispered.

"But he is all right, isn't he?" Robin's large, sad eyes were questioning.

"Yes. The bullet only grazed his shoulder. Still, they insisted on taking him to the hospital." She paused, then added bleakly, "Unfortunately I don't know any of the details."

"If he hadn't stepped between us and Chad—" Robin broke off again, sounding on the verge of hysteria.

"Don't, honey. Don't torment yourself anymore," Janey pleaded, trying her best to keep herself together and comfort her daughter. That was hard, when what she wanted to do was crawl into a closet, curl into a fetal position and nurse her own emotional wounds.

From the moment she realized her daughter was at the mercy of her ex-boyfriend with a gun, she'd been absolutely beside herself. Then, to have to stand by helplessly and watch as Dillon staggered backward, was almost more than her heart could take.

But she hadn't passed out. She had managed to remain upright, though only because her legs felt like chunks of cement, which made any movement impossible.

Dillon had taken a bullet, but it hadn't stopped him. In the split second after Chad saw what he'd done, he had hesitated. And that split second was all Dillon had needed.

He'd lunged for the gun, and had it in his possession before Chad could grasp what had happened. Then Chad dropped to his knees and began sobbing.

Pandemonium immediately broke out. The cops had been the first to go into the school, though the gathered parents had soon followed. Later, Janey didn't know where she found the strength to grab Robin, but she had. They had clung together, both sobbing.

When she had finally pulled back and regained a semblance of control, she had realized Dillon was nowhere in the room. Her heart seemed to stop. She was suddenly terrified that he might be dead, and that she'd never have a chance to tell him...

She'd been about to enquire as to his whereabouts when she'd overheard one of the police officers tell another parent that Dillon had been shot, but not badly, and had been driven to the hospital, even though he hadn't wanted to go.

Because the policeman had been smiling when he'd talked about Dillon, Janey's breathing had resumed.

Now, as she sat beside her daughter, having replayed that nightmare, she had to stifle her desire to grab Robin and crush the breath out of her.

She would have liked to do the same to Dillon, but that was not to be. Tears gathered in her eyes, but she refused to give in to them, at least in front of her daughter.

Robin had suffered too much trauma already. Heaping more worry on her would be selfish. Later, Janey would have to come to terms with her own private hell concerning Dillon.

This time belonged to her child. It could be no other way.

"Mom."

"Mmm?"

"What will happen to Chad?"

"I don't know, darling. He'll have to suffer the consequences of his actions, that's for sure."

"I can't believe anyone I actually cared about would go totally ballistic." She paused and shivered. "It's too scary."

"Hopefully he'll get lots of counseling and love."

"Does Dad know?"

A sudden attack of guilt hit Janey. "Lord, no. I'll go call him right now." Janey lunged off the bed. "You want him to come over?"

"You wouldn't mind?"

"Oh, honey, of course not. I've told you countless times, your relationship with your dad has nothing to do with me. I want you to be with him, as long as…" Janey's voice faded, and she looked away.

"As long as he's not drinking," Robin finished for her.

"That's right," Janey responded.

"I understand, Mom. I feel the same way."

Relief and pride rendered Janey speechless once again. "Oh, honey, if anything had happened to you…"

"It didn't, thanks to Dillon."

Janey gnawed at her lower lip. "I just hope he's going to be all right."

"Why don't you go see for yourself?"

Janey gave Robin a startled look. "Oh, I don't think that would be a good idea."

"Why not?"

Janey opened her mouth, then shut it.

"I know you love him."

"I wish it were that simple."

"Why not?" Robin asked with the innocence of youth.

Janey leaned over and kissed Robin on the forehead. "I'll explain it to you sometime."

"Mom, you're just too stubborn for your own good."

Janey smiled through her tears. "Think so, huh?"

"I know so. You've always told me to go for the gold. I suggest you do the same."

Tears ran down Janey's face. If someone had told her she would ever be having this kind of conversation with her teenage daughter, she would have responded, "No way." How quickly situations could change, and for the better, too. "I love you," she whispered.

"I love you, too, Mom."

That was when Janey noticed her daughter's eyes fluttering. "You sleep, and I'll go call your dad."

By the time Janey made it to the door and turned, Robin was already asleep. Janey stood for the longest

time and stared at her, eternally grateful that her
daughter was alive.

Shuddering, she eased the door shut behind her
and walked straight to the phone. She called Keith
and learned he had just heard about the incident over
the news. But since no students' names had been
released, he'd had no idea Robin was involved. Once
Janey had told him his daughter was okay, he'd opted
to call her when she awakened.

After she replaced the receiver, Janey continued to
stare at the phone, tempted to pick it up again and
call Dillon. And say what? she asked herself, feeling
hysteria surface.

But, dear God, she ached to know if he was okay.
If only she could see for herself that he'd suffered
no serious injuries from the gunshot. Another hard
shudder shook her body. She loved him so much,
and wondered how in the world she was going to
live the rest of her life without him.

Robin was important to her, but so was Dillon.

Her stomach churned, and she grabbed it, hoping
to ease some of the pain. If only things had been
different.

But they weren't different, she reminded herself
brutally. She had to face facts.

Even so, she had to see him. Right or wrong, she
had no choice.

Dillon walked to the window and watched the rain.

He hadn't even realized it was cloudy until he'd
heard the rain hit the skylight. But from the menacing
look of the lightning, the area was in for a bumpy
ride.

He should be rejoicing. The gloomy day fit his

mood to a T. While his mind was definitely cluttered with the horror he'd just survived, it was Janey who had his guts in a turmoil.

Although he hated to admit it, thoughts of her took precedence over everything else. He wanted to see her so badly, he actually felt a physical ache. If just once more he could kiss her, touch her, he would be all right. That kiss, that touch, would suffice for a lifetime.

Desperate.

That was what he was. And he didn't have a clue how to combat that feeling. It was as if he were trying to fight a grizzly bear with a switch instead of a club.

When he'd boldly walked into that gym before the police arrived and had seen that Robin and Janey were being held hostage, he'd come closer to losing it than he ever had before.

His reaction to seeing his wife in another man's arms didn't compare to the devastation that had sprung to life inside him at that school. His need to spare Janey further heartache had jolted him into action, providing the motivation for his brazen responses.

Even though he was being touted as a hero, he'd brushed that aside, claiming he'd just been doing his job, which was taking care of the kids under his watch.

After leaving the emergency room, he hadn't bothered to go back to the school. Classes had been dismissed for the day, and there was still a lot of tidying up to do. Besides, the doctor had threatened to keep him overnight if he didn't agree to go straight home.

A bad idea.

He had nothing to do but coddle his own misery. Allie had rushed to his side, of course, but once he'd been pronounced good to go, she and Mike had gone back home. She'd pleaded with Dillon to come stay with them, but he'd said no, that he preferred to be alone.

Now he wished he hadn't been so hardheaded. Maybe he should have gone to the farm. Better yet, maybe he should have gone over to Janey's and made her listen to reason. He'd walked out of her life far too quickly and foolishly. Anything worth a damn was worth fighting for, and he'd given up like a yellow-bellied coward.

Disgust replaced his desperation. So what did he intend to do about it? Get the lead out of his ass and go see her. She wasn't coming to him—no way.

Hurling curses through the air at random, Dillon was halfway to the door when the bell chimed. He pulled up short, and narrowed his eyes. If that was another reporter, he swore he would wring his bloody neck. Enough was enough.

He jerked open the door, his expression fierce, only to freeze.

Janey stood on the steps.

"May...I come in?" she asked in a barely audible voice.

"Uh, sure," he responded with equal nervousness, then cursed silently. This was what he'd longed for, *prayed for,* so why was he standing here like an idiot at a loss for words?

He stepped aside and motioned for her to go ahead of him, the blood drumming in his temples. When she reached the middle of the living room, she swung around, tears glistening in her eyes.

"I had to see for myself that you're all right and thank you for saving Robin," she said quickly.

"Was that the only reason you came?" he asked grimly, unable to hide his disappointment and despair. He had hoped...

"No."

It took him a second to get his mind back on track. "What's the other reason?" he asked thickly.

"I wanted you to know that I love you."

Every muscle, every bone, every nerve seemed to fuse, and he was able to move again, striding to close the distance between them.

"Please, don't touch me!" she cried, her body turning rigid under his eye.

He stopped and asked in a tormented voice, "God, Janey, that's crazy, when that's all I want to do—forever. I want to marry you now, if you'll have me."

"Oh, Dillon, you just think you want to marry me. But I can never give you the children you want."

For a second he stared at her in disbelief. "Surely you—"

"Let me finish," Janey pleaded. "Even if I wanted to have another baby, I can't. I've wanted to tell you that for so long now, only things kept happening and I never got the chance. And I was so scared to...." A sob tore loose from her throat. "I'm so sorry."

Dillon grabbed her then and pulled her against him. "You have nothing to be sorry about, you hear me. I don't give a damn if you can have children or not. I'd rather have you." He kissed her hard. "I'd rather have you any day than a child."

Dillon laughed and kissed her again. "Besides, I

have nearly a thousand kids. That's enough for any man. Too, we can look forward to Robin giving us grandchildren in the future.''

"Dillon, Dillon," she sobbed, holding him tightly.

He lifted her into his arms, carried her down the hall and gently placed her on his bed. But that was the only gentle thing he did. He quickly and roughly discarded their clothes. Moments later, his hot lips and tongue were on her skin.

"I want you!" Janey cried, taking his shaft and guiding it to the edge of her warmth.

Completely at her mercy, he thrust into her and rode her harder than he'd ever ridden any horse.

They climaxed at the same time, their cries filling the air.

When their breathing allowed them to speak coherently, Dillon pushed her damp hair back and stared deeply into her eyes. "I love you, Janey Mayfield, now and forever."

"And I love you, Dillon Reed, now and forever."

They both giggled like teenagers.

"What about Robin?" Dillon asked in a sober tone.

"She's all for us getting together."

Dillon gave her an incredulous look. "You're puttin' me on."

"No, I'm not."

Janey explained the conversation that had taken place between her and Robin after Robin had broken up with Chad.

"So you see," Janey added, "my daughter's already rallying on your behalf."

"That's my girl."

"But it won't always be sunshine and roses,"

Janey whispered, her eyes shadowed. "With Keith always in the picture, there'll be some hard times."

"I'm up to the challenge," Dillon said, cupping the still-pulsating spot between her legs.

He heard her breath catch, and Janey asked, "What about the job?"

"I turned it down."

"Are you sorry?"

"There'll be others. If not, I'm perfectly content to remain where I am, so you can keep Sweet Dreams."

"What if the store doesn't make it?"

He increased his pressure between her legs. She jerked, her gaze heating up. "Let's just cross that bridge when we come to it," he said huskily. "But I'm betting on you."

"Are you sure you're okay about not having a child?"

He rolled her on top and eased her down on his erection. She moaned and closed her eyes. For the next little while, only their mutual groans of pleasure filled the silence.

Later, as she lay beside him, Janey whispered through tears of happiness, "You never answered my question."

"You're all I want," he said around his own tears.

*An artist's sudden blindness is diagnosed as psychological
trauma—but what is it she doesn't want to see?*

FOX RIVER

Fox River is a world where Thoroughbreds and fox hunting are
passions, not pastimes. The community is rocked to the core
when a beautiful heiress is murdered. The trauma has particular
resonance for Julia Warwick—her lover has been charged with
the crime. The result for Julia is that she plunges into a world
without sight.

Blindness has darkened her world, but it has opened her eyes.
Julia listens as her mother reads to her from her novel in
progress. A story emerges, a forgotten memory returns and the
secrets of Fox River are revealed.

EMILIE RICHARDS

USA Today Bestselling Author

Available June 2001 wherever paperbacks are sold!

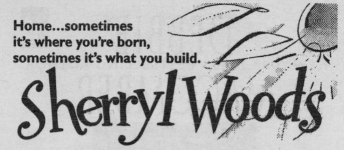

New York Times **Bestselling Author**

LINDA
LAEL
MILLER

ONLY FOREVER

Once married to one of baseball's superstars,
Vanessa Lawrence has coped with betrayal, divorce and
the tabloids. So when ex-football hero Nick DeAngelo takes
to the playing field that was once her heart, Vanessa's not
about to let another sports-crazed womanizer ruin her life.
But Nick's not prepared to let Vanessa get away. Because
the day he saw Vanessa, he knew he'd found his destiny....

**"Sensuality, passion, excitement...
are Ms. Miller's hallmarks."**
—*Romantic Times Magazine*

Available June 2001 wherever paperbacks are sold!

MARY LYNN
BAXTER

66588	SULTRY	___ $5.99 U.S.	___ $6.99 CAN.
66523	ONE SUMMER EVENING	___ $5.99 U.S.	___ $6.99 CAN.
66440	HARD CANDY	___ $5.99 U.S.	___ $6.99 CAN.
66417	TEARS OF YESTERDAY	___ $5.50 U.S.	___ $6.50 CAN.
66300	AUTUMN AWAKENING	___ $5.50 U.S.	___ $6.50 CAN.
66289	LONE STAR HEAT	___ $5.99 U.S.	___ $6.99 CAN.
66165	A DAY IN APRIL	___ $5.99 U.S.	___ $6.99 CAN.

(limited quantities available)

TOTAL AMOUNT $_____
POSTAGE & HANDLING $_____
($1.00 for one book; 50¢ for each additional)
APPLICABLE TAXES* $_____
<u>TOTAL PAYABLE</u> $_____
(check or money order—please do not send cash)

To order, complete this form and send it, along with a check or money order for the total above, payable to MIRA® Books, to: **In the U.S.:** 3010 Walden Avenue, P.O. Box 9077, Buffalo, NY 14269-9077; **In Canada:** P.O. Box 636, Fort Erie, Ontario, L2A 5X3.

Name:_____
Address:_____ City:_____
State/Prov.:_____ Zip/Postal Code:_____
Account Number (if applicable):_____
075 CSAS

*New York residents remit applicable sales taxes.
 Canadian residents remit applicable
 GST and provincial taxes.

MIRA®